# The Dark

*BOOK 2 OF THE EBON KNIGHT CHRONICLES*

## James Wood

# Also by James Wood

## THE EBON KNIGHT CHRONICLES

### NOVELS

The Ebon Knight

The Dark Witch

The Arch Mage

### SHORT STORIES

The First Fury

The Lord Commander (Coming soon!)

**For the most up-to-date information, go to
authorjamesdwood.com**

*For my wife.*

*Ava has absolutely nothing on you, my love...*

*(particularly the mind reading part)*

# Acknowledgments

This book would not exist without the help of a lot of people. Thank you again to my editor, Elizabeth Cartwright, at EC Editorial; you did another fantastic job! Again, I take full responsibility for any errors left in this story, as I'm probably too stubborn to heed all of your sage advice.

I also want to thank my awesome cover designer, Alerim, at 99designs—you did another remarkable job with the cover and really did justice to the Dark Witch. Thanks again to Mark Rivera, Paul Adams, and the Book Writing Cube team for helping me get the second book in this series successfully published.

Again, many thanks to the great folks who play Elvenar. So many of you have embraced this project, and I'm honored by your support. A special shout out to my guildies at "Maximum Effort" on Arendyll, "Twisted Grotto" on Sinya Arda, and "Forest Dwellers" on Winyandor. You are all amazing people!

A big thanks to Mike Stackhouse for my website design and maintenance—I would still be totally lost without your help.

Thank you so much to my beta readers; your feedback kept me on the right path and motivated me to keep on writing!

My special thanks to Angela Null and my mother, Kathy. You both went above and beyond this time, and I truly appreciate it!

# Contents

# Prologue

It was a cold night.

Ryka was glad that her Dark kept her warm, but she still shivered in sympathy for what she *should* have been feeling. Glancing over at her Sisters standing stoically in the light snow, she reminded herself again that she needed to toughen up. Sometimes Ryka worried that she didn't really belong in the Sisterhood—which was impossible, of course, because once in, she was in. She had passed the only test that mattered when she survived her first battle. Still, she sometimes had doubts about her suitability as a Fury.

It didn't help that as one of the newer entrants into the clan, Ryka still had a long way to go—for everything, it seemed. What made a Fury a Fury did not come easily to her, and Ryka often felt like a weight that her Spearmates had to deal with. They were very sweet to her anyways, even as they often beat her half to death during their daily training sessions.

Ryka was extremely grateful that her healing prowess seemed up to snuff, at least—because she needed to rely on it quite a lot.

"Don't look now, but I think Ryka is having an existential crisis," Falen stage whispered to Micheline.

The tall woman looked over at Ryka, grimacing at Falen's words.

"I told you not to look. Now we're busted!" exclaimed Falen again in a hoarse whisper. "Just act normal."

Micheline shook her head. "Falen, stop being weird. Again." The tall woman sighed, walked over to Ryka, and put her arm around the shorter woman's shoulders.

Ryka leaned into her gratefully and mumbled, "I'm fine."

Micheline kissed her on the forehead. "Sure you are."

Turning Ryka to look at her fully, Micheline raised a finger in admonishment. "No Fury your age can perform the way Furies like Falen and I can. I've told you this several times now. Be patient."

"Yeah," interjected Falen, "...cause we're all super old and creaky and stuff. Be happy in your youth; don't let your summer slip away into fall."

"Really?" asked Micheline incredulously, turning to look at the other Fury. "You're bringing the seasons into it now?"

"Define *it*," challenged Falen.

"Her worries and feelings of inadequacy—which are *not* valid, by the way," Micheline added hurriedly, turning back to Ryka.

"Hmm, sounds like a crisis of confidence then. Maybe almost like an existential crisis, perhaps?" Falen had an impish grin on her face, and she winked at Ryka behind Micheline's back.

Micheline and Ryka both laughed.

"Ok, moving on," Micheline said, releasing Ryka and turning back to the freeway that was the artery between east Sparks and a desolate drive through Nevada into Utah.

The land here was nothing like Ryka's homeland in India. She had been awakened for about a decade, so she was still a novice in the Sisterhood's ranks. It was strange to think that the people she knew back home were still alive and kicking—just a tad more mature-looking. Ryka still looked exactly as she had ten years ago.

Aging *very* slowly was a benefit she liked, along with maintaining a constant body temperature. The constant temperature was key because Furies didn't tend to wear a lot of clothing. There was no taboo against clothing or anything, and it was not like they had a Fury dress code where everyone had to be in skimpy stuff; it was just a matter of practicality. Every time a Fury raged, anything they were wearing (except around the chest and buttocks) would probably get shredded or, worse, restrict their transformation *just* enough to hinder them in combat.

Turning into a raging demonic monster was kind of a drawback, sure, but it was also freeing. Being thrust into an eternal war with *very* unclear battle lines was a definite—and quite often fatal—minus, though.

Sighing audibly, Falen turned back to the road, and Ryka followed suit (minus the sigh), but she felt like it. Ryka knew what was bothering Falen—it was tough being out here in the dark and snow when such incredible things were happening in the city. The three Furies stood atop a large stone outcropping about a hundred yards from the road. They were just one Spear out of many that were fanned out all around Reno and Sparks. They also had the dubious honor of being the farthest out along I-80, almost an hour from where the action was.

The call came in earlier, full of dire import and worry. The three Sisters had listened in disbelief to the tale of what happened at the airport hangar where three Sisters died engaging a Royal. It was the way the other two Furies had reacted to the news that had started Ryka down the path of self-doubt. They had known one of them—Ivey—and respected her, but Ryka hadn't and only knew of Ivey through her legendary reputation within the Sisterhood.

Ivey had been the leader of Princess Ava's Spear, and she had also been instrumental in securing a chance for the Princess to escape from the Dark Court three years ago. Even though their true enemy—the "Other"—had labored to sideline the Furies that day, Ivey had helped to outsmart it. Or them. Or… whatever it was. As a matter of fact, Ryka wasn't sure anyone knew what the Other was.

Ava was still alive because of Ivey, and since the Princess was of the utmost importance to the Sisterhood, that meant a lot. The Sisterhood's splintering from the greater Dark had actually been set in motion by Ivey yesterday, and she had been one of the very few capable of initiating it. To know she had fallen mere hours later was a heavy blow indeed.

As the Furies attempted to pull back from the Dark and escape, hundreds were dying, with likely hundreds more over the next few days. Ivey was, by far, the greatest of them that had fallen though. It was heartbreaking to keep up with all the deaths, and it was extremely hard on the Sisterhood to feel so many disappearing. Ryka believed that Falen's ribbing was perhaps a coping mechanism they all needed. Humor to counter the horror.

Still, Ivey had been a giant within the Sisterhood, and even on the night when so many were dying all over the world, her death stood out. Besides, the way she had died was horrible. Two nearby Spears had reached the hangar about the same time as Ava and saw the ruin that was Ivey for themselves. They had also seen Ava's reaction to it.

It was well known that Ava and Ivey were close, and Ivey had often said that she loved the youngest Princess of the Dark as if she were her own daughter. That was physically impossible, of course, because every combatant on either side of the Conflict was either sterile or barren. Or maybe they weren't. But neither the Dark nor the Light allowed children to be born into the Conflict, so having kids was a moot issue for all—with one known exception.

Ava's mother, the Queen of the Dark, was that exception. By extension, it could be argued that Ava's father was an exception as well. It didn't matter, but the bottom line was that only those two could have children, and they'd had *many* over the years, of which the vast majority were as evil and malicious as could be imagined. In the Furies' opinion, only Ava had turned out well, and she had been banished, exiled, and hunted by the Dark as punishment.

Even Ava had a dark side, though. Those two Spears that had joined the remnants of Jesslyn's and Ava's guard also witnessed the receding manifestation of her other self—and that was enough. The Princess did not often descend to such a state, but when she did it was… memorable. The Sisterhood had a name for Ava when she embraced this darker, more unstable side of herself—they called her the Dark Witch.

Ava was not more dangerous when she was the Dark Witch, just more apt to do *anything* in the throes of it. Much like the Furies themselves when they were angered. In their rage, the Furies were the same women (albeit with demonic features, elongated and powerfully strong legs, arms, nails, and so on), but they were a *lot* wilder. Being more in tune with the darker parts of themselves made them implacable and fearless foes, but they could get a little overzealous when in such a state.

Ryka had to admit that raging was both scary and exhilarating. Like most of the Sisterhood, she feared and longed for it in equal measure. It was like riding the world's most dangerous rollercoaster with a frayed seatbelt; the possibility of tragedy and unintended consequences was there, but the excitement the ride offered was worth it. Every time a Fury raged, the rollercoaster she rode was herself.

Ava apparently took that to the next level when she embraced her darker side. She was more controlled than the Furies, but her power was so vast that the Princess had zero room for error. Ava was the best the Dark had ever produced, a perfect blend of grace and lethality. Ryka had never met her personally, but she knew pretty much everything about her. Every Fury did.

Ava was the hope of their clan. The Dark that drove them all, that gave the Sisterhood their unique powers and skill sets, also instilled in them a need to use those gifts to serve a cause. That need had been met over the last three hundred years by becoming the traditional guardians of the Royal Family, but that had

6

changed about twelve hours ago. Now, they were the enemies of the Royals—except for Ava. She was their *only* beacon now, and they flocked to her.

*All* the Furies from *all* over the world were on their way to Reno and Sparks, Nevada. It was almost laughable that such a mighty force could descend on any one place; and this particular area didn't have a whole lot going for it other than Ava just happened to be here.

So, they were coming.

The Splintering had happened, and death stalked the clan. So, too, a potentially fatal break with Ava. Something unexpected had happened in the aftermath of Ivey's death. The Princess had shocked the Sisterhood by giving them two ultimatums, even as three Sisters lay cooling on the ground at Ava's feet—all having died for her welfare. It was an incredible turn of events that threatened to put the final nail in the coffin of the Furies, one and all.

The first requirement was that they had to *always* keep the Princess in the loop from now on. This seemed a simple condition on its face, and Ryka actually agreed with it. The Princess was easily more formidable than any five Spears, so why keep her in the dark about any foes or dangerous situations? Both would arise more frequently now, and Ryka believed the Sisterhood needed all the help it could get.

Unfortunately, this was not how the elders viewed Ava's ultimatum, and they were sorely put out by it. They hadn't had a choice. One of Ava's personal Furies had vouched that the clan would agree to Ava's terms, and the eight other Sisters with her had as well.

What nine of their dwindling number had promised was to be done. The elders were in quite a tizzy over it though, and Ryka was sure they would try to weaken the agreement or add layers of difficulties to foul it up. That certainly wouldn't go over well with the Princess, but if push came to shove the elders would give in. They had no other choice.

Really, what was the point of trying to keep Ava safe by keeping her ignorant? Ryka grunted in frustration, which went unremarked on by the other two. She bet they were mulling over the exact same events she was and, hopefully, coming to similar conclusions—at least when it came to the first of Ava's demands.

Ava's second requirement, though? It was anyone's guess if it was even still valid and in effect.

In the span of about two days, the Princess had apparently fallen in love. This possibility, in and of itself, was not particularly alarming or even rare. People fell in love all the time, and this held true for the natural and supernatural world. People could also fall in love quite quickly. Ryka could understand the whole "love at first sight" phenomenon herself because it had happened to her. At the Fury's thought, she cast a little glance over to Micheline, who smiled as she felt Ryka's eyes on her.

Turning back to the freeway, Ryka smiled to herself as well.

The issue was—no, the *problem* was—with whom Ava had fallen for. He was a Knight of the Light, and something like this was just not done. The Light and the Dark did not mix like that, and frankly, Ryka had no idea how it could possibly work. The opposing powers that made them both would kill each other off if given the chance.

Ryka shook her head in frustration while her eyes idly picked out a mass of headlights a few miles away heading towards Reno—of little interest other than as something to look at to break the bleakness around her. It didn't help. Ryka still couldn't believe that a Princess of the *Dark* could fall for anyone of the *Light*.

"How?" she muttered in disbelief.

"I know," Falen agreed.

Micheline just nodded.

All three women were thinking the same thing—it *was* kind of impossible, wasn't it? How could they ever really relax around each other? How could they ever sleep together? In both the act and in reality? Ryka just couldn't see it.

Worse, though, was that the Knight was now infamous with the Furies, even though none of them had known him before tonight. The greatest warrior they ever had, Kiasa, had disappeared a year ago. She had inexplicably walked away from her Spear Sisters and Ava one day and was never heard from again. Why she did this was still unknown to the Sisterhood, but, three months after her disappearance, they felt her die.

Kiasa had blocked them all out for the ninety days that she had been missing, but on her final night, she had rejoined their collective consciousness just long enough for them to feel her one last time before she disappeared forever. Her death had rocked the Sisterhood to its core, but no one knew where she'd fallen or to whom.

Last night, they discovered some of what had happened to her, or at least *who* had happened to her; the *who* being the same Knight that Ava now loved.

Ava had approached the Knight recklessly and for reasons still unclear. By all accounts, he was weak—or so it had been believed at that time. Her Furies had been surprised but not really concerned until she had discovered Kiasa's soul mark on his arm. How the Knight, *any* Knight really, could have brought down Kiasa was beyond comprehension. That he had was undeniable, however. Amazingly, Ava had forbade her Spear from avenging Kiasa then and there, and instead accepted a duel challenge.

In hindsight, the Furies now knew that this was all just subterfuge on her part because the next thing they knew, she was actively seeing him and even went out on her first date (ever) with him! Truthfully, Ryka didn't begrudge the Princess her happiness, not even if it was with the Knight. War was brutal on both sides and if Kiasa's soul mark rode the arm of the Knight, then it had been life or death for him as well. His mark would assuredly be nested on Kiasa's arm if he had not prevailed.

Ryka believed that most of the Furies would eventually come around to her way of thinking. It was easier for her because she had never met Kiasa; but for those who had, it was a devastating pill to swallow. Their champion had died to the new love interest of the Princess, and that put them all in a challenging position. All of that could have eventually worked itself out—except for what happened not even an hour after the pact was struck.

The Princess had made it *very* clear that he was not to be harmed by *any* Sister or *all* of them would be dead to her. Ava further promised that anyone who touched him would be killed by her own hand. The shock and hurt of her ultimatum struck the Sisterhood to its core, and some were resentful and angry about this pact. A few even decided to disregard it.

The unusual light source on the freeway was quite a bit closer now, and Ryka's enhanced vision discerned that it was a long convoy of cars following some of the big rigs that transported goods back and forth on the I-80. Had the trucks hemmed in the cars behind them? If so, there was probably more than enough road rage to go around down there. She would be interested to see what exactly was going on when they passed her position in a few minutes.

Ryka's eyes tracked the convoy's progress as she finally confronted the crux of the problem tonight—at least when it came to the Princess and the Sisterhood. A promise had been made to Ava to safeguard the Knight, but within thirty minutes the Furies had broken that promise.

One of the very few in the Sisterhood with the temerity to consider disregarding the new pact happened to run across the Knight by chance out in the middle of nowhere at a dilapidated farm. That he was there rescuing a Childe of the Dark, a future Fury even, had not been enough to save him from the wrath of the Furies in attendance.

Seven whole Spears, twenty-one women in total, engaged the Knight in direct defiance of Ava. That they would do so at all was an aberration. The women of the Sisterhood had honor and would typically never engage an enemy with such overwhelming odds—if at all—*particularly* if that enemy was actually there to save one of their own.

All the stars had aligned just wrong to allow it to happen. The Furies were off balance and grieving over the constant deaths that were registering with them minute by minute as Sisters fell all over the world. The Knight was alone but acted completely unafraid and even dismissive of his predicament. Most critically, though, the leader of that Warband—a storied Fury in her own right named Lilly—was also one of those who deemed the pact ill-advised and foolish. Predictably, disaster was the result.

In the history of the war, a single Knight had never fought against so many Furies at once. That he had, and won, was unbelievable. More fantastical even than that feat was that he had done so *without* using lethal force. The Knight's love for the Princess and his determination not to destroy her guardians demonstrated that he'd sacrifice his own life to ensure Ava's continued safety. If that wasn't true love, nothing was.

A more honorable and skilled foe had never been known by the Sisterhood—and a bigger blunder had not been committed by them either—than when those twenty-one attacked him. The fear among the Sisterhood now was that Ava might declare the agreement null and void whether he died or not. It was reported that he was grievously wounded and not likely to see the morning sun, making it likely that the Princess would cut them all loose.

Ava had almost died in the barn herself, appearing to use a facet of her gifts to follow him through the very doors of death. The Princess had brought him back, but just barely. Tragically, she had made it very clear that she would not live without him— and if that were true, she might soon be dead herself. Why she was so set on being with the Knight, in life *and* death, was a mystery to the Sisterhood.

Ava loved him; it was clearly known and undisputed now, but there was something more at play. Perhaps a previously unknown weakness in her formidable armor had developed. Some unbearable weight that only the Knight could help her with, maybe? In any case, it was now a huge mess with the potential to blow up in all of their faces. What would happen to the Sisterhood if she died? What if she cast them all away for breaching the pact?

The twenty-one were now acting strange and had been banished from Ava's service for attacking the Knight. Where would they go, and what was to be done about them? The Childe that the Knight had come to save had actually defended him at the tail end of the battle, pitting her Dark against her future clan. Such an action was unprecedented, and Ryka had no idea how that would play out either.

So many questions, so few answers.

The young Fury's musing was cut off suddenly as her intuition was pricked. The convoy was almost upon them, and Ryka started to feel that something was strange about it. At nearly that exact moment, her two Sisters did as well. All three were now intent on the approaching cluster of lights.

There were a hundred or more vehicles in the convoy of all makes, models and sizes. Trucks, cars, even two motorcycles— all of them bunched closely together and approaching at the same speed. This was what made their progress interesting to Ryka and her Sisters. What made the convoy forbidding was that every vehicle seemed to be going at the *exact* same speed. To Ryka's eye, there was zero variation among *any* of them.

As the convoy started to pass a chill ran up her spine, followed by an immediate adrenaline spike.

Not only was every single vehicle going at the exact same speed, but they were all trundling down the road at sixty or seventy miles per hour with six inches or less from bumper to bumper. Perfectly in unison, the convoy began streaming by them on the otherwise deserted highway. And they were only an hour from the outskirts of Sparks—where Ava was.

Falen was already on the phone before half the convoy had passed. There was no doubt in any of their minds that what they were witnessing was a threat to the Princess and the Sisters currently with her.

As soon as the convoy completely passed, the Furies would make haste back to their own vehicle hidden behind an outcropping. They would follow the mass of vehicles at a safe distance.

Ryka's body thrummed with anticipation at the thought that a battle would surely be joined tonight.

Even as Ryka thought this, the last vehicle in the convoy pulled over onto the shoulder directly in front of the three women. The car turned off, and the lights faded as a lone figure emerged.

"Bows," whispered Micheline.

Instantly, all three women held weapons, their Dark awakened by the threat. They kept silent and still for a moment as the lone figure made its way around the front of the vehicle and towards them. Ryka's eyes sharpened, and she began to stretch, seconds away from her combat form and black rage.

It was a female. Ryka's superior vision picked out the woman's features as she made her approach. Two more females got out of the car behind the first and stood next to the vehicle, looking up at the three Furies at the crest of the hill.

Falen gasped. "It's Jiren!"

At her words all three hesitated. Jiren stopped and looked up at them, a mere fifty yards away. She had been one of the three Furies who had accompanied Melhmut the Sorcerer to Utah to investigate a significant incursion by the Light. But there was nothing to fight over, so why was the Light even there? It was strange and concerning. Worse was that the Warband of nearly four dozen had all disappeared en route, and all contact had been lost. Even the three Furies before them had become unknowable to the Sisterhood. However, they had not been killed, either. They had just disappeared… until now.

The utter dark of the night, only fitfully lit by the moon, did not reveal the details of Jiren's face, but even so, Ryka knew there was something wrong with her.

"Micheline—" Ryka began worriedly before Jiren interrupted her.

With song.

"If you're happy and you know it, clap your hands!" she sang in a voice of madness and unknowable distance. Every syllable and word almost unintelligible yet, at the same time, suffocatingly intimate. Jiren clapped twice.

"If you're happy and you know it, clap your hands!" she sang again and clapped twice once more—but this time, the two Sisters standing behind her clapped too—in *perfect* unison.

"If you're happy, and you know it, and you really want to show it, clap your hands!" the thing that had once been Jiren extolled. To Ryka's horror, both Falen and Micheline no longer had bows summoned. Falen's hands actually twitched like she wanted to clap along, and Micheline's eyes were wild and unfocused.

Ryka's rage was doused in utter disbelief and dread.

"If you're happy, and you know it, stomp your feet!" sang the Other in front of them and stomped twice with the two behind her still following along in perfect unison. And Falen.

"If you're happy, and you know it, stomp your feet!" the

harbinger crooned again, voice now like honey and so sickeningly sweet. They all stomped along now. Even Ryka stomped next to the Other, and the Other near that one.

"If you're happy, and you know it, and you really want to show it, stomp your feet!" sang the one who had once been Ryka in perfect unison with the other five. As she stomped her feet in glee, perfectly in time with her other selves, she finally felt like she belonged. It was her last independent thought.

# Chapter 1

In the Knight's house, the tension in the air was thick enough to cut with a knife. The youngest Princess of the Dark, Ava, and her elite guard of Furies stood frozen in a face-off with the Arch Mage of the Light and her High Lord Paladin. In any universe, that was a surefire way to guarantee several deaths within a few seconds. To make matters worse, the Princess and her guardians had their arms full—with 250 pounds of dying Knight. It also didn't help that there was no space between the two foes—they were literally eyeball to eyeball in Kelso's lunchbox-sized front room. Chandra could have reached out and ruffled the Arch Mage's hair if she'd really wanted to—if she had no more interest in living, that was.

How could this be resolved without pretty much everyone dying? Ava wasn't sure. She briefly considered that Argenta had double-crossed her, but there was really no other path open to them. Kelso *needed* healing—right now and without delay. The Princess couldn't afford to retreat from Cassandra or fight her either, so she was stuck, watching as Kelso's life drained away by the second.

Did Kelso know something she didn't? Even mortally wounded, he was shaking in either anger or fear as he beheld the tall blonde.

"Bitch," breathed Kelso weakly, his one remaining eye locked on the Arch Mage. *Well,* Ava thought, *she now knew he was shaking from hatred.* That gladdened her a little.

"Ah, Kelso. I'm so sorry for leading you on, truly." Cassandra didn't look particularly sorry, but her tone was sympathetic. "I will try to explain what happened later, if you survive. You do want to survive, don't you?"

Kelso said nothing as he glared at her. If looks could kill the Arch Mage would have been in serious trouble.

"I'll take your silence as an affirmative if you don't mind. My ring is almost spent, and Argenta is ready to give up the ghost, too, if you know what I mean. This way, ladies. I realize none of you know your way to his bed. I do, though, so I will be happy to lead." Cassandra's face was bland, and her tone solicitous, but the glance she threw at Ava spoke volumes.

The Arch Mage wanted the Knight, too.

Gritting her teeth, Ava carried Kelso into his small bedroom and deposited him on his bed.

"Right here," instructed the beautiful blonde super killer. "This side is the most comfortable. Charlie likes to sleep on the other side. Which is kind of a pain, really…"

The Furies were frozen in dismay and shock, just going through the motions while their brains tried to catch up. Ava knew they had not yet picked up on the fact that the Arch Mage—the hands down deadliest person in the world—was taking shots at the Dark Witch, who just happened to be one of the *other* deadliest people in the world. When they figured that out, it was going to get… tense.

Ava could not allow that.

"Let's go, my warriors. Give her some space and go back to the front room." Ava started to usher her Furies out quickly, before the shock of meeting the leader of the Light wore off, and they began to examine what Cassandra had said—and who she was saying it to.

"Yes. I need the privacy," agreed the Arch Mage, again needling Ava.

"No," said Kelso suddenly. His voice was weak but firm. Iron. "She stays with me, or you can take your healing and leave."

"Even knowing that your inevitable death kills her as well? Would you truly turn me away?" Cassandra looked at Kelso curiously, her face a strange mix of true puzzlement and perhaps just a tiny smidge of hurt.

The Knight hesitated. Ava was paralyzed with indecision—she wanted more than anything to stay with Kelso, but she was afraid the Arch Mage would let him die out of pure spite if she did. While Ava had no real experience in these matters, she felt that Cassandra was more of the "If I can't have him, no one can" type.

Cassandra hesitated herself.

"Fine," she muttered finally. "She can stay."

Unceremoniously, she unbuckled Argenta from the Knight's chest and effortlessly lifted him to pull the sword out from underneath. Kelso shivered slightly in apparent revulsion at the Arch Mage's touch. Cassandra pretended not to notice, but Ava could tell that she had.

With a little more force than necessary, the Arch Mage tossed Argenta carelessly to the far corner, where the sword clattered loudly against the wall before miraculously coming to rest hilt upright.

"Since you're staying, you might as well help," said the Arch Mage, casting a critical eye over Kelso's wounds. "These rents are actually worse than I imagined."

"It sounds like you knew he was going to be wounded," Ava said suspiciously as she approached and knelt beside her Knight.

"I did," said Cassandra distractedly. "Put your hand here." She swiftly grabbed Ava's hand, pressing it firmly on the bandage at his side. Ava's Dark recoiled from the touch for a split second but rallied and held firm against the Light of the Arch Mage. A massive shock jolted both women, which also served to shock Kelso.

The Knight's breathing faltered for a second, and his eye fluttered shut. Unconscious again, he slumped bonelessly deeper into the bed.

Cassandra smiled grimly. "We're going to lose him if we keep at it. I'll banish my Light if you do the same to your Dark. We will both be exposed and vulnerable, which makes it interesting at least. On your word?"

"You have it," said Ava quickly and suited her actions to the promise by immediately reigning in her Dark. Her only thought was of Kelso, and she knew he absolutely could not take another shock from them.

21

"Wow. You're quite smitten with the grim Knight, aren't you?" Cassandra said derisively, but she also quieted her Light.

"Yes."

Cassandra produced a pair of medical scissors from... somewhere. Honestly, Ava didn't have a clue where she could have been hiding them due to the skimpiness of her outfit, but they were suddenly in the Arch Mage's hand. The blonde woman started cutting bandages off the Knight quickly and efficiently, her brow furrowed in concentration.

Ava stayed silent as Cassandra worked to uncover the Knight's injuries. As the extent of them became clear to the Princess, tears formed and silently traced their way down her cheeks. Ava couldn't understand how he was still alive.

The Arch Mage was quiet as she worked, but Ava saw her face tighten as she uncovered more and more of the Knight's wounds. Kelso's leg was an absolute mess, and his face was a ruin. His Light had given up and was nowhere to be seen, but at least he was not bleeding anymore. The wounds had been staunched well, but he was still oozing from his ruined eye. Ava wanted to throw up in horror at how badly he was maimed there. A jagged gash ran down his face, starting at his scalp and going clear through his eye and into his cheek.

It looked like a dagger or sword had caught him, probably by the scarred Fury back at the barn. Ava felt a surge of hate for that woman, and only her promise to Kelso kept her from vowing to kill that Fury the moment she had a chance.

Ominously, the Arch Mage leaned back with a sigh. Her beautiful and pixie-like face marred by a frown.

"Do you want the good news or the bad news?" she asked Ava suddenly, eyes still locked on Kelso.

Ava was at her breaking point; it was an easy choice.

"The good news."

"Well, I think I can save him. Barely. It will take all my power and skill to do so, but it can be done. I think." Cassandra sounded a little unsure, in direct opposition to her words.

Ava's heart sank. "And the bad news?"

"I can save his eye or his leg. Not both."

That was also an easy choice.

"Save his leg," Ava said without hesitation.

Cassandra looked up at her sharply. "Are you sure? He will be hideously disfigured and blinded in that eye." The Arch Mage searched Ava's face as she spoke, measuring her.

"I don't care how he looks," Ava said truthfully.

"Really?" Cassandra seemed a little doubtful.

"I would much rather he be able to walk, to stand, to fight. If Kelso feels crippled, if he feels like he is a burden, he will be lost." Ava remembered the conversation they'd had in his mind— what his first objection to coming back to her had been. Yes, Kelso had worried that his destroyed face would embarrass her,

23

how he would not be worthy of her, but his first concern had been that he would be an anchor.

"I'm impressed, Princess, and I agree," said the Arch Mage grudgingly. "To add to the good news, then, I believe that when I heal him *this* time, he will walk pain-free and without a limp."

Ava's hand flew to her mouth as she looked up at the blonde in sudden hope. "Really? Why?"

"Because the first time I tried to heal him, it was from a wound caused by Argenta." The Arch Mage glanced over at the sword with another frown. "Her wounds are not meant to be healed. It was all I could do to keep her from eventually killing him, in fact."

"What's different now?"

"Ironically, his leg has been shattered so thoroughly by your Furies that Argenta's damage was destroyed as well. It's like an old scar that was improperly stitched has been reopened and now can be stitched correctly." Cassandra stood swiftly and went to a small backpack on Kelso's computer desk.

Rummaging around, the Arch Mage pulled out a wand about a foot and a half long with a blunt point. It was a beautiful artifact, runed all the way around from the base of its handle to its tip. It fairly thrummed with power.

"What is that?" Ava asked, awe coloring her words.

"A very rare item. It is my bonded." Cassandra held the wand lovingly, turning it over in her hands so Ava could see it better.

24

"What does it do?"

"Among other things, it draws power—permanently—from a willing host and allows that power to then be redirected in any way the bearer desires. All of Kelso's wards, his weapons, his armor, everything... was done with the help of this wand." The Arch Mage hurried back to Kelso, dragging the chair behind her.

"Permanently?" Ava asked with a small sense of alarm.

"Yes. It is not the most pleasant of feelings, and what you give up stays gone. You can regenerate your power again, but it is a slow process, and you are weakened in the meantime." Cassandra paused. "It took me weeks to get back to where I was the last time I visited Kelso. I gave him so much that I felt vulnerable for the first time in hundreds of years."

"So, the wards around this house are actually made up of your own Light?" Ava was surprised—and secretly impressed—that the Arch Mage had been willing to sacrifice so much for the Knight. The Princess ruthlessly squashed that budding admiration by reminding herself that the blonde woman had done so because she had the hots for Kelso, too.

For a gimpy stone-faced Knight, he certainly got the ladies. Somehow. He owned a stinky but kind-of-cute dog and a tricked-out but sort-of-old Jeep. And that was about it. How, then, did he still manage to attract some of the most beautiful and powerful women on the planet? Literally! Ava was going to chastise him thoroughly once he got better. She would need to keep an eagle eye on him from now on before some other supermodel-type appeared out of nowhere, lusting after him.

It was ridiculous and maddening.

Unbidden, a memory of Argenta flashed in her mind. *You got to be kidding me,* she thought. There was no way Argenta was warming up to her Knight, too, was there? Argenta wasn't even human!

Cassandra laughed suddenly. "Your expression is telling. I totally know what you're thinking." She glanced over at Kelso's ruined visage for a moment. "I don't think his face will even hinder him, really. Maybe we're attracted to the Knight because he has some secret gift? I've seen stranger powers over the course of the war. Still, it's too bad. It would take the unique healing of a Fury to save that eye now. Once I expend my power on fixing his leg, the eye will be beyond my prowess."

Ava nodded dully. Her decision was sound, but she knew Kelso was going to be horrified by his new face. It didn't matter, and there was nothing she could do about it anyway. Ava wasn't attracted to the Knight due to some strange gift of his—she was attracted to Kelso because he was Kelso. Only that, and she didn't care if he was scarred. That Cassandra could even wonder about his worth, even in passing, meant her affection for the Knight was nowhere near Ava's.

Kelso was *her* Knight, and he always would be.

"I need to summon my Light now, so you have to let him go. Take a break and make sure that your Furies and my Paladin are playing nice in the other room. I haven't heard any explosions yet, so that's encouraging at least."

Ava nodded again and released Kelso with one last squeeze. She stood up and started to make her way out of the room.

"Ava," said the Arch Mage suddenly, almost nervously.

The Princess turned to look at the dangerous blonde who had promised to mend her Knight.

"I'm going to be weakened after I do what I must to save Kelso, and…"

"You want to make sure I won't strike at you?" Ava kept her face smooth and inscrutable as she looked back at Cassandra.

"Well, yes."

"You're saving Kelso; you have my word." Ava turned to make her way out again but then stopped and turned back. The Arch Mage was already beginning to draw power from herself, her lips twisted slightly in discomfort. The runes on the wand began to glow with her Light, brightening steadily as she drew more into it.

The question that had come to Ava died on her lips. It was stupid anyway, and the Arch Mage was already busy. With a sigh, Ava opened the door and walked out into the room.

She immediately pictured the old western stand-offs in movies, where combatants sized each other up before everyone drew down and started blasting. Ava was certain that the only reason she and the Arch Mage had not heard 'explosions' aplenty was because Carmen and Charlie stood directly in the middle of the room between two clearly incensed and glowering factions.

On one side stood her three Furies, staring death at the Paladin. As exhausted as they were, Ava knew they were one small trigger away from raging. Only the dog and Carmen had stopped them from doing so already.

For his part, the Paladin was favoring the three clearly furious women with a malevolent grin. An enormous warhammer rested on his shoulder, clutched tightly in his right hand. Ava knew he could bring it to bear in a quick second should he choose to, but it wouldn't be nearly enough against her Furies.

The Paladin was clearly insane. To intentionally antagonize three already frayed Furies was just outright stupid. Ava didn't care how powerful he thought he was; two of those three Furies were some of the deadliest in the entire Sisterhood. If the Paladin didn't watch himself, he was going to find that out the hard way.

Quickly, Ava stepped into the middle of the room too, her back to the Paladin. "My warriors—" she began to say warningly before Chandra broke in, nearly spitting in anger.

"Do you know what he said, Ava? He said he knew that many of us were dying the world over, and that was a good thing because it was less work for him."

Ava was shocked. That her Furies had not already attacked was almost unbelievable. The sheer crazy bravado and arrogance to say something like that to them was… well… she had no words. It was also stunningly cruel.

"Are you the only one who can honor and love their friends?" asked Ava over her shoulder while still pinning the Furies with her eyes where they stood. She allowed the disgust she felt at the man to freely color her question.

The Paladin laughed. "Your Furies are savages; what do they know of true friendship? Hell, they turn into demons! Please. They wouldn't know a true friend if one came up and bit them on their scantily clad asses."

"Insult them again, Marcus, and I will kill you myself." Ava had rarely been as furious as she was right then. On top of everything else that had happened tonight, this was just too much. Suddenly, she was directly in front of him, just a foot from his face. The Princess didn't even remember moving.

Unbelievably, the small man smiled. "Big mistake, gorgeous."

"Marcus," said the Arch Mage, her voice verging on annoyance. "Stand down."

The Paladin's eyes twitched almost imperceptibly at Cassandra's command. "You're lucky, Princess. You have no idea..."

Ava realized that she really didn't have any idea of how "lucky" she was, or at least why he would think that. Something was *really* off with the Paladin—so she read him.

Instantly, the Princess knew what her mistake had been and how to overcome it. Apparently, the Paladin was an unstoppable juggernaut in close combat—his gift made him invulnerable in hand-to-hand battle. The closer you were to him, the stronger he was. Ava would be killed if she engaged him for any length of time at less than twenty feet. Marcus was cocky in his standoff

29

with the Furies because they were all in an enclosed area, and, so he would absolutely clean the floor with them.

*Good to know.*

It also occurred to Ava that Marcus was a unique foil to a raging Ebon Knight. He might just be the one combatant on either side of the Conflict that could dismiss Argenta's lethality out of hand. Now Ava knew why Cassandra had brought the clearly unhinged man: he was her insurance policy.

In seconds, Ava knew everything she needed to know about the Paladin, and she absolutely could kill him if she had to. If she wanted to.

The Princess leaned in, and Marcus's grin returned.

"Princess, attacking me will be the last thing you ever do. I promise." His arrogance and desire for her to try was peaking. *Time to burst his bubble.*

"My warriors," Ava said, never breaking eye contact with the man, "if he doesn't shut up and obey the Arch Mage like the puppet he is, feel free to kill him."

The Paladin outright laughed at her instructions.

"Just retreat about, oh, thirty feet or so and bring down this arrogant coward with your arrows. Keep at least that distance between you and him at all costs. If he attacks in here, just take out a wall on your retreat. I'll replace it." Ava got a *lot* of satisfaction from the look of startled panic that instantly replaced the Paladin's gloating leer at her instructions.

"How—" he started to say, but Ava interrupted him.

"My Knight called you an asshole, and I see his description was very accurate. I also know why Kelso recognized you. You were sent to keep an eye on him whenever he mingled with others of the Light, yes? Instead of befriending him, or at least treating him like a fellow warrior, you goaded him. You *wanted* him to attack you. I know what you *think* you can do against him if it comes down to a fight. A fight you want." Ava's voice was ice, but her eyes were embers of utter disdain and anger.

She leaned in even closer.

"It won't be enough," she whispered in his ear. "I'm with Kelso now, and I *will* bring you down with Fel Spikes at a distance before you can engage him. It won't even be hard." Ava straightened away from the Paladin, eyes searching his to make absolutely sure he understood she could kill him without effort. Sweat rolled down his bald pate, and his eyes were wild. Inside, he was panicked and unsure, frantically questioning how she could possibly know his secret.

"Ava," came the Arch Mage's voice again, "that's so not cool."

Ava laughed bitterly. The Arch Mage didn't even sound upset that Ava had so easily neutralized her "ace card," which meant she had other contingency plans in place if this shindig went south.

It was an uncomfortable hour. They all watched Kelso's smallish big screen, volume turned low. Ava sat in one of the chairs, and the Paladin sat next to her in the other. Carmen was huddled with Charlie in her lap near the fire. The three Furies stood directly behind the Paladin, itching to kill him—at least when not working the phones with the other Spears tasked with coordinating their continuing retreat from the Dark worldwide.

Ava could only imagine what they wanted to do to him, how many daggers they wanted to sink in his back. Marcus was unaffected by their hate and proximity, though, and why wouldn't he be? They were so close they could have touched him if they wanted to, but he was completely at ease, safe in his invulnerability.

On the outside, at least.

Inside, Marcus was terrified. Never had any of the Dark ferreted out his secret gift, and now he was feeling vulnerable, which was something he had never felt before. The Paladin's doubt was not helping with his already tenuous hold on sanity, and his thoughts were distracting and unsettling.

Ava pretended to watch the TV show, as did all others in the small room, but she was certain none of them could recall what they had watched this past hour, so furiously were they all plotting. Even Carmen shot the man quick glances of distaste when she thought the Paladin wouldn't notice. Unfortunately for her, he had. Marcus was upset that he had let the girl and the dog stop him from rolling toward the Furies earlier when Ava and Cassandra were in the other room. The Paladin was sure he could have killed all of them before Ava intervened.

Ava agreed.

She knew her Furies would be no match for him in close quarters; no one was. The Princess herself was not, nor was Kelso with Argenta in hand. Now, though? Ava had every confidence that the Furies could take Marcus out. They would understand that her instructions were key to that battle even if they didn't know why.

If Marcus fought any of them, alone or together, the outcome would be the same. They would live. He would die. Everyone, save him, would live happily ever after: The End.

But *would* they get to live happily ever after, dead Paladin or not? The Knight could still die, and with him, Ava. That would splinter the Furies further, but at least Ava knew Chandra, Jae, and even Misima would care for Carmen no matter what. It would make letting go just a little easier when the time came. *If* the time came.

Ava fervently hoped it wouldn't come to that, but she had never realized just how desperate she was for a particular kind of companionship until she met Kelso. She was a desert, and he brought the rain.

Now Ava was at a loss for what to do. Even exhausted, she fretted that she should be doing *something* of worth, but there really wasn't anything she could think of. Her senses were finely tuned, listening for anything from the room that held her Knight and the Arch Mage while also alert to counter any sneaky attack from the unbalanced Paladin beside her.

The Princess knew who the Paladin was, or perhaps more aptly, she knew *of* him. It was hard to label any of the Light as butchers or madmen, but Marcus was one of the few exceptions. He was a legend in his own right. Seemingly reckless, the small man next to her was infamous for leaping into large groups of foes, swinging his intimidating hammer with abandon. Now she knew why.

His massive armor protected him from most long-range attacks, and he was always quick to close the distance and engage. When he did his gift was potent. Based on the snippets of thought she had picked up from Marcus, his power drained and weakened an attacking enemy the closer that enemy was. At a certain point, typically within seconds, his Light literally *melted* the enemy he engaged—the flesh would turn waxy and run in rivulets to the ground as his hapless opponent died screaming.

Marcus had killed many of the Dark over the years, and Ava suspected his arm was nearly solid black with the weight of all he had harvested. His gift was devastating, yes, but his Achilles' heel was dramatic, and Ava didn't fear him as a possible foe. His fighting prowess and gifts were not her concern, though—his spiraling madness was.

Barely held in check, Marcus was a loose cannon ready to blow at any minute and at anyone with zero warning. Being around him was tedious: she couldn't let her guard down for a second. Marcus had even considered engaging the Arch Mage a few times. His diseased mind turned over and over on itself in constant and dizzying motion even as he sat utterly still, pretending to watch TV just like everyone else.

Why in the world had the Arch Mage brought him? It was

folly to rely on someone in Marcus's state of mind. She must know how close he was to going off his rocker, so there had to be another reason she'd brought him other than as a counter to Kelso.

It made no sense.

Almost as if summoned by Ava's gloomy thoughts, Cassandra suddenly opened the door and stuck her head out of the room. "Ava, could you ask your guard to leave the house for a few moments, please? We will be getting visitors shortly, and I think it... best... if they were not in here. Take the dog, too."

Ava turned to her Furies and nodded. With one last venomous look at the still-seated Paladin, they gathered Carmen and the bulldog and went outside. Ava felt immeasurably better now that her Furies had gained some distance from him and almost sighed in relief when the door shut behind them.

"Marcus, please sit tight for a few minutes longer. I will be back out shortly." The Arch Mage smiled warmly at the Paladin, but Ava could tell it was a forced smile. *She knows he's about to lose it entirely*, Ava thought.

The Paladin didn't even acknowledge the Arch Mage's words as he sat stone still, eyes glued to the television while his mind raced and raced.

"Come see your Knight," Cassandra said in a low voice, eyes still locked on Marcus while she moved aside to let Ava pass. She watched the Paladin as one might watch a snake.

Once Ava was fully in the room, the Arch Mage hurriedly shut the door. Cassandra's overwhelming and incomparable Light was long gone. She had expended an enormous amount of power on Kelso, and Ava could tell she was barely on her feet.

"What were you thinking, bringing him here?" hissed Ava in a low voice as soon as the door closed.

The Arch Mage didn't answer her immediately, and Ava forgot her irritation for a moment upon reaching Kelso's side. Tears poured from her eyes in a weird mixture of sympathy and gratitude. Her sympathy came from seeing the state of her Knight's face—it was truly disfigured. Ava worried how Kelso would view himself once he woke and knew she would have to work *very* hard to show Kelso that her affection for him could never be diminished by something as trivial as a torn-up face and lost eye.

Ava hiccupped a small sob at the thought. It was all true, but the Knight wouldn't believe it. Kelso would always be self-conscious around her, even more so than he was now. He would also feel uncomfortable around *anyone* who saw him too, human or otherwise. Only time would make him feel more at ease, and time was something they did *not* have. The Princess saw a very dark road ahead with him, but it didn't matter; she would see it through.

Ava also cried with gratitude, however. Nearly all of the Knight's other wounds, large and small, were gone, fading, or healing rapidly. It was amazing. Not quite to a Fury's potency, but close enough.

He would live, and he would walk.

36

"Thank you," Ava said fervently, tears still dripping down her face. "You managed to do much more than I thought possible. I am in your debt."

The Arch Mage sniffed. "Nonsense. We both know I did it more for Kelso than for you. Much more. I do appreciate the fact that you haven't slaughtered me out of hand, however. I'm pretty spent at the moment, so it's probably crossed your mind, right?"

"Twice. No, scratch that, three times now," Ava confirmed, eyes still glued to her Knight.

"Well, you gave your word, and I believed you would uphold it. Because of that belief, I expended my power recklessly on his behalf—much more than I had originally anticipated or planned." The beautiful blonde paused for a moment in thought. "I actually can't remember the last time I was this weak. Over a thousand years, at least."

"You're really that old? Why would you be after my Kelso? Isn't he a little young for you?" Ava couldn't keep a bit of sarcasm from coloring her words; she sounded very accusatory, even to herself.

The Arch Mage startled Ava by laughing. "I'm the cougar of all cougars, apparently, but I never really thought about it like that." She moved next to Ava and stared down at the Knight as well. "I'm a woman too, and like you, I am mostly human. Well, maybe a bit more exotic than you are, but we are reasonably close in power. I came here a few months ago to help him because I owe him—probably more than I can ever repay. Falling for him... a little... was never the optimal plan, but I couldn't

37

help it. There is something about Kelso that makes me want to protect him—even if he could never understand it. I don't think he will ever give me the chance to get close to him again, though."

"You're right," agreed Ava happily. "He really does despise you. Sorry."

"You don't sound very sorry," the Arch Mage observed dryly.

"Yeah."

The other woman sighed and sat down next to Kelso on the bed, pulling her legs up to sit crosswise. Apparently exhausted, the blonde woman placed her head in her hands morosely.

"So, I know you're happy with my work, but there are a few things to keep in mind." The Arch Mage didn't look at the Princess as she spoke, staring instead at her now dormant wand lying next to Kelso's head.

"What is it?" Ava asked, a momentary dread descending on her. *How much more bad news could she take tonight?*

"Well, he will walk again. Probably as soon as he wakes up, in fact. I don't believe there will be any discernible limp or stiffness in his knee or leg anymore. The damage wrought by Argenta was indeed overridden by what the Furies did to him, and thankfully, I could heal what the Furies were capable of—brutal as it was." Cassandra sighed again and ran her fingers through her hair. Ava almost felt bad for her; the woman seemed so exhausted. Almost.

"Ok, not seeing an issue here yet," Ava prompted.

"He is healed, yes, but he picked up quite a lot of scars even then. His face, leg, ribs, and several other points around his body are going to be marked up pretty good for the rest of his life. I'm not a Fury. I don't have their unique powers when it comes to healing. His leg, in particular, is going to look a little rough. It will be perfectly useable, but it will be very obvious that almost his entire bone was sticking out of it once upon a time." The Arch Mage paused to allow Ava to process what she had just said.

The Princess smiled confidently. "Chicks dig scars; I heard that earlier tonight in a country song. So, I'm ok with it. The more scars, the better, from our point of view."

"I never knew that. Well, good for us!" The Arch Mage smiled ruefully. "I'm going to bet that the singer was a male, however."

"Good guess!" Ava confirmed. "To be fair, the song is really catchy, and I can't get it out of my head. Kelso might have a better shot than he believes at converting me to his country cult. Don't tell him, though, please; he'll just get all arrogant about it." At Ava's words, the wise and deadly blonde woman just looked at her in disbelief.

"Maybe you *are* a better fit for him," she murmured under her breath.

Ava shrugged. "I think so."

The Princess really wanted to reach out and touch Kelso, but the Arch Mage's Light was still all over his body, healing and repairing, reknitting, strengthening, and just generally putting him back together right before her eyes. It was very impressive.

"Well, ok, then. I think my job here is done…" the Arch Mage said, readying herself to leave.

"Just stop," Ava said, still not looking up from the rapidly healing Knight.

Cassandra paused and looked up at Ava questioningly.

"I know I'm young, particularly compared to your decrepit butt, but there's no way you're just going to leave. Get on with the next act, please. What else is there to do?" Ava looked the Arch Mage in her eyes challengingly. "Something has to be done about your Paladin, and I don't think you actually brought him here as a foil to Kelso. You knew I would never allow that." She looked back down at the Knight's face, "And I also think you believe there is something that can be done for Kelso's eye. What is it?"

The Arch Mage laughed lightly and clapped in delight. "Ah, I am so pleased you caught on. Bravo! I loved it all—except for the decrepit shot."

"Spill it."

"Which part do you want me to answer first?" queried the blonde, settling back down next to Kelso.

"Let's go with the easy one first. Why is Marcus here?" Ava met the green eyes of the Arch Mage fearlessly, seeking to ferret out any half-truths or deceptions as soon as they were uttered.

"To die," answered the Arch Mage promptly and without any hint of remorse.

"That's really cold of you, but I can't say I'm displeased at all. Why not kill him yourself if you want him dead?"

"I don't want him dead, but no other path is open to him now. I have taken Marcus as far as I can and have constantly interceded on his behalf to even get him to this point. Now that *you* have chosen *this* path, Marcus's fate is sealed. He dies tonight." The Arch Mage didn't blink or shrink from Ava's inspection at all. She was telling the truth.

Since it was now almost three in the morning, Ava figured that *tonight* meant much later on… several hours at least. Truthfully, the Princess wasn't 100 percent sure that the Furies would let him live that long anyway.

"Ok, we can get into that more in a minute. How about my second question? Can something be done with Kelso's face? And if so, what?"

"We're not quite at the point yet where I can guarantee his eye and face can be… healed. I guess that is the best term for it, yes."

Ava was verging on awe with what the Arch Mage was apparently revealing. "So, you see the future, or something like that? Is that part of your gift?"

"Yes. I see many, many paths all the time, with only one sure ending. Before that ending, there are as many variables as grains of sand on a beach. And you have a decision to make very shortly that will determine if Kelso *might* have a chance to be healed fully. I cannot tell you more, though." Cassandra was either a master liar, or she was still telling the truth. If Ava had to bet, she would wager that the woman sitting comfortably next to her Knight spoke truth and nothing but.

"What decision?" asked Ava curiously.

In response, the Arch Mage just smiled and shook her head. A few seconds passed before she inexplicably put a hand to her ear like she was listening for something. Exactly as she did this, Ava felt a wave of worry flow through her bonds. Her Furies were uncomfortable about something. Very uncomfortable.

Chandra, standing in the front yard, called to Ava, "Princess, can you come out, please?" Even muted by the walls of the house, her voice sounded startled, unsure, and sad.

At her words, the Arch Mage grabbed her wand and then got up and opened the door for Ava, left hand sweeping across her body in the classic "after you" gesture, a sardonic grin on her face.

With one last look at Kelso, Ava made her way to the door but then stopped and looked up at the taller woman. "You knew this was going to happen, right?"

The blonde woman nodded.

"So, you follow prophecy? Or are you the source of prophecy?"

The Arch Mage snorted indelicately. "Prophecies are for chumps. Let's go."

# Chapter 2

Both women moved to the front room, where the doomed Paladin remained motionless in the same position Ava had left him in. His eyes were slightly glazed, and a small ribbon of drool hung unnoticed from the corner of his mouth.

Ava didn't need to read him to know that the Paladin was shut down with terror. Her knowledge had apparently been just enough to push him off the ledge of sanity. It looked like he was spinning round and round in his head, spiraling deeper into his insecurities as he went. Ava had no interest in reading his mind further; she was afraid of the hellish landscape she might witness within.

Her experience with Kelso had been necessary but terrifying. The Princess had never delved into someone's head as completely as she had the Knight's, and she now realized that there were dangers in doing so. The Princess feared being drawn into the Paladin's world as a result, particularly with what she now knew about her gift.

Both women stopped and inspected the Paladin silently for a moment.

"I won't leave him in here with Kelso," Ava stated firmly, eyes still glued on the small man. A part of her actually felt sorry for him, in spite of him saying such horrible and hateful things to her Furies. The Princess knew without a doubt that Marcus had not been fully in control of himself when he had goaded them on so viciously. Subconsciously, a part of him probably wanted to die.

"No, I agree," said the Arch Mage, eyes sympathetic as she examined him too. "Marcus was once a great and honorable man, but his madness has taken him over piece by piece for hundreds of years. The effort and time I have spent getting him to this point would startle you; I have done absolutely everything I can for him."

"He's not infected by the Other, is he?" Ava's blood ran cold at the thought, and she wondered why she hadn't considered that possibility before.

"No," said Cassandra again. "We aren't Gods, Ava. Sometimes, we succumb to infirmities in mind, spirit, or body. His madness is his own. It doesn't make it easier to accept, but..." she trailed off and sighed.

"I feel sorry for him," Ava admitted, almost guiltily. "Is there no hope? Can he not be restored?"

The Arch Mage shook her head.

"His course is set. I will tell you this, though. He will be redeemed at his end. I have managed to get Marcus to this point in the hope of that small mercy. And I believe his death will have meaning and honor."

Ava nodded. Even as both women discussed his end, not fifteen feet from where Marcus sat, he was oblivious to them, lost in his own madness.

Cassandra cleared her throat loudly. "Lord Commander, I

need your services. Let us sally forth, Marcus."

At her words, the Paladin shook himself awake and glanced over at the women. When his eyes met Ava's, he visibly flinched. It was heartbreaking to see him so thoroughly beaten and cowed merely by her knowledge of his vulnerability and her threat to exploit it. He was a dangerous man who had menaced her Furies, but he was not a predator and never had been. As such, Ava held no unbending animus towards him.

The Paladin was just really sick. Ava regarded Marcus much as she would a rabid animal that needed to be put down—the need to do so was absolutely necessary, but it was not the animal's fault. Ava's eyes prickled slightly at the thought. Very slightly.

"Steady, Princess. Stay the course. We all die eventually, and his death might well be glorious indeed," whispered the Arch Mage featherlight in her ear.

The Paladin stood. His movements reminded Ava of a puppet. It was like he was not quite in control of himself, and his body acted solely through muscle memory; the higher intelligence that made him who he was now fled.

"I don't know what you have planned or what you think you see," Ava turned her head to look the Arch Mage in the face, "but it will all come to naught if he threatens my Furies again. I *will* kill him myself."

"I know," Cassandra answered blithely. "It could have happened like that, sure. It won't now; that path is closed. We do need to get outside, however."

Marcus followed them mutely out into the cold night. It was moderately snowing, and the scene outside was idyllic. A car turned at the corner and made its way slowly down the middle of the street. Its headlights illuminated close to seventy women standing silently in the frigid weather, most in bare feet and all only wearing stretchable shorts, sports bras, and the like. Some had been standing motionless for so long that snow had accumulated on their shoulders and heads. It was a surreal sight, and Ava stopped short midway down Kelso's driveway, trying to reconcile what she was seeing.

The driver of the vehicle was a sleeper, oblivious to the true nature of things, and, as such, never even slowed as their lights illuminated woman after woman on the street. The mass of Furies pressed up against the ward line in three distinct groups, not quite touching it, but close enough to do so if they wished.

That much of the scene alone was a little unusual but not extraordinary. What was different about this grouping of Furies chilled Ava to the bone. The seven Spears she had exiled were standing between the two larger groups. The outcasted ones, led by their scarred warrior, were staring at Kelso's house intently. All twenty-one were present, and they stood closer to the line than any, as if determined to push in no matter the cost.

The other fifty or so Furies surrounded the outcasts, one group to each side. These women were not looking at the house. They were staring silently at the Furies Ava had banished, and none looked happy to see them here.

Contrary to everything Ava knew about the Sisterhood and the Furies in general, the mood in the street seemed tinged with possible violence, as if battle could break out between the groups at any moment.

The Princess was shocked.

Ava had made it *very* clear to the twenty-one women that they were never to be near her again. Why, then, were they standing in the street, not forty feet from where Kelso lay recovering in his bed? An ember of anger blossomed in her heart. Had they come here to try to finish the job?

The Princess drifted forward with the snow until she stood five feet in front of their scarred leader, planting herself firmly between the Fury and Kelso's home. Utter silence descended as the close to eighty supernaturally fast and strong beings, all accustomed to violence and well suited to it, stood perfectly still—hardly breathing.

Well, eighty warriors and one English Bulldog.

Behind Ava's Furies at the rear, Charlie broke free of Carmen's light grip as she stood transfixed by the scene. Instead of heading back inside the house to snuggle with Kelso, the dog inexplicably beelined to Ava. He sat down quite deliberately next to Ava's feet and calmly regarded the scarred woman who had almost killed his master only a few hours earlier.

Remarkably, his presence broke the mood that had settled over the women, and several from all three groups turned their heads to watch him. Some of the women even smiled slightly, which seemed to be Charlie's gift: anyone who met him liked him.

The scarred leader of the ostracized group tracked the dog as well, but she didn't smile. That same woman, whom Ava had specifically and unambiguously warned to stay away, looked at Charlie for a moment in puzzlement, then up to Ava.

"Is there something wrong with your dog, then?" she asked with a thick Irish burr.

"What?" Ava was caught completely off guard by the question and spared a quick glance down at the dog near her feet. Charlie was sitting on his butt facing the Furies, his two back legs ridiculously extended past his front two. His tongue was out, completely ruining his otherwise distinguished face. "No, he's fine," Ava's eyes settled back on the woman again. "Why?"

"His tongue's out." The large Fury jerked her head quickly towards the dog since she couldn't raise her arm to point without losing it to the ward line. At her words, several other women from the three groups looked at the dog, too. Charlie realized he was the focal point of dozens of eyes and wilted a little under their combined stare.

Ava came to his defense with the only thing she could think of.

"It's Tongue Out Tuesday. Obviously." The Princess almost winced. Never in her life had she wanted to physically claw back words even as they left her mouth. There was nothing to do now but roll with it, however—it was already out.

The large woman frowned. From one of the other groups, a

Fury whispered, "It's Saturday, isn't it?" Several women nodded at her words, but no one else spoke.

Ava cleared her throat. "Well, it's Tongue Out Tuesday somewhere. Charlie knows. Time zone changes and such." Ava was going to wring Kelso's neck over this humiliation later, when he was better.

Several more women now looked at the Princess with varying degrees of disbelief and even worry. The Arch Mage cleared her throat behind Ava, but it sounded suspicious: like she was actually holding back a laugh. The whirling snow should have melted mid-flight within a five-foot radius of Ava, such was her embarrassment. Kelso was in BIG trouble for this!

Time to move on.

"I commanded you to remove yourself forever from my presence. You no longer serve me. I made that very clear, did I not?" At her words, all the Furies snapped out of the spell Charlie had woven and refocused on the matter at hand. Still, the mood was not nearly as precarious as it had been.

"You did," agreed the large Fury calmly, face unperturbed.

"Then why are you here, in complete opposition to the directions I gave you?"

"Because we no longer serve you." The woman stood easily, and confidently, and her words made perfect sense—to her and her cohort at least. Ava and the rest of the Furies were confused.

"I don't understand. You attacked my Knight; you lost. I

banished you from my person and instructed you to find another to serve. I will no longer have you. Why, then—again—are you here?"

The large woman's eyes tracked back up to the house and even to the room where Kelso lay. Her voice was serene. "We have come to serve *him*, Princess. If he'll have us."

If the silence had been deep before, it was nothing to the complete absence of sound that now settled over the street. Ava was frozen in shock, as were all the Furies, except for the twenty-one mad women in the center.

"You... can't?" Ava was so off-balance that her statement turned into a question instead.

"Why not? Has he died, or is he going to die?" The Fury was still calm, but her question carried an undertone to it that belayed her casualness.

"No. He will live." At her words, a tenseness that she hadn't even recognized fell away from the Knight's would-be guardians. A few even smiled in relief.

The large Fury just nodded. "That is good indeed."

"Look... you. What is your name, anyway?" Ava was completely discombobulated; *this wasn't really happening, was it?*

"Lilly."

"Look, Lilly, why would he take you on? Why do you want to serve him in the first place? Why should I allow it?" Ava could see so many issues with this mad course of action that she hardly knew where to begin.

Lilly looked away from the house and met Ava's eyes calmly. "I don't know that he'll accept us. If he doesn't, well then, it's onto plan B." Her eyes fell slightly. "We want to serve him because he has both honor and skill. He's brave and filled with faith. The Knight is worthy of the likes of us." Lilly's eyes fell farther to the ground between her feet, and she no longer sounded steady. "You should allow us the chance to accompany him. His eye is... rent... and he'll be needing more than just you to guard his blind spot."

Ava saw red for a moment and closed her eyes. She breathed deeply. Without opening them again, she whispered, "It *was* you, wasn't it?"

"Aye, it was," the large Fury agreed sadly, "and I would pledge my life and my death to make it up to him."

"We're all to blame, Princess," spoke another of the twenty-one. "We all bear that burden. Please give us the chance to ask him."

Ava opened her eyes. She had regained control of her rage, just barely, but there was no way she could hang around with Lilly day after day—along with the rest of them—while they self-righteously babysat the Knight they had maimed. Her Knight was down an *eye* because of them!

Sighing in distress, she glanced back to read the expressions on her Furies, but instead, her eyes were drawn to the Arch

51

Mage. Cassandra had a slight smile on her face as she stared at Lilly, and in her right hand, she held the Wand. As Ava's eyes fell on it, the Arch Mage tapped it once against the palm of her left hand.

The puzzle came together rapidly then. Ava had almost asked the Arch Mage if a Fury's Dark could be drawn into her wand much as Cassandra's Light could, but hadn't, thinking it was stupid. The Princess had *not* given up on the thought entirely, though, particularly because the Arch Mage had kept mentioning the Furies' healing prowess.

Cassandra had been dropping hints all night in preparation for this moment. As soon as the Princess realized this, her eyes flew up to meet the Arch Mage's. The incredibly sexy blonde woman winked at her.

Numb with the possibilities, Ava turned back to Lilly once more.

"You said you wanted to serve him, even unto death, because his eye was torn out, yes?" Ava folded her hands over her stomach to keep them from shaking.

Lilly was confused. "Aye. He is diminished by my actions, and I want to make amends. More so because he's worthy of us to try."

"Ok," Ava nodded, "what if you could help him to heal? What if it hurt to do so and weakened you in the process?"

Lilly frowned. "Sure, I would. We all would, but that's impossible."

"It's not," declared Cassandra suddenly, stepping forward to stand next to Ava. "I can facilitate the regeneration of his eye—with you and yours helping, of course."

The large Fury inspected the beautiful blonde standing next to Ava with obvious distaste. The Princess could almost read her thoughts even without the use of her gift: the Fury was *not* pleased that one such as Cassandra had any interest in Kelso at all.

Ava's estimation of Lilly inched up just a smidge.

Cassandra smiled. "I really can help the Knight with your assistance. I swear it."

Lilly dismissed her with a snort. "Princess, who is this blonde home-wrecker standing next to you? She's after your Knight; it's written all over her. You know this, right?"

Cassandra shook her head and grimaced.

Ava didn't know what to say, so she just went with the truth.

"This is Cassandra, and I am aware of her interest in Kelso. However, she has now twice directly saved his life, including earlier tonight when she repaired *all* of the damage done by you and yours, save for his eye."

Many among the Furies looked at each other in disbelief and back towards the tall, willowy blonde next to Ava.

Lilly snorted again. "I wish that was true, so I do." She appraised Cassandra again quite rudely. "There's no way this woman... this *cailín*... could have the power to heal your Knight.

She's not weak, but she's nowhere near strong enough. I'm sorry, Princess, I just don't believe it." Several among the assembled Furies murmured assent at Lilly's words. They could all sense the strange woman's power and knew she didn't have the juice needed to do what Ava was attributing to her.

Cassandra sighed and muttered, "Go ahead."

Ava sighed too. Behind her, she could feel her Furies tense up as well.

"Well, that's just it. She doesn't have the power to help him anymore. She used up almost all she had to save his life, so there was nothing left for her to spend to fix his eye. Even if she did, though, it would only lessen the severity of the damage *you* wrought upon him. Cassandra can't heal his eye fully; she needs a Fury's healing prowess for such as that."

"I see." Lilly turned back to Cassandra. "Thank you so much, ya bonnie lass, now please depart and get out of our way."

A rumble of agreement came from all around at Lilly's words. Ava realized that the Furies—one and all—did not care for the idea of a sexy blonde hanging around Kelso when he and Ava were so obviously pairing up. Nothing good could come out of it. Ava agreed wholeheartedly. Sometimes, she *really* loved her Furies.

Cassandra rolled her eyes and looked at Ava. "Just tell them already... time flies."

Lilly turned to look back at Ava curiously at the blonde's words. Many of the Furies refocused their attention on Ava as well.

Subconsciously, Ava reached down with her right hand and patted Charlie lightly on his big head. She needed the comfort. *This should be fun,* she thought.

"Cassandra didn't spend just some of her power; she spent almost all of it. Do you understand what that means? She is formidable still, yes? Which means she had a *ton* of power to spend in the first place." Ava looked around at the sea of questioning faces, not one of which was putting two and two together.

*To hell with it.*

"Peace," Ava warned. "She is friend, of sorts, to us... an ally. I introduce to you Cassandra St. Augustine, Arch Mage of the Light."

# Chapter 3

Ava wasn't sure what she expected—but what she got wasn't it.

The Furies digested her information for a moment, all eyes studying the tall blonde woman. For her part, the Arch Mage just stood quietly with a half-smile on her lips and let them look. Ava was confused.

"Shouldn't you all be raging, or upset, or at least... I don't know... I can't think straight anymore." Ava shook her head to clear it. "Why are you all so calm? Remember the Boogie Man of the Light? The mysterious Arch Mage? You know, the *leader* of our enemies? Why does no one seem to care?"

One of the women spoke, "Probably because we aren't with the Dark anymore. Do you still consider yourself part of the Dark armies, Princess?"

Ava turned to regard the speaker with thoughtful eyes.

Lilly now: "Also, it's a wee bit tricky for us to get riled up when she's literally standing right next to you, still breathing." The scarred Fury's tone left no doubt that she thought Ava was making a mistake by allowing that to happen. "I mean, you could just kill her now." The large Fury grinned at the Arch Mage. "Ah, no offense, but someone who strolls about in an outfit like yours is sort of inviting trouble, ya know?"

The Arch Mage was miffed. "I'm wearing more than you are! Than any of you are, actually!"

56

"Ah, I see. So, you grow a couple of feet within a few seconds quite often, too? My apologies, lass; I had no idea." Lilly put her hands on her hips and shook her head in disapproval. "We dress as we do because we must. Trying to wear something like that—" she looked the Arch Mage up and down "—would mean we would just run around naked after our first rage."

"Why are we talking about this?" Cassandra responded tersely. "We have more important things to do, like saving the Knight's eye. That's all I care about." She paused and then immediately made a lie of her words. "I have lived for over a thousand years, and no one has *ever* called me a home-wrecker. You're kidding, right? Are Ava and Kelso going to put money down on the home of their dreams and raise a family behind a white picket fence? Is that the kind of home you're talking about? Because we all know that's not going to happen."

Lilly was silent at the rebuke.

It was true. No kids were born to those of the Conflict—ever—except to Ava's own parents. And that was a shame because Ava could not imagine a more unpleasant and wicked family.

Ava could also testify—due to personal experience—that growing up in the Struggle really sucked. It was dangerous, terrifying, and depressing. Without her gift, she never would have made it past twelve—if that far. How her brothers and sisters had survived was largely a mystery to her. Apart from her, and maybe her youngest brother, it was too bad that any of them had.

"Enough of this. Kelso's grim, but he has honor and strength.

He's unyielding but not harsh. What's not to like? He *is* a little rough around the edges, though." At this, Cassandra looked over at Ava in apology. Ava just shrugged; she'd thought the same thing more than a few times.

Kelso's face *was* stern, stark, and intimidating. Admittedly, it looked like it was carved from stone most of the time. Those features, coupled with his honorable bearing and broken wing, might serve to attract supernaturally gifted women from both sides of the Conflict. Hadn't that already happened? The Princess was a little jealous of the Arch Mage over her history with the Knight, but was pleased nonetheless that she had not mentioned Kelso's silly humor and quick wit in her run down. In direct contradiction to his looks, Kelso was *really* fun to be around. Since Cassandra didn't know that, it meant Kelso had not shared that side of himself with her, and Ava absolutely loved that he hadn't.

"I agree with the Arch Mage. Just let it rest. She can help Kelso if you're willing to assist her, and that's all that matters, but it won't be pleasant." Ava wasn't sure how unpleasant it was actually going to be, but there was no way to know until they started.

Cassandra shuffled uneasily. "Um, it's actually going to be a bit... uncomfortable. My wand is made to channel my Light. It's *my* bonded. These wards, his weapons, everything you see with a glow, basically, is all me. I pulled some of my power away and gave it to him. You notice I didn't say I *lent* my power to him. What you give is gone."

Every eye was upon Cassandra, and a few of the twenty-one nodded in understanding and acceptance. "How much is used? Can we replenish it later?" Lilly hadn't nodded, but her questions zeroed in on the two most important parts.

The Arch Mage turned to look at her directly. "I would say that the wand typically takes about twice as much power as it should to do what I want. There is a price to pay, and so it keeps some of my Light, eats it, or dilutes it somehow. I have no idea what your conversion rate will be, for lack of a better term. My wand was not designed to siphon the Dark, but I believe it can. How long you take to regenerate depends on you and how much I have to take in the first place to get the job done."

Ava knew that the Arch Mage was lying. Cassandra didn't 'believe' that the wand could convert their Dark. She knew it for a fact because she had scried it already. She had come out with Ava specifically to give this speech, and probably nothing that had happened tonight had been a surprise to her. Briefly, Ava wondered how the taller woman could live like that—and for so long, too. What was there to look forward to, anticipate, or even wonder about? Was there any mystery at all left for Cassandra?

The Arch Mage's only joy—or challenge—was probably to facilitate the outcomes she most wanted, which also meant that she could never *ever* be trusted. It was all a grand manipulation on her part. She picked the winners and jettisoned the losers. Ava suspected that anyone in the Arch Mage's orbit was just another chess piece to her. Cassandra moved them here and there until she finally released her hand and made the play she wanted to make.

It was unsettling to consider.

Ava was on pins and needles around Cassandra for a multitude of reasons, but the fact that she had probably orchestrated everything that had happened, was happening, and was going to happen tonight was truly intimidating. The Arch Mage's gift made Ava's own admittedly formidable gift pale in comparison. Ava could read *minds*; Cassandra could read *timelines*.

"Are you in or are you out?" Ava asked the Fury. "If you're out, then there's no need to ask for Kelso's permission to serve him. It's a no from me."

Lilly stopped her suspicious perusal of the Arch Mage and turned back to Ava. "Princess, it was always a yes, and you know that too. I just wanted to quiz the temptress over yonder about the details, so I did, and no offense."

"None taken," Ava answered shortly and looked up at Cassandra. "Now what?"

"Now I'll invite in the Spears that hurt Kelso," answered the Arch Mage distractedly, still shooting daggers at Lilly due to the Fury's constant needling. For Lilly's part, the bland expression plastered on her horribly scarred face did not quite hide the satisfaction she was getting by poking the most powerful individual in the world. True, the Arch Mage was considerably weaker than she had been just a few hours ago, but she could still mop the floor with Lilly, should she choose to. Why did Ava feel like Cassandra was playing with possibilities even now to get the opportunity to do just that?

After inviting the seven Spears past the ward line, Ava and Cassandra left them bunched up in Kelso's driveway as just the two of them made their way back inside to prepare.

Ava had her own guard stand watch outside as well. She wanted to make sure that the Paladin's 'blaze of glory' didn't involve leaping into the fifty or so Furies still milling around on the street. With his gift, he would decimate them all in about a minute.

"Sorry about that. Furies can be fiercely protective and somewhat direct," Ava said. Since the Arch Mage had done wonders for Kelso—and would do yet more before the night was through—she felt a little obligated to make peace on their behalf.

"I know Furies," Cassandra said shortly, but not out of anger. She seemed to be struggling with herself a little bit as they walked into the room where Kelso still lay unconscious.

"Sifting timelines, are we?" asked Ava distractedly, eyes glued to the rent in Kelso's face. The pain must have been overwhelming, yet he had joked about wanting an aspirin on their drive over from the barn. Ava was proud of him, of his courage and stoic nature, but she wanted nothing more than to heal him and take the pain away. The desire to do that cut her to the quick.

"I know you aren't foolish enough to try and read me again, so good guess," the Arch Mage confirmed, sitting on the chair next to Kelso's bed.

"It wasn't a guess. What are you trying to ferret out?" Ava's voice was not accusing; she could understand more than most the allure of using a gift constantly—even to the point where it might be considered a crutch.

"Well, I'm trying to decide how much more power I should expend tonight. A lot... or a lot more." Cassandra didn't appear to be joking, but Ava looked over at her sharply anyway.

"You don't have much power left; I don't think you need to worry about it." Ava's blue eyes searched the other woman's green ones with concern. "Just how tired are you? Can you even get this done?"

"I have more in me than you think. I *am* the Arch Mage, you know." Cassandra frowned and looked at Ava. "If I do what I want to do, what is best for him... and you... then it will leave me quite weak. I don't know how much help I will be for the coming trials."

"What trials? And why would you care to help me?" Ava was confused. They weren't technically enemies—Ava wasn't really with the Dark anymore, and neither were the Furies—but the two women were definitely rivals; both were used to being in charge and being the most powerful in the room. Alphas often didn't get along well until one acquiesced to the other, and Ava certainly wasn't going to do that unless it was to save Kelso. That was different, though, and she knew Cassandra would recognize any malleability on the Princess's end for what it was—temporary and transitory.

The Arch Mage sighed. "I have already lost Kelso. No matter what happens from this point on, he will never look at me as anything other than an untrustworthy complication—at best. A lot of what I have coming for me I deserve due to my actions and decisions, at least when it comes to him. I'm trying hard to remember that as I consider which way I'm going to go tonight with you, Ava." The Arch Mage's brow furrowed with thought; the Princess could almost see the calculations being tallied behind her eyes.

"I'm sorry," she said simply.

Cassandra looked up at her wearily. "For what?"

"That you already know the things that are going to happen to you, at least to some degree. It probably makes the unpleasant things you're going to experience even more so because you know it's coming." Ava smiled tentatively. "If you care to share, I could do my best to advise you. I promise to do so truthfully if you trust in me enough to confide. No reason you should, of course, but the offer stands."

The blonde woman was silent for almost a minute, eyes searching Ava's as she thought.

"Ok, I'll give you a very small glimpse of the three choices I have to make tonight." Cassandra smiled herself now, but it was not a reassuring smile at all. "One of them is about you."

Ava nodded. "I'm game."

"I need to recharge the ring on Kelso's finger. The power it lent to him is one of the reasons he's still alive. But look." At her words, she lifted Kelso's hand for Ava to inspect.

On his right ring finger, a beautiful silver band faintly

shimmered. The large face had an exquisite black sword as its signet, pointed away from Kelso. The ring's power looked weak and spent.

"You gave that to him?" Ava guessed.

"Yes. I saw that this night was a possibility when I was last here, and I knew that Argenta herself would not be enough to keep him alive if he ended up in that barn. Even with my boon it was iffy, but it was his only chance *if* he ended up on this path." The Arch Mage put his hand back down and smiled grimly. "I know he will need it again, too."

"God, please don't tell me he's going to be wounded like this once more," Ava whispered in horror, eyes darting back to Kelso's ruined visage.

"He could be; it might even be worse. He might die. There are so many variables that have to play out before I know for certain. I do know that battle awaits him at every turn and on every path, so he must be made whole to survive it." Cassandra grimaced. "What I see is not an exact science, but as choices are made, the path continually narrows. Previous paths close and others open, and the percentage of certain things happening goes up until there is no other possible way forward."

Ava nodded. "I see."

"You really don't." The Arch Mage laughed. "No one could. But to give you an idea, I didn't realize he was going to end up in the barn until he almost was, but I saw that future becoming more and more likely since 2 AM yesterday morning."

"What happened then?" Ava was intrigued.

"He met you," Cassandra said, eyes sympathetic.

The Princess felt like she had just been slapped. "You mean I put him on the path to the barn? To what happened to him?"

"No, not totally. You did increase the chances of it happening, but so did many other factors as well. Anyway, once you two met, it seemed prudent for me to be ready. As the variables that led to the barn became more and more likely, I had to arrange to be here. And I had to be here in just the right way so that we didn't kill each other when you walked in. That, too, was a possibility, but not a very high one. For example, sitting with my back to you, petting Charlie, drinking coffee, all of that was done intentionally to ever so slightly decrease the chances that you and I—or my Paladin and your Furies—would just go at it the moment you walked in. Does that make a little more sense?"

"Unfortunately, yes."

"Well, that's why I really should recharge his ring, but to do so requires power I can ill afford to spend at this time, and it also opens up other pathways that are not… optimal. To not do so raises the chance he will be slain." She grinned humorously. "I must also ward his eye. I need to place a barrier around the wound to keep the Furies' Dark in check. There is a fairly high probability that if I don't, their Dark will end up warring with his Light and—"

"He'll die again," Ava finished dully.

"Yes."

"That's two of the three things you need to do, so what's the third? Something to do with me?" Ava looked at the Arch Mage impassively, but inside she was a ball of curiosity and dread.

"Yes. What I *could* do for you is the third decision I must make. I am loathe to do it for several reasons, not the least of which is you might refuse me." For her part, Cassandra met Ava's eyes with no discernible nervousness or fear, but maybe with a hint of sympathy.

What could be so unsettling to the Arch Mage that she would look at Ava so? The Princess felt like she had a large stone in her stomach, but outwardly she showed no sign of her disquiet.

"Well, what is it?"

"I would need to give you some of my power," the other woman answered promptly.

Ava laughed. "How? Why?"

"I would tattoo some of my Light upon you, and I would do so because there is a... chance... that you will suffer mightily and die without it. I'm unsure if I should, though, because expending even more of my power means some unpleasant paths open up for me as a result." The Arch Mage didn't blink as she held Ava's eyes with hers, searching.

"If it's unlikely, then why would you? Why take the chance at all?"

Cassandra was silent for a moment.

"Because if that future finds you, the indignities and

66

humiliation that would be done upon your person would be too horrible to describe. Your death would be excruciating and prolonged. Just seeing it as a possibility makes me want to weep or kill you myself in order to spare you that fate—at least if I was sure that was the route you were truly destined for. I don't know that yet. But if it did happen to you, I'm not sure I could ever forgive myself. We are not friends, although unbelievably, there is some possibility of that too." Cassandra paused. "Have you ever heard the expression, 'I wouldn't wish that upon my worst enemy?' Well, there it is. That's why."

Ava felt cold and distant. She had an inkling of what the Arch Mage might see in her future. "I would end myself. You needn't worry."

"Have you not been listening to anything I've been saying? I already know that. I know what you intend, and in some of the possibilities, you do exactly that. In others, you don't, or you're not successful in your attempt. In many more still, you never have to make that kind of choice at all, and those are the ones I would most like for you." She paused. "But understand this—I am not in nearly as much control as you think I might be." The Arch Mage slapped her wand against her own palm in frustration and fell silent.

After a moment, Ava said softly, "Why do you want to help me at all if there are so many other paths? Particularly if doing so opens you up to jeopardy?"

Cassandra sighed and looked down for a moment before meeting Ava's eyes again. "Because the possibilities are shifting dramatically towards that worst-case scenario. I'm sorry."

***

Ribbons of diluted and steaming red cascaded off of Jesslyn's exhausted body as she cleaned up in the shower. It always felt so luxurious after a night of killing to wash away all the blood and ichor—she truly looked forward to it. How many had she killed tonight, though? Quickly, she recounted her escapades: two at Carmen's house, then three at the hangar, followed by the woman whose car she had stolen, and then the two young men in this motel room. So, that was five sleepers and three Furies put down. Nice! It had been a fairly productive night, all in all.

She had gotten very messy with Carmen's parents and with the Furies, and some of the blood she had all over her was even her own. That had not happened a whole lot in her life, and she didn't like it one bit. One of her brothers and two of her sisters loved pain, and she had obliged them all from time to time, but that was one vice that had skipped her completely. One of the *very* few that had.

Jesslyn had originally planned to flee town entirely; it was getting to be a little more dangerous than even she was comfortable with. Her fixation on the Knight had goaded her to stay, however, and so she did. More the fool she was for doing so, but that had its own allure, did it not? To be reckless in pursuit of a worthy goal was not something she had done often.

The Furies would be looking for her, of course, and they knew her tastes—well, any Royal's tastes—for the finer things in the mundane world. Expensive hotels, food, cars, and entertainment were all part and parcel of what made a Royal a Royal. They would start searching for her with that in mind. So, Jesslyn had made the very difficult—but ultimately necessary—decision to downscale by staying at a moderately priced hotel.

It had been a simple matter to beguile the two twenty-something men who had rented a room here. Whether they were a couple or whether they were just friends on the hunt for companionship, she didn't know or care. All she had wanted was their room.

Once inside, she tested each of their beds and pondered for a moment as the men stood stupefied behind her. She decided that the one farthest from the bathroom would make the most sense to kill them on because she wouldn't have to maneuver around their bodies to go to the bathroom during the night. She often got up at least once.

Helpless in the throes of her Dark, the men had cried silently and steadily while waiting for her to decide how they would die and how long it would take. It didn't take long, and Jesslyn felt sure they were both grateful—at least on some primitive level—to be granted quick and mostly pain-free deaths. The Spider was not in the mood for playtime or an extended and drawn-out session. She was too tired and sore to bother with it and had other things on her mind.

So, they were actually quite lucky in that respect.

Jesslyn instructed them to lay down on the bed and roll themselves over in the blankets as far from her bed as they could. Once they had snugged themselves against the far wall, completely cocooned in their bedding, she simply deposited a drop of poison Dark in both. She was so eager for a shower that she didn't even pause to see them shudder and shake as the poison had its way with them, nor did she hear their last wheezing breaths. Jesslyn was a connoisseur of 'death rattles'— she had certainly caused many throughout her long life. Tonight, though, she just couldn't work up any interest.

From a dispassionate point of view, Jesslyn knew she was twisted, corrupt, and probably a little crazy. She didn't care. The problem was that she was bored and had nothing to believe in or work towards. Yes, of course, she believed in the Dark, and she knew her powers had been gifted to her for a purpose. They were gifts best suited to subjugate and degrade those who crossed her path, and so she used them as such.

However, as decade after decade rolled by, she'd found herself descending further and further into debauchery and sadism. Again, she didn't really care except that there wasn't much further to fall. What would happen to her when she hit bottom and there was nothing else to excite her, to push her yet deeper into sin? That this would happen was of little doubt. Already, the Jesslyn of a hundred years ago would be horrified at the Jesslyn of today. And the Jesslyn of one hundred years ago would have been alien and frightful to the Jesslyn one hundred years before that.

Where, then, could she go when she hit rock bottom?

Jesslyn was terrified that the last frontier would be herself. She would explore damaging and hurting herself out of sheer desperation for stimulation. That she could even imagine herself doing this when she hated to be in pain was very concerning. And once she grew bored with sharp instruments, bludgeoning, slicing, peeling, breaking, and more common forms of inflicting pain on herself, what then?

Would she become a student of the more esoteric ways of harming herself?

Boiling, stretching, burning, and poisoning might then keep her amused for another ten years—but at what cost? Even with her impressive healing abilities, she would slowly grow infirm and sickly as her experiments, torture, and self-mutilation added up. She had seen it already with one of the sisters, Andeve, who adored pain even more than Jesslyn enjoyed inflicting it. Andeve was a mess now. Her once stately features devolved into horror after over a hundred years of encouraging damage to her body. Andeve looked old and fragile, but her eyes were still feverishly intrigued whenever Jesslyn cornered her.

They'd had some good times together since they both got what they wanted, but that didn't mean Jesslyn could understand Andeve at all. She didn't want to, either.

And that was the issue, wasn't it? Jesslyn was finally becoming afraid of herself because she knew the last mystery for her, the last way of being interested, could only be found in death. Jesslyn didn't want to die, and she certainly didn't want to be the cause of her own death either, but she could see the end in sight. For years, this feeling of hopelessness had plagued her subconscious, and only now could she recognize it.

One factor—introduced to her just yesterday—helped her to realize just how close to the bottom she really was. Ironically, it was the Knight, Kelso.

He was interesting to her. He was a challenge for her, too. Jesslyn felt that if she could only make Kelso hers, his company alone would add many years of excitement to her life. Just the carefully planned and choreographed descent she would help him make would take decades to realize. A small part of her hoped that by seeing him getting enjoyment from the lesser evils, she might find some true enjoyment in them again, too.

Maybe he could save her even as she showed him the dark wonders only she was privy to.

As she washed her hair for the second time, watching the suds flow down her body, Jesslyn realized that he would be her opus, her oeuvre, the be-all and end-all of who she was and what she wanted to be. Jesslyn was smart enough to know that the other side of her, the Spider, was slowly winning, and soon there would be nothing left of Jesslyn herself—unless she did something about it.

For the last few decades, her absolute obsession with Ava had blinded Jesslyn to just how close she was to a point of no return. The constant daydreaming of the horrors she would inflict upon her youngest sister had masked the likelihood that Jesslyn would inflict those same horrors on herself in the not-too-distant future.

Turning off the shower at last, Jesslyn dried off and wrapped her hair in a towel. Naked, she made her way to bed, fluffing the pillows before covering herself up gratefully. It never even occurred to the Spider to glance over at the two bodies not ten feet away as she felt sleep finally overtaking her.

Before she went under completely, Jesslyn made two promises to herself. The first was that she would capture Ava, and she would make that exquisite creature hers, body and soul, before ending her in a spectacular and excruciating fashion. Ava would thus become the capstone of her descent because Jesslyn could go no further down without risking herself. She thought it fitting—and almost poetic—that Ava's demise would serve to lift Jesslyn back up into some form of sanity and self-respect.

The second promise was that she would find a way to ensnare Kelso, and she would treat him preciously when she had him. Jesslyn would guide him and help the Knight to become stronger still than he already was. She would remove the weaknesses from him as impurities were removed from metal before being shaped by a blacksmith's hand. Jesslyn would be the blacksmith, and Kelso would be the unforged metal she would shape. The Knight already had a deadly sword in Argenta, so Jesslyn felt that she should shape him into something greater yet.

A scythe.

Jesslyn smiled slightly as she drifted off to sleep. She could not remember the last time she had felt so at peace with herself.

# Chapter 4

Kelso dreamed.

Deeply unconscious and on death's door, he once again returned to the night almost a year ago when his life changed forever. He had dreamed of this night constantly since his ascension into the Conflict, and now he returned to a much more vivid version than ever before. He knew more, too, and as the scenes replayed themselves in his mind, a part of him stood aloof, seeing things from a different angle and realizing how much he had failed to understand.

One constant of this dream was that it would become a nightmare by its conclusion. Kelso would awake from it as he always did, with a terrified and sickening feeling clawing at his heart. Kelso did not expect that to change in spite of what he now knew from Argenta, but her knowledge did spur him to examine more closely some of the details that he had perhaps overlooked before.

Kelso had picked up his sister Amber and her son Ben from their home in Denver, Colorado, for a three-week stay at his small home in Sparks. Amber had given Kelso quite the business about the trip, wondering why they should leave their modest home in Denver for his "hovel." She was joking, of course. Kelso was taking her away from Denver simply because Amber needed to get out of town for a few weeks—the destination really didn't matter much.

Her boyfriend of several years, Dennis, was moving out of the house they shared. He was a police officer with Denver P.D. and wasn't a bad guy by any stretch. Kelso held no personal animus towards Dennis because he had done nothing to warrant it. He wasn't a drunk, hadn't cheated (at least to Amber's knowledge), and had never mistreated Ben or Amber. They had just grown apart. After a few years, it had become clear to them both that they didn't work anymore, and neither was getting any younger. One night a few weeks ago, home at dinner, they had just opened up to each other about where they were as a couple and where they wanted to be.

It was what it was, and Amber had a lot of personal time saved up with the county. She worked for the housing commissioner and had a great relationship with everyone in her office, so when she needed to take a few weeks off for personal reasons, they green-lighted her with little fanfare.

Kelso was excited to play host for a while. The only minor disagreement was regarding Charlie, Amber's rescue English Bulldog. He was Amber's pride and joy (right after Ben), but Kelso had forbidden her from bringing him. Kelso had no interest in having that stinky beast in his Jeep or his home and told Amber that Charlie needed to stay behind.

Amber had argued, but Kelso had won by reminding her that they would be on the road for three days in his Jeep, suitcases in tow, and there just wouldn't be room for the dog anyway.

Amber had reluctantly agreed, to Kelso's relief, and it had been made even smoother by Dennis being ok with Charlie hanging around. He promised to care for and feed him while she was gone. It was indeed a mild and dispassionate separation, which ironically was probably the reason behind their parting in the first place. In any case, Charlie would be fine, and that was what mattered to Amber.

Oh, how she doted on that dog! Amber had about as many pictures of him on her social media accounts as she had of Ben. For his part, Ben was crazy about Charlie too, and had convinced his mom to let Charlie sleep with him from the first night on. Amber and Dennis had even modified Ben's bed by taking off the legs so that Charlie didn't have to struggle to get up at bedtime. Ben couldn't lift Charlie, as the dog weighed more than Ben did by a good ten or fifteen pounds, so Amber had reasoned that if you couldn't bring the dog to the bed, bring the bed to the dog.

Kelso secretly thought it was ridiculous how much they did to accommodate Charlie, but they seemed happy to do it. Sleeping with a dog—particularly *that* dog—was just crazy, though. Charlie was a funny dude, but a stinky and slobbery one too, and Kelso constantly washed his hands whenever he visited Amber. Charlie was a lover boy and needed constant human contact. He was also persistent, so he always ended up with his paw on you or his head in your lap or some such. Kelso didn't dislike the dog; that was impossible, but he just wanted a bit of space—which he didn't get when Charlie was around.

Charlie had been one of several bulldogs seized from a filthy puppy mill. Amber initially had her heart set on saving one of the little mamas that had more or less been bred half to death, determined to give whatever little lady she ended up with a beautiful second half of life.

When Amber went down to look at the dogs, she cried freely both in relief that they were rescued and with sadness upon observing some of the still-present tells of their abuse. She'd sat down on a small bench to collect herself and regroup. It was visiting day at the shelter, and many dogs were out in the enclosed run, excitedly meeting everyone and playing.

Amber had smiled through her tears at their antics but noticed one dog sitting quietly off by himself. He watched the other dogs playing and prancing with calm and sad eyes. He was young, barely more than a puppy himself, but already filling out. A light-tan-brown boy with interesting eyes: one brown and one a mix of brown and blue. He noticed Amber staring at him, and when she leaned forward to put her hand down to his level, he came over, gently put his face in her palm, and closed his eyes. And just like that, it was done.

In the intervening years, Amber's love for Charlie had only grown. During the drive to Kelso's house, she had already called Dennis about four or five times to check up on the dog, and both she and Ben had talked about him forty or fifty times. Kelso couldn't understand it.

On the few occasions they were not talking about Charlie, the two siblings passed the time by ribbing each other constantly. It was a time-honored tradition with them; their childhood had not been the easiest, and humor was a great coping mechanism. They had grown up in the foster care system, their mom having died in a car crash when they were both young. Kelso could hardly remember her face, and Amber had only a dim memory of her.

At the time of their mom's death, their dad had been an unknown in their lives since he was serving time for manslaughter. They had no other family except an aunt in New York who was deemed unfit to adopt them, so both had grown up in the system. They were lucky on two counts. The first was that nothing bad had ever happened to either of them growing up with the families they had stayed with, and the second was that they had always managed to stay together.

Eventually, their father was released from prison, but the family reunion was short-lived. He was a stranger to them both and, within a year of his release, killed himself. Kelso and Amber were informed a few days after the act, and Kelso honestly had trouble identifying him at the coroner's office as their father. Amber had waited out in the hall.

Neither cried over their father's death—they had hardly known him. He also didn't seem like a very good man, and Kelso was just relieved that the sickness that had caused their father to shoot himself in the head with one of his prized Magnum revolvers (which he was not supposed to have) had been the only life he had taken on his way out the door. Their father's "inheritance" had been depressingly pitiful. He had six dollars in his wallet, a few guns to turn over to his kids, some clothes, some secondhand furniture (which they promptly took to the dump), and nothing else.

Amber had gifted Kelso the guns, saying she had no desire to have them. Kelso took them with a healthy dose of trepidation, but they were beautiful weapons, and a small voice inside suggested he should. Kelso gave Amber the six dollars, and they called it even.

Time passed, but brother and sister stayed tight and friends to the end. When Amber got pregnant, and it all went south with Ben's father, Kelso held her hand during the labor. Eventually, Kelso left to take over an old friend's private investigation business in Nevada, but the two siblings talked daily. Now that Amber had broken things off with Dennis, she was visiting Kelso to check out the housing market in Sparks and Reno; maybe it was time for her and Ben to make a move.

Kelso hoped so; it would be great to have her around again, and he would love to see Ben grow up. Ben knew there was a second agenda to this visit with his uncle, but neither Kelso nor Amber was sure how feasible it might be. That didn't stop them from coming up with all sorts of "pros" and "cons," though.

Long shadows leapt away from the headlights and across the landscape as the Jeep sped along the winding highway. Kelso's fingers tapped the steering wheel in rhythm with the radio, the melody of a country song filling the air around them. Amber sat in the passenger seat, one arm propped up on the door.

"You know, Kelso, I'm not so sure I wanna see that ugly mug of yours every day."

"Well, the window to turn my nephew into an incurable gambler is quickly closing. We need to take Ben to the casinos before he turns ten if we want any hope at all."

Amber laughed. "At least Charlie will have a second yard to do his business in. I'll bring him over whenever I can."

Their banter was interrupted by the young passenger in the back seat. Ben leaned forward, curiosity gleaming in his eyes. "What are you two talking about?"

Kelso swiveled slightly in his seat to address Ben. "We were just discussing how we're going to turn you into a world-class gambler! You're almost ten, right? It's high time we got you on the path to easy riches."

Amber shot Kelso an exasperated look, her head shaking gently in disapproval.

With a mischievous glint in his eye, Kelso leaned toward Ben in the back seat. "I'm going to spot you twenty bucks in gambling seed money. I'm getting older, Ben. You need to win me a lot of money so I can retire in style."

Ben looked unconvinced and rolled his eyes at his uncle's nonsense. "Would I lead you astray? Look, they build those casinos really big so everyone can easily come in and win money whenever they want. Isn't that obvious? I mean, why else would they build them, right?"

Amber interjected, her voice laced with a hint of amusement. "Ben, honey, don't pay too much attention to your uncle. As a kid, he ate more than his fair share of lead paint chips, and he's a little soft in the head."

Ben had simply sighed, mumbled something about both of them being crazy, and popped in his earbuds. Amber and Kelso had laughed like hyenas at Ben's exasperation, giving themselves high fives, but then fell to squabbling over who had won the round.

Before they could quite settle it, Kelso noticed a truck stop ahead on their right. He was hungry and asked Amber if she was up for a late dinner. She was. Amber pulled out one of Ben's earbuds and told him the plan, and of course, he was up for it too. What nine-year-old boy wouldn't be?

"Can I have chicken tenders, Uncle?" Ben asked, excitement lighting up his eyes. "With extra ranch?"

Kelso put on a face. "Sorry, dude, they're all out of ranch. We can get you taco sauce, though—as much as you want."

"How do you know they're out of ranch?" the boy wanted to know, eyes narrowing suspiciously. "And I hate hot sauce."

Kelso painted on his most sincere look and met the boy's eyes in the back seat where he sat leaning up against a suitcase, a pillow behind his head. "I called them earlier to warn them we were coming. They told me they were out of ranch right off, but they offered taco sauce as an alternative. You can trust me."

Amber sighed and stage whispered to Ben, "He's lying. Again. What did I tell you about your uncle?"

"That he ate a lot of paint chips growing up?" answered Ben, eyes glued on the approaching oasis of light.

Amber looked over at Kelso triumphantly and wiped an invisible tear from her eye. "That's my boy," she rasped.

Kelso pulled up to the front door and parked. The diner was empty but still open, and the truck stop was deserted, which was to be expected. It was late, and they were smack dab in the middle of a desert on a Tuesday night in Nevada.

"Classy place you picked, Kelso. I bet there are about forty different ways of ordering a grease burger and not much else," Amber remarked, unbuckling her seat belt. "Put on your coat, Ben, it's cold," she added.

"I'll have you know that this is a five-star rated restaurant according to Michelin. Don't hate, please." Kelso got out and shrugged into his jacket as well. Glancing around at the barren hills that ringed the truck stop was depressing. Who would want to work out here in this God-forsaken place? He was sure the view in daylight was just as bleak as it was at night because there never was any real detail to any of Nevada's hills—just dirt, rocks, and sagebrush.

Ben got out, zipping up his coat as he did. Kelso closed the door behind him and walked with his nephew to the front door. "Hold it open for your mom," he instructed quietly, and Ben rushed to follow his uncle's instructions.

Amber swept in regally, arms out as if she was flying. She looked back at Ben and winked, though, and he grinned, showing a couple of gaps that his adult teeth were trying to fill. It would still be a few more months.

Kelso winced when he read the menu—Amber had nailed it, and he knew his sister well enough to know that her retribution would be swift and merciless. Sure enough, she moved to stand right next to him, casually resting a hand on his shoulder.

"Hm… well, lookie there. How many ways can they destroy a burger? They seem to be connoisseurs of the craft, for sure." She patted him on the shoulder several times and gathered Ben up. "Hey, kid, let's go find a place to sit before all the tables are gone."

Ben looked around in confusion at the empty restaurant but moved to join his mom at a table next to the front windows. Amber slid in first, Ben right behind. Kelso took a couple of menus back with him and, sighing, sat across from them both.

"Well, at least they have chicken tenders," he muttered sourly, eyes looking everywhere but at his sister. For her part, Amber lounged like a queen, a smile of knowing benevolence painted on her face.

Kelso handed her a menu with another sigh. "Ok, just get it out, Amber."

"What do you mean?" Amber said innocently, taking the proffered menu daintily. As she took it, a large truck pulled up right next to Kelso's Jeep, even though the parking lot in front of the restaurant was completely empty.

Kelso could never understand why people did that. He was opening his mouth to gripe about it to Amber when his complaint lodged in his throat.

The man who exited the truck was enveloped in silver-white armor of dull light, and wisps of light trailed behind him as he walked into the restaurant. It almost looked like he had recently been on fire and hosed off, yet tendrils of smokey white still followed in his wake.

Kelso was not sure what he was seeing, but his foreboding shot through the roof when the man turned to look at Kelso directly and smiled. It was not a friendly smile.

Amber and Ben looked over the menu, oblivious to the man, until he hooked a chair with his foot at the table next to them and sat, aggressively angling toward Kelso. Amber looked up in puzzlement for a second, which quickly turned to alarm as she took in the man's bearing and face. Ben was still looking at the menu.

"Found you," said the man sitting just a few feet from Kelso. "Thought you could outrun me, did you?" The man smiled again and glanced over at Amber and Ben. By this point, Amber had snaked an arm around Ben and pulled the boy tight against her.

Kelso was uneasy, confused, and boggled by both the man's words and his translucent armor. Kelso looked mean: his face could have been used to hammer nails when he wasn't joking or laughing. He certainly wasn't doing either now, yet the man seemed oblivious to Kelso's intimidating looks. Kelso also outweighed the stranger by thirty pounds at least.

"Hey, man, I've never seen you before. I think you've got the wrong guy." Kelso held out his left hand, palm down, in a placating gesture. It didn't work.

"I know you haven't seen me before, but I have seen you. In my dreams." The man spit on the ground at Kelso's feet. "You're awakening, and that cannot be allowed to happen. You've been identified to me as a traitorous weakling who would betray the Light at the first opportunity. I will not allow that."

"What?" Kelso asked, mind racing. Amber had pulled Ben over as far away as she could from the strange man and had plastered herself against the window. Her eyes were wide with fear, and Ben looked utterly terrified.

The man merely looked at Kelso much as someone might look at roadkill. His face had an ugly sneer, and his eyes looked a little wild.

"I don't even know your name. How could you know who I am? Let's just dial it down for a minute and talk, ok?" Kelso was desperate to find a peaceful resolution, but a small part of him screamed that there was no chance of doing that. He didn't know why, but a voice inside him was hollering that he needed to get up and run. No doubt the angry man would follow him, which was fine because Amber and Ben could then flee the other way.

Even as he thought this, he glanced over at Amber. At that exact same moment, she also cut her eyes to him and nodded slightly. She knew what he needed to do, and she would be ready when he did it. Kelso started to look back to the man but hesitated as he spotted a pack of wild-looking people—male and female both—walking quickly across the parking lot. Some seemed *dark* to him, like they were wrapped in shadows—and all looked dangerous.

Kelso's inner voice was haranguing him to do something: to move, to protect his family, to draw the man away—something, anything. Try as he might, he stayed frozen with indecision and turned back towards his immediate adversary, mind-churning. He watched the large group approach with mounting dread from the corner of his eye.

The man laughed. "You don't know who I am? Worm. I'm the Ebon Knight, Roil. I have come for thee on advice from the Arch Mage." His gaze sharpened on Kelso with malevolent intent.

"I don't know what that means. I don't know who—"

The man who had named himself Roil exploded to his feet. His chair flew back with power as he effortlessly flipped the table he had been sitting at into the far wall. It was like the table weighed nothing to the man.

Spittle foamed on his lips as he screamed in Kelso's face. "YOU'RE NOT WORTHY! You're as weak as she told me you would be! The Light would be better off without your kind polluting our ranks!"

Kelso stood quickly, hands out placatingly as he backed away. Kelso was strong and in good shape, still young enough to throw down with the best of them if need be, but the man in front of him was completely out of his league. The strength he had demonstrated simply by flipping the heavy table over and sending it crashing against the wall almost thirty feet away was supernatural. Kelso was well versed in self-defense, which was a requirement for his line of work, but there was absolutely nothing he could do against the man who now stalked him as Kelso stepped backward—away from Amber and Ben.

Clad in ghostly armor, Roil followed a few steps after Kelso before halting as the horde of men and women that Kelso had tracked across the parking lot filed in at the crazed man's back. They were covered in black armor and carried weapons of shadow, but Kelso knew they were not allies. Even in his shock, he knew they were just as dangerous to him and his family as the crazed Knight.

Roil looked over his shoulder at them for a second as they entered. Kelso cut his eyes desperately back to Amber, but she wasn't looking at him, her mouth open in surprise and fear as she looked over the gang of rough people pouring into the diner like ants. They took up stations around the room, some even jumping up on chairs, booths, or tables as they came.

Kelso realized they stood between Amber and the door, so she couldn't run with Ben unless she was willing to try to go through the horde. Kelso thought that would be a terrible idea, particularly since some of them were sneaking glances at her and Ben even as they menaced the Knight. They were not friendly glances; their eyes were wild, excited, and vicious.

"Ah, so you laid a trap for me, did you?" asked the Knight as he turned back to Kelso. "So, not only weak in the Light, but also a traitor."

Kelso started to shake his head frantically, but then the Knight's eyes rolled up, and in a terrible voice of indifferent bleakness, Roil said, "There's only one punishment for traitors, right, Roil?"

The Knight's eyes refocused on Kelso. "Absolutely. Traitors

87

die."

The sound that issued from Roil's lips next was meant to be a laugh, but Kelso thought it almost sounded mechanical. Like someone had once copied someone laughing and was now playing it back through Roil.

It was terrifying.

Behind the man who had apparently decided that the mass of killers at his back were less important than Kelso himself, several of them suddenly stopped, smiles fading as they, too, were taken aback by Roil's actions and the strangeness of his voice. It sounded like something other than Roil was speaking—and laughing—using the Knight's vocal cords. It was utterly alien, but before Kelso could say anything, a tall, fit woman partially hidden by the door jamb screamed, "For the Dark! Kill him and embrace your destinies!"

At her words, the night-clad would-be assassins flowed toward the Knight, led by an older, sinewy man with a large hunting knife bizarrely held out in front of him like a spear. Kelso had a split second to register that the woman who had encouraged them to attack didn't move forward to engage the Knight herself, but she now held a bow made entirely of shadow, an arrow of pitch black to string.

They all moved so fast! It was like Kelso was stuck in quicksand while they all moved freely. To his perceptions, Roil was just suddenly facing the other way. He effortlessly caught the maniac with a knife by the throat and used him as a shield against a hurled missile of some type—maybe an axe?—that was flung from the rear flanks.

The axe hit the older man in the back, and its impact was such that blood flew out of the man's mouth and misted Roil as he held his "shield" aloft with one hand at his throat, the other at his wrist. Kelso watched in horrified fascination as the Knight raised the old man's limp hand to his shriveled throat and cut deeply with the knife. Fresh blood fountained from the gash as Roil sawed in, and the thoroughly dead man's head lolled grotesquely backward.

With a powerful shove, the Knight threw his temporary shield at the mass of crazies still scrambling forward. Such was the strength of the Knight that the dead man himself became a weapon as he hurtled through the ranks of his erstwhile companions, killing some outright and knocking several more aside before crashing through a far window and out into the parking lot.

Kelso was staggered by the power of Roil, and he knew without a doubt that he would die if the Knight laid a hand on him. Even as this certainty flew through his mind, Roil reached out and caught yet another axe in his armored fist. Grey sparks flew from where black axe met white armor.

With deceptive ease, Roil flipped the weapon around and immediately threw it back at its owner, the axe burying itself deeply in a large man's face and knocking him backward into a booth. The axe winked out of existence as the man died.

From the left, an older woman dove at Roil's side with a long spear of night. Hardly even bothering to look at her, Roil caught the spear and yanked the slight woman towards him so violently that her feet left the ground. The crazed Knight turned and clotheslined her as she reached him, and Kelso heard the bones in her neck break as she fell to Roil's feet, dead.

The rest of the mob hesitated as Roil glanced up from the dead woman. Kelso could clearly see them reassessing the Knight, and many had undisguised fear in their eyes. Any further examination of them was snuffed as Roil turned back to face Kelso, his face a mask of hatred and contempt.

"Time to die, trait—" the Knight began, but a black arrow of the deepest pitch took him in the back and slammed him into the wall right next to Kelso.

Kelso didn't hesitate.

Without conscious thought, he leapt over the woman lying at his feet and bounded toward Amber and Ben. Amber was crying but prepared to bolt as well. Ben seemed to be frozen in terror, his face buried in his mother's chest. Kelso reached them and grabbed at Ben roughly, intending to tear him away from Amber so she could get up and run with him to the door.

The path to freedom was momentarily clear except for the tall woman with fierce eyes that he had noted earlier. Somehow, she didn't look as crazy as Roil nor as unstable as the mob she led, but Kelso wouldn't hesitate to bowl her over if she didn't move out of his way.

Impossibly, Roil was suddenly next to Kelso. Before he could even begin to figure out how Roil could have appeared out of thin air, a crushing backhand sent Kelso flying right back to the wall he had left just moments before. He hit hard, and the breath was knocked out of him as he slid to the ground, dazed. Desperately, his eyes sought out his sister's eyes, and they locked gazes.

Amber, still crying, was petting Ben's hair as she looked at Kelso from behind a mask of ageless sorrow. She knew what was coming before Kelso did. She had always been much quicker than he to grasp things.

A stark white blade, seemingly made out of brilliant light, suddenly entered Kelso's vision as Roil slid the sword effortlessly through Ben and Amber. The force of his strike drove the blade into the seat behind Amber, where it lodged for a second. Amber's face contorted in pain for a moment, and blood burst from her lips as she stared at Kelso. Ben merely shuddered once as the sword impaled him through his back, and then he lay still against his mother.

Kelso screamed in horror as Roil withdrew the blade.

Amber slumped over dead, still holding Ben.

The world broke.

Kelso was cast headlong into despair and grief as everything slowed down, time stretching out and thinning. Dimly, he was aware of the Knight approaching him, calling Kelso a murderer. *Of who? Of his own family? Was he the cause of their deaths?*

He had one moment of horrified self-loathing before his world was shattered yet again by the worst agony he had ever felt. The sword that had just slain his family had slashed his leg open at the knee. Sickeningly, Kelso caught a glimpse of his own severed tendons and gleaming bone before a rush of red concealed it all as his blood burst forth from the deep cut.

Kelso gasped in pain and clutched at his leg, the world turning grey around him as he struggled to stay conscious, trying in vain to staunch the blood. He worried for a second that he might pass out and die from blood loss, but really, was that so bad? Kelso glanced up at Amber and Ben. He could catch up to them before they got too far, couldn't he?

His contemplation was interrupted by the woman he had seen standing at the door. She was carefully picking her way around bodies and upturned tables as she strode to the center of the room. She was carrying a large two-handed sword of black fire and mist, and her eyes sought him out with a look that might have been sympathy as she stopped and waited in the now quiet restaurant. Besides the two of them, only the dead remained in the building—the mob and workers had fled.

Kelso could not remember where the others had gone or when, but the Knight must have followed them in pursuit. Roil. A deep rage blossomed in Kelso as he thought about the face of the man who had done this to him, to his sister and her child, and he no longer wished to follow his family. Not yet. He first wanted to slay the man who had killed them.

Kelso could no longer protect them, but he could avenge them.

As new resolve hardened within him, the woman's expressionless face somehow conveyed approval. She could obviously read the determination in his eyes and recognized his desire to balance the scales.

Before she could say anything—if she was going to say anything—Roil broke the momentary calm as he strode back into the wrecked dining room, whistling tunelessly. The sword that had killed Kelso's family was held carelessly over his left shoulder as he sauntered in and stopped, eyeing the woman still standing in the center of the wreckage and bodies.

She broke eye contact with Kelso to turn towards the Knight, sword raised and held crosswise in front of her body.

There was silence between them for a second before the Knight said with a snicker, "I saved you for last because you hurt me, and you were wise enough not to run." He paused. "Why aren't you a monster yet? I like killing monsters. Won't you change for me?"

"You're the only monster here," the tall woman said, her voice dripping with contempt.

"You will fall to my blade either way, but at least if you rage, you might last a little longer. Do it." The Knight lifted the sword off his shoulder and shook it at the woman a few times, encouraging her to... what exactly? Kelso wasn't sure, and he didn't care. His eyes locked on the face of Roil, and hate blossomed in his heart.

The woman answered boldly, "I'll fall to Argenta but not to you." At her words, the woman launched herself into the air, the huge sword over her head in a two-handed grasp. She jumped impossibly far in the blink of an eye, coming down directly in front of where Roil had been standing a moment ago.

Her sword cleaved empty air and struck the floor hard enough to shatter tile and rattle the tables and chairs.

Roil had teleported away from her killing strike. He faced Kelso for a moment—and winked—before spinning quickly with his own sword held out horizontally at the waist, intending to decapitate the woman's upper half from her lower.

She anticipated him and followed her strike down with knees bent almost to the floor. Roil's blade whizzed overhead, missing by mere inches and ruffling her brown hair with its passage.

Without pause, she spun in a blurring counter sweep that looked like it was going to connect a split second before Roil teleported again. But, this time, away from the woman and only ten feet or so from where Kelso lay on the ground, holding his leg together.

The woman rose to her full height easily, sword trailing her as she stalked forward; black lightning following close behind in the sword's wake. It was beautiful.

Kelso could not see Roil's face, but he could tell by the uncertainty with which the Knight held himself and his heavy breathing that the battle had turned against the crazed slayer. Kelso's eyes started to search around for a weapon of his own.

His momentary distraction caused him to miss the furious start to the fight as the woman engaged the Knight head-on. Within seconds, Roil was driven back half the distance to Kelso, fighting desperately against the deadly woman who gracefully wove herself in and out of her attacks, almost as if she danced to a rhythm only she was privy to. Kelso frantically tried to keep up with what he was seeing, but her strikes flickered in and back so quickly that it was impossible.

Roil was forced back a few more feet and now stood braced against her onslaught right at Kelso's legs. Just as Kelso was resolving to kick the Knight's knee in from behind, the woman's sword shattered on the blade of the Knight, and his weapon cut deeply into her chest. Somehow, she still managed to drive the jagged remnants of her blade down through Roil's arm. It fell at Kelso's feet, cleanly severed from his body—still holding the sword.

Blood fountained from the Knight's arm as he stood in shock, and the woman fell backward onto her knees, clutching her chest.

Kelso's eyes were drawn to the sword. It was the most beautiful thing he had ever seen, glorious and deadly. It was also the implement that had been used to slay his family. Kelso hated it, but time was fleeting, and his revenge could be had if he was only bold enough to take the sword out of the hand that still held it.

The dying woman looked at him, steely vengeance in her eyes.

It was never a choice. He leaned forward to pry Roil's lifeless fingers off the pommel of the sword with shaking hands. The Knight never moved; mouth still opened in an O of shock. For his part, Kelso was struck with numbing dread as a door in his mind slammed open and… something… entered. He somehow felt that he had just made the biggest mistake of his life.

It didn't matter anymore. What was done was done.

Holding the sword awkwardly, Kelso could only manage to swing it with moderate force at Roil's knees. The blade bit into its previous master with ease, neatly severing both legs clean through. Roil's upper body collapsed, and he spasmed in pain as he hit the ground, blood spurting out of the three separate appendages that had been severed from his body.

It was a fitting end for a monster, Kelso decided, as he watched the Knight quickly bleed out and grow still.

A sudden pain seared Kelso's left forearm at the wrist, and as he turned his arm over to look at it, he was struck by the small half-inch-by-inch mark of white now resting on his arm. A chill ran through Kelso as he realized the mark's color was the same shade and intensity as the aura of the Knight he had just slain. Kelso had the strangest suspicion that a small piece of his vanquished enemy now marked his own flesh.

Lights flashed into the parking lot as several cars entered the truck stop. They were not police because no sirens flashed or wailed. Still, before he could wonder who they might be—and before he could fully sink into the battle shock that was now descending over him—a slight sound from the woman kneeling only a dozen feet away pulled his attention back to her.

She was still kneeling, but she now held a small amulet in her hand, and even as his eyes settled on her, she broke the amulet and smeared the liquid it had been holding over her chest and heart. It looked like more blood. Whatever it was, it mingled with her own for a moment before she suddenly raised her head and looked Kelso in the eyes.

Kelso was still holding the sword out with both hands, blade shaking in a strange mix of exhaustion and adrenalin. His gaze locked with hers, and she snarled, a black dagger of Dark forming in her hand. Kelso was terrified of the woman... and for the woman. He wanted to plead with her not to attack, that he was not her enemy, but it was already too late.

The woman launched herself at him, not nearly as quickly and gracefully as before, but still faster than he could track. Horrified, he felt the impact of her body as she was impaled neatly through the heart by his sword. He wanted to drop it, to pry his hands from the pommel, but he couldn't.

A great being of death strode across the landscapes of his mind, and a dirge of woe followed in its wake. A film of red veiled his eyes, and crazily, he wanted to stand, to go out and meet the inhabitants of the cars that were pulling up to the restaurant. Maybe he should go check them out—and slay them all.

Before he could pull himself up, the dying woman impaled upon his sword reached out and covered his hands with her own.

Her touch snapped him out of his fever dream, and Kelso's eyes refocused on the world and her. She held his hands steady for a moment before whispering something to the sword too low for Kelso to hear. *Something* in his head howled with rage, and he saw black stars. He flinched back at the pain of it, and this time he was able to pull away from the woman.

She slid off of his sword with a sigh and fell to her side, facing him. A discomfort drew his attention down to his right arm, and when he turned it over, Kelso saw that he had been marked again, but this time with a black mark the exact hue and density as the woman's sword. Did Kelso now carry a piece of her as well?

Tears spilled down his face at the thought. His eyes sought her out just as she took her final breath. Numbly, Kelso looked up as several men and women with grim faces swarmed into the restaurant. They were armored in light and carried weapons of power in their hands. They saw him and made as if to approach, eyes steel, but noticed the sword and stumbled to a stop, looking back and forth among themselves with uncertainty. Kelso didn't care; his eyes sought out his sister and nephew again, and the world swam behind his tears.

Suddenly, a woman's voice, cruel and evil, boomed in his mind as words came to him. He could hear them as clearly as he could hear anything else: "*Greetings, Ebon Knight! I am Argenta, the greatest weapon in the Conflict! We shall dance across the battlefields of this world, bringing death and despair to all. Rejoice! We are now bonded until your death, and the world will remember your passing for all time.*"

Kelso leaned over and retched onto the ground.

# Chapter 5

Kelso woke with a start, bathed in sweat. The dream was always the same, and he had relived that night—and the circumstances leading up to it—every day since his ascension. He feared that he would never escape the recollection of it and dreaded the thought.

It appeared to be just after dawn based on the weak light seeping in from under the shades. In the dim illumination, Kelso's eyes focused on a form bent over him. He was disoriented and groggy, but his heart seized for a second as he realized it was Ava, her beautiful eyes leaking tears as she stared at him in sympathetic grief. Her distress was so terrible that it seemed like she was actually struggling to breathe. *Why was she so sad?*

Then he remembered.

The kidnapping of Carmen, his pursuit, the fight in the barn, his grievous wounds, the strange dream-like sequence in his head with Ava, his return home, and Cassandra. All of it hit him in a rush, and he grunted.

Now Kelso knew why she was so upset and sad—he had been crippled and blinded, his face a horror. The two of them could have had a chance at a life together. Now, it was all torn asunder. He fully expected her—even wanted her—to run away from him as fast as she could. He would only be a burden to her now; just recovering from his wounds enough to sit up would take weeks. She could not be expected to wait around until he did.

Ava shook her head in denial, and a small sigh escaped her even through her tears.

"Hi, Kelso, let's get you up," she said with something close to exasperation.

"Are you insane?" Kelso demanded before he could stop himself. That he was alive at all was a miracle, but to think he could stand up? Already? No force on this earth could have healed him so well as to allow that, nor stir him from his bed.

Ava moved, pulling him up quickly as she stepped back, and Kelso unceremoniously found himself sitting up, a shocked expression on his face.

The beautiful Princess hovered protectively a few feet away, examining his face with concern, lips pinched. "Brain damage?" she muttered to herself, then shook it off.

Kelso was in complete denial. How could he possibly sit on his own? Where had all the endless oceans of pain he had drowned in gone? The Knight actually felt good. His lips felt slightly numb from the surrealness of it all, and he looked up at Ava in wonder.

"So..." she said, rocking back and forth on the balls of her feet, "how are you feeling?" Hastily, she reached up and rubbed her face and eyes clear of the tears that had been there. At the same time, her face broke into a small grin. Kelso couldn't understand how she could be so sad yet so happy.

"What's going on?" he asked, completely flummoxed.

"Nothing much. It's nice to *see* you again. Are you happy to *see* me, too?" Ava's emphasis confused him for a moment, and then his mouth fell open.

"I can see you!" Kelso blurted in astonishment, surging to his feet. "I can stand too!" He announced in wonder.

"Yeah, but can you dance a jig?" Ava mused. "No, better yet, can you take me dancing? Teach me how to line swing and cowboy dance and all that?"

"You know I can't dance, Ava. Not with my bum leg." Kelso was a little disappointed that she was mocking him, but the complete absence of pain more than made up for it. "And it's called 'line dancing' and 'cowboy swing.'"

"Ok, so let me get this straight. Are you saying that you won't take me dancing?" Ava folded her arms over her chest and cocked her head at him. Her eyes seemed dangerous but also amused somehow.

"Ava, no, that's not what I mean. Of course, I would take you if I could, but I can't. Does that make sense?" Kelso wasn't even sure what he said made sense to him—Ava just muddled him up so easily.

"Are you sure about that, Sir Cowboy?" Ava asked skeptically, quite obviously looking him up and down—eyes lingering for a moment at his... waist.

Kelso froze. In utter dread, he looked down, and yes, he was quite, quite naked. Not a stitch of clothing anywhere to be seen. With a yelp, he snatched a pillow from the bed and covered himself, his face burning bright enough to be seen from space.

Ava smiled sweetly up at him. "Aw," she teased. "I was enjoying the view. Looks like I picked the right guy, at least." She winked.

Kelso wanted to die. If his embarrassment could have taken physical form, it would have strangled him to death right then and there. His mind was whirling, but then two things finally intruded at once: one, he could see, and two, he could stand without pain. Kelso had already acknowledged both but had not truly realized what that meant.

He did now.

"Finally," grumped Ava, eyes searching his face again as he took an internal inventory.

"How?" he finally asked. "I don't understand."

"Well..." Ava paused uncertainly. "Cassandra had a lot to do with it."

Kelso's jaw tightened at her name.

"Look, Kelso..." Ava paused again, and Kelso got the distinct feeling that she was carefully choosing her words. "Some things have changed... and it might take a little getting used to."

"What's changed?" Kelso wondered briefly if her feelings had changed towards him, but he didn't think that was it. Then why was she acting so weird? "I'm grateful for my sight, and I'm happy to be out of pain for the first time in a year, so why am I feeling uneasy?"

"Because you're not stupid or naïve," Ava answered promptly. "You were a mess, Kelso, you know that. Extraordinary measures were taken to save your life, to heal your leg, and to fix your eye. Not all of what was done on your behalf will be easy for you to accept. I just want you to know that we did the best we could."

Kelso looked down at his leg, holding it out in front of his body and peering at it as he did so. Ava whistled at the display but quickly swallowed it back down at his quick glare.

"Really?"

Ava shrugged unapologetically.

Kelso returned his attention to his knee. It wasn't easy to ascertain since he was kind of hampered by having to hold the pillow in front of his privates, but it seemed like he had full motion again. How could that be? He balanced for a second on his left leg, something he never could have done before without excruciating pain. He felt nothing.

He looked back up at Ava in wonder. "Am I truly healed?"

"Yes," she confirmed with a smile. "And I wasn't kidding about dancing either. I expect you to take me."

"It's been a long time," Kelso murmured, flexing his leg and bending his knee. He felt good. The Knight hadn't realized how much pain he had been in before this moment. How had he endured it for a year? The absence of it was heavenly, and he almost wanted to weep with gratitude—until he remembered who had healed him, and his joy withered somewhat.

"Yeah, well, dancing is like riding a bike, right? You'll pick it right back up, yes?" Ava seemed strangely fixated on dancing, at least to Kelso's reckoning, and he stopped his ministrations for a moment and looked at her suspiciously.

Her face seemed a little flushed, and he realized she was nervous. About what, he had no idea.

"Do you even know how to dance?" He paused. "For that matter, do you even know how to ride a bike?"

Ava sighed. "No to both." But then, in a smaller voice, she added, "Would you be willing to teach me?"

The uncertainty in her voice moved him deeply, and he started forward to put his arms around her before remembering that he was completely naked except for a pillow. He pulled up short and felt his face heat up again.

"Look," Ava said, "hold on."

The Princess circled him and headed to the small bathroom that adjoined his bedroom. Kelso circled with her so as to keep the pillow between them at all times, trying to be casual about it. Ava turned on the light and grabbed a towel off the rack. She threw it to him and turned her back for a moment so he could wrap it around himself. All his clothes seemed to be gone, but Kelso realized that he was still covered in dirt and dried blood.

He needed a shower.

As soon as the towel was wrapped securely around his waist, he headed towards the bathroom, intending to ask Ava for a little privacy so he could wash up. To his surprise, she spun around quickly as he approached her and held out her hand, palm facing him.

He stopped uncertainly. "What?"

"So, I told you we did our best, right?" Ava said and waited for his nod before continuing. "Well, your leg has a pretty good scar, and frankly, you picked up lots of little ones to complement that monster on your leg." She shifted gears suddenly. "And I need you to be more careful next time. What were you thinking? Haven't you ever been taught how to duck? Or block?" She was glaring at him accusingly, hand still out to keep him from entering the bathroom.

"Well..." Kelso said carefully, "It was about twenty to one. I did the best I could?" His last statement turned into a question as he watched storm clouds gather in her dark blue eyes.

"You could have died! You should have died!" Ava's hand started to shake a little. "What the hell were you thinking playing patty-cake with them while they were trying to kill you!? I know your reasons, and they mean so much to me, but..." She started to tear up, eyes brimming. "I really need you to live, ok? If someone attacks you, no matter who they are, fight to win! Please."

Ava's hand dropped, and she covered her face with her other.

Kelso's own eyes misted, and he leaned in a little, dropping his face next to hers. "I'm sorry. I beg your pardon, Princess. I promise to fight like a demon the next time I'm jumped by twenty Furies again. So… like tomorrow, probably."

Ava choked out a laugh behind her hand and raised her eyes to look at him. "You *did* fight like a demon. Your skill and bravery have changed a lot of opinions about you. In fact…" she trailed off, thinking about something for a moment, her eyes distant. Then they snapped back to him and sharpened. "So, you didn't answer me about the dancing. And riding a bike. Will you teach me or not?"

Kelso's confusion deepened. *Why was she so set on this?*

"Err, yes… I could pick up dancing again for you—it would come back naturally, like riding a bike, I'm sure. And yes, before you ask, I will also show you how to ride a bike too. Fair enough?" Kelso was beginning to think that Ava had another angle to this line of questioning; it was just too random.

Ava flushed again.

"Yeah, ok, good." She paused. "You have promised to teach me things I don't know how to do yet. Good talk." The Princess seemed very flustered. *What was going on?*

Ava's face reddened yet more, but she stepped aside to let him enter his small bathroom. He started forward, marveling at the lack of pain and stiffness as he did so. Brushing by her, his eyes fell on the shower greedily; he couldn't wait to sluice all the dried *stuff* off him.

Turning to ask Ava to leave so he could start immediately, his eyes found himself in the mirror and he froze in shock.

His reflection was still him, but also not. The left side of his face, from mid-forehead to mid-cheek, was covered in Dark—it looked like he had been tattooed with night. His eye was healed, which was a miracle, of course, but the line of Dark marched right around it from both sides.

To his horror, he saw that the Dark was moving, almost as if he himself was of the Dark now—in that location at least. The line that stretched down his face was about an inch thick and four inches long. Even though the flesh was unblemished, and his eyesight completely restored, he was marked by the power that had healed him.

He looked positively sinister.

"What in the hell have you done to me?" he whispered in fascinated horror, eyes fixed on his new face in the mirror.

"Besides saving your life, we restored your leg and eye. Oh yes, we also managed to patch up the other gazillion wounds you had in the process. Aside from that, not much. Why?" Ava's tone was light, but she was looking up at him with concern.

"Gazillion is not a real number, you know," he said absently, eyes still glued to his face. "It's completely arbitrary."

"Ah," Ava said thoughtfully. "Well, thank you for the lesson, Sir Professor, but you actually just proved that gazillion was exactly the right term for how many wounds you were sporting. Because you had a very large number of them." She shook her head and sighed. "And so I have arbitrarily decided gazillion comes closest to encompassing them all. I can do this because

107

I'm a Princess and have that kind of power. Naturally."

"Ok, point to you. Now, why do I look like an assassin out of some video game? You do understand that I'm sporting a black mark down the left side of my face, right? I'm not the only one seeing this, am I?" Kelso tore his eyes away from his reflection to look at her for confirmation that he was not, in fact, going insane.

Ava met his eyes a little nervously. "Yes, I see it too. Um... anyone that can see us for what we really are will as well."

"Oh my God," Kelso breathed and turned back towards the mirror. "I'm hideous."

"Well, I wouldn't go that far," Ava began, turning to look at him in the mirror as well. "You do stink a little bit, but not too badly, all things considered. Also, you need to shave and clean up your goatee. All easy fixes." She paused as his eyes locked on hers in the mirror in complete disbelief of what her idea of hideous was versus his. "Ok. Yes. I didn't want to say anything, but you really need a haircut, all right? The eighties called when you were out; they want their mullet back."

Kelso felt like he was starring in a supernatural version of candid camera and resisted the urge to look around for the hidden recording device. This could not be happening. His face looked like it was tattooed with pitch, and Ava was talking about how he styled his hair. He expelled his breath in an annoyed rush and mentally calmed himself.

"Ava," he said mildly, "I'm not talking about anything else but this damn mark across my face. I wasn't a friendly-looking guy in the first place. This—" he gestured to his face in the mirror "—makes me look like a tatted-up Viking with a chip on his shoulder. I look scary."

"I know," Ava said dreamily, "you're so freaking hot."

This could *not* be happening.

Kelso turned to look at her full-on; he was already sick of looking at himself. "Come again?" he said in disbelief, sure that he had completely misheard her.

"I said you're hot." Ava was staring up at him avidly, her lips curved in a small smile.

"Are you swooning?" the Knight asked in horror. "What's *wrong* with you?"

Ava laughed lightly and moved in a little closer. "Kelso, can you think logically for just a minute?" She waited patiently for his reply, and he nodded uncertainly.

"So, your eye is healed. You can see. How we did it is a story for a bit later because there were a few complications—" Ava broke off and frowned at him as Kelso jerked a finger up to point at the mark on his face with raised eyebrows. "No, that is not a complication. We will talk more about the true complications facing you in a bit."

Kelso just stared at her.

"I told you to think logically. Listen, you said you look like a tattooed Viking or assassin with an attitude, right?" She waited for him to nod again. "Well...," she drawled, "I agree. And it's very attractive. Women are going to start throwing themselves at you—at least from the Dark side. And in case you forgot, I grew up in the Dark. You were never a pretty boy, and I love that about you. But this?" She leaned up to get a better look at his face. "My God, you look like a pissed-off emissary of death with a toothache. And yes, I like it a lot... and I won't be the only one either."

Kelso didn't know what to say. He glanced at himself in the mirror again; he still hated how he looked, but, if he was being completely honest, the black line of Dark looked almost natural on his hard face. He looked ridiculously intimidating, yes, but he could also see. He had questions about how it had happened—who had given their Dark to him, and how his Light had not rejected it entirely—but it could wait.

Right now, he just wanted to take a shower and round up some clothes.

"Ok," he agreed. "I'll stop clutching at my pearls over it. I'm grateful that I didn't lose my eye, so however you got it done, thank you."

Ava nodded distractedly, still looking up at him. Her cheeks were coloring a bit. She was so amazingly beautiful, he felt like his heart could break. He had to admit, it was kind of nice that she found him "hot" now. Ava wasn't evil in the least, he thought, but her tastes might still be a little *dark*, even so.

Kelso needed to screw his head on straight, black mark or not, and find out what had happened while he was down.

"All right," he said with more enthusiasm than he felt, "if you will excuse me, I need to shower before I give Charlie a run for his money in the stink department."

"Yeah, ok," Ava said, still looking up into his face. She didn't move.

"Err..." Kelso was at a loss. Again.

"How long has it been?" she asked suddenly, face intent.

"Since what?" His eyebrows furrowed together.

"Since you've been with someone." Ava's cheeks reddened again, but her eyes were very direct. She seemed determined.

Kelso froze in shock. Was this conversation going where he thought it might be going? The Knight gazed into Ava's deep-blue eyes for a moment. Except for Cassandra, it had been over a year. His time with Cass didn't count, he decided, and he would do his best to forget it. The Arch Mage had manipulated him horribly, and Kelso wouldn't allow what she did to him to affect his relationship with Ava. It wasn't fair, and it wasn't right.

As he thought it through, Ava nodded slightly in encouragement and understanding, almost as if she knew what he was thinking about and agreed with his conclusions regarding it.

"A long time," he said at last. "In some ways, at least since before the night of my ascension."

For some reason, at the mention of that night, she flinched. Kelso had not told her about how he first donned the mantle of the Ebon Knight; it was a part of his past that he tried to keep hidden. Why, then, did she look so uncomfortable—even sad—when he referred to it?

"I'm sure that was a horrible time for you," she murmured, shyly reaching out for his hand. "I would love for you to tell me about it someday. If you want to, that is."

Kelso nodded; her touch felt electric.

"So," she continued, taking a steadying breath, "it's been over a year since you were… intimate… with someone? Is that right?"

Kelso nodded again, his mouth going dry.

"Hmm," she said thoughtfully. "Tell me, is it like riding a bike?"

Kelso almost smiled, even as enthralled as he was with her. The Knight now knew what she was doing earlier—she had been setting him up. For this.

Ava looked like she was fighting a grin, too, and she reached out with her other hand to lightly trace his Dark mark, eyes drifting over his face as she did so.

"Well, yes," Kelso answered, clearing his throat, "I have heard that the, uh, act… comes back quickly and easily. So, I guess it is like riding a bike in that respect."

"I've never ridden a bike. I wouldn't know." Ava's eyes locked on his now, and she cupped his face in both hands as she looked up at him.

"I could teach you," Kelso offered, his voice trembling a little.

"I love you, Ava. You know that don't you?"

"I do, and I love you too, Kelso." Ava rose on her tiptoes and whispered in his ear, "Please teach me everything… my Knight."

# Chapter 6

Jesslyn woke up about an hour after dawn and stretched. It had been a long time since she had slept so soundly, and she realized it was because she had a purpose again. She now had another worthwhile goal—other than entrapping her sister—and she felt the new challenge would do her a lot of good.

She padded into the bathroom and prepped for the day, her mind turning over various plans before finally settling on one. It was risky; her new allies meant to crush the renegade Furies tonight, and that was fine, but they also meant to kill Ava and Kelso—and that was not. Ava's capture would usher Jesslyn into her new life, and she needed Kelso alive to enjoy it.

She wasn't completely sure Kelso had survived last night—that arrow he'd taken towards the end looked like it hurt—but she would just have to trust that her baby sister got to him in time. Ava was not stupid, and Jesslyn believed she would figure out how to keep the Knight alive. She had to, or Jesslyn was doomed.

Humming happily, Jesslyn rummaged through the dead men's toiletries until she found a toothbrush, liberally applied toothpaste to it, and brushed vigorously. Mint. She loved mint… Today was already shaping up to be a great day—although she was nervous about the step she was about to take.

The allies she had made recently were eerie and weird, which was really saying something coming from her. Jesslyn suspected that they were a faction of the Light, perhaps disillusioned with how the war was going. Maybe a secret cabal of their mages had banded together to ingratiate themselves as her ally in order to form something better on the corpses of those who couldn't see the big picture.

Jesslyn was not as nearly opposed to that now as she would have been just a few days ago. After all, wasn't she interested in a Knight of the Light? Maybe he could be the leader of this new third power, and she with him, always by his side. Yes. She liked the thought of that a lot.

Putting on her ripped and bloodied clothes sucked, but she had cleaned them as thoroughly as she could in the shower and left them hanging overnight to dry, so they weren't completely disgusting. She would need to pick up some new clothes today.

Finally, she could put off the call no longer.

Sitting on the bed again, Jesslyn dialed her father. He picked up on the second ring.

"Yes?" he said in his deep voice; she could imagine the little frown on his face at her audacity. To call him directly was quite out of the ordinary, but Jesslyn knew she needed the King himself to greenlight what she had in mind.

"Your Highness," she said formally, "I have a report to make."

"Oh? Does it have anything to do with my wayward youngest daughter and the traitorous band of Furies now flocking to her in Reno, Nevada?" His voice was tight, clipped, and controlled.

Quickly, Jesslyn reshuffled her strategy. The King's foreknowledge of what was happening here put her at a disadvantage. "Yes, my lord, it does," she answered, mind racing.

"Well, I already know. So, goodbye, Jess—"

"The Ebon Knight has appeared!" she blurted. "He is here with Ava." Jesslyn held her breath and waited. Silence came from the other end of the line, but he had not hung up.

After thirty seconds, he asked, "And you know this, how?"

"I have seen him, Sire. He accompanies the Dark Witch and—"

"Never use that name for her again, or I will cut your tongue from your useless mouth. Do you understand me?" Her father hadn't even raised his voice, but Jesslyn shivered at his rebuke. She knew he meant every word and would follow through with his threat if she should forget.

A few hundred years ago, in a fit of crazy hubris, Jesslyn had sought to hide herself away in his quarters. To this day, she was not sure why she had decided to spy on her father or what she would do with any information she gleaned. Looking back, maybe she was just bored. In any case, it had ended badly for her—very badly.

Wrapped within her gift, confident in her ability to confound the senses of even the King and Queen, Jesslyn had slipped in and waited in their room for them. They had eventually returned, her mother trailing her disgusting Dark as always, her father walking next to her as they entered through the oversized door that led to their bedchambers.

*Maybe,* Jesslyn thought, *I could even hear the Queen speak.*

Once inside, her father made his way across the floor, angling towards Jesslyn but not looking at her. Her mother had stopped abruptly and was looking out into space, for all the world unconcerned with, well, anything really.

Jesslyn had but one quick moment of alarm before her father had her by the throat and effortlessly lifted in the air with one hand. His face was completely impassive as he stared in her eyes; her mother didn't even bother to look at her at all.

Jesslyn's hands flew to her throat, and for one second, she considered injecting her poison into her father, but a small voice warned her that she would be killed—painfully—if she did. Gasping for air, feet dangling over a foot off the ground, Jesslyn had managed to rasp, "I'm sorry, Father. I meant no harm. Please forgive me."

At her words, his face finally softened—into a sneer.

The King pulled his daughter close, still dangling, until she was only inches away from his face. "If you ever call me father again, I will kill you. You will always address me as your King. Do I make myself clear?"

"Yes… Sire." Jesslyn was seeing stars and had barely enough strength left to murmur out her affirmative. She glanced over at her mother briefly, but the Queen still stared into space, uncaring about the tableau taking place not thirty feet from her.

His hand loosened on her throat just enough for her to draw in some air, and she staved off unconsciousness by mere moments.

The King put her down on her feet, still holding her by the throat, but lightly.

"Now, then," he said, face expressionless again, "let's begin your punishment for daring to enter the King and Queen's room, shall we?"

Jesslyn's eyes widened just before the first open-handed slap caught her across the face. She hadn't even seen him move. Eyes tearing, she managed to look at her mother—hoping to see *something* from the Queen that might ward off the beating she was about to receive.

Her heart fluttered with hope for a moment because her mom had indeed turned to look at her and the King, but another slap, this one a backhand, knocked her sideways, and her mother was no longer in view. The next slap jerked her face back to the other side once more, and she could see her mom again. Jesslyn's blood ran cold at the sight, even as the King backhanded her yet again the other way.

The Queen had been smiling.

She had been beaten almost to death. Slowly. Since that day, Jesslyn lived in fear of them both, and she never again made the mistake of addressing her father as anything other than her King. All of those memories rushed through her now at his threat, and she swallowed hard.

"Of course, Sire. My apologies." Jesslyn paused, afraid that this rash and desperate gambit had backfired on her spectacularly. "I know where they are, but they are well fortified behind runes and accompanied by many guards."

A full minute passed, and then another. Jesslyn almost asked if he was still there but was too terrified to do so.

Finally, the King asked, "What do you need in order to root them out?"

***

"Make way, out of my way!" Janus bellowed as he plowed through the crowded foyer.

The guards knew him well. Paladins all, they merely watched as he pushed and shoved through the crowd of Childer and others of the Light that perpetually seemed to mill around in the Temple—even at this early hour. They made no move to stop him as he commandeered an elevator, pushing a couple of Priests out of the car bodily in his haste.

Hurriedly, Janus fished out the sacred key from underneath his shirt and inserted it into the cleverly hidden hole accessed by pulling the sixtieth button out and away. He turned the key left once and back, then right twice, and the elevator rose.

Janus watched the light as it flickered through the floors with barely contained frustration: *twenty three, twenty-four, twenty-five...*

"Come on, come on..." he growled to himself as the elevator steadily made its way up—and past—the sixtieth floor of the high rise. To all but a select few, the sixtieth floor was supposed to be the top floor, but it was not. Another ten seconds brought him to

119

the actual uppermost level of the building, and he exited.

In front of him lay a grand foyer with marbled columns and expensive water displays. The air was cool and sweet, and despite his hurry, he approached the opposite end of the large room at a stately pace. This was not the kind of place to act as anything but proper—at least if you wanted to keep your head attached to your body.

A cluster of Knights, Paladins, and Priests waited on the other side for him, almost a dozen pairs of eyes watching his every move. These several were the personal guards of the Council of the Light, and the men and women who made up this elite guard had no tolerance for fools who lacked decorum. Unlike the rabble on the ground floor of the Temple, these adherents of the Light expected all who entered to act with appropriate deference.

"Peace under the Light," Janus said, bowing deeply to the large man in front of him, blazingly armored and armed with a large poleaxe of wondrous beauty. The man held his weapon loosely in one hand, the weapon butted firmly on the ground, and Janus couldn't help but admire it for a second. The deadly axe gleamed under the overhead lights of the Temple, its wicked edge sharp enough to cleave armor, bone, sinew, and flesh without perceptible friction.

Its owner, Baston Tijeran, was infamous as the unofficial enforcer of the Light's precepts. He was a zealot of unbreakable faith and towering skill, and it was whispered that he had killed more of the Light than he had of the Dark. If you were smart, you paid him proper respect.

Janus was smart.

"And peace unto you, Janus," responded the man in a deep baritone. "What brings you to Las Vegas and the sanctum today?"

"An urgent message for the Council. May I present my seal?" Even though none of the warriors present had made the slightest move towards him, Janus knew well that he would be slaughtered out of hand if he made any move that could be construed as threatening. As such, he held perfectly still with his hands open at his sides. His palms were sweating as he waited for the inevitable—and dreaded his unavoidable response.

"What message do you bring that would require me to allow you to interrupt the Council?" Baston asked lazily, his index finger tapping the shaft of his weapon.

"I'm sorry, sir, I'm not at liberty to divulge the information I carry to any except the Council themselves, in person. Once again, may I present my seal?" Sweat broke out on his forehead as Janus saw a few guards on the periphery of his vision turn his way, squaring up with him ever so slightly. Hands drifted towards weapons, and the room's temperature—previously cool—became cold to Janus's reckoning. He was certain that the sweat now breaking out all over him was steaming in the air.

What would they do if they felt his nervousness was anything other than benign and understandable? He was afraid he knew the answer.

Baston just stared at him for a moment, jaw clenching and

relaxing a few times as he considered. "Very well," he finally said. "Present your seal."

Janus almost sighed in relief. Carefully and slowly, he reached into his pocket and pulled out a thick silver seal stamped with a pyramid and an eye. He held it in his hand palm up to Baston and willed his Light to awaken it.

The seal began to glow softly, and Janus pinched it in his fingers and held it high for a ten-count, turning it this way and that so that all the guardians could see it for themselves.

Baston nodded once after Janus lowered his hand.

"So be it," he said. "Follow me."

The executioner of the Light turned on his heels and strode away towards two large silver doors laced with platinum runes. They glowed with inner power, and occasional flashes of lightning arced from the doors randomly. Janus hurried to catch up with Baston, seal still clutched in his hand as a priest would clutch a crucifix in uncertain lands.

This was not the first time Janus had come to the Temple to deliver messages of dire import to the Council, but it was the first time he had been here since the Arch Mage himself had... defected. A new force was afoot in the lands, and it had claimed their mightiest before it had been discovered.

The Light was in an uproar over it, and many among them feared that the loss of the Arch Mage was the last nail in their collective coffin. Emerie had retained a remarkable strength despite his advanced age. However, in the last century, his frailty had grown to the point where he frequently relied on the support of his young niece, Cass.

Janus had thought her amazingly beautiful on the few opportunities he had seen her—with short platinum blonde hair and a shapely, willowy figure. Her intellect was rumored to be keen, but her power was very mediocre, barely strong enough to allow her to enter the Priests. She had been missing and presumed lost in the battle that ended Emerie, but Janus had information contradicting that. It was why he was here—to report on her survival and location.

The Council had put out an edict to look for the young woman, and it was easy to understand why—she had been privy to the Council's inner workings for over a hundred years. That type of knowledge could not be left unfettered.

It got better. Apparently, she was in the company of Marcus Dain, Lord Commander of the Paladins—also someone who was presumed to have died in the battle with Emerie.

That both he and Cass lived was amazing, but that they had not seen fit to return to the fold was ominous. Janus wondered what the Council would do. As a Knight Courier, he was tasked with hand-delivering messages of the utmost importance gleaned from the many sources—both mundane and supernatural—that he was privy to, but this message was perhaps the most important he had ever carried. There was even a push to expand the Courier network due to the nature of the force that had recently entered the field.

Some were calling it "the Other," and Janus supposed that was as good a name as any. The Other was chaos itself: insidious and *catching* was perhaps the best word for it. An infected member of the Light became something else altogether within a few weeks of exposure, and the disease—or possession, or whatever it was—made the affected victims even more powerful than they'd been originally.

Such had happened to Emerie. The Arch Mage apparently went berserk in the council rooms one day, and the subsequent battle had resulted in the demise of several great heroes within the Light before Emerie was brought to bay. It was whispered that once shackled and subdued, the Arch Mage had screamed obscenities at the Mages, and his madness had forced them to put him down.

It was an ignoble end for one as storied and powerful as Emerie, and the loss of a few dozen other luminaries within the Light only added to the distress felt by all. Worse, many of the fallen had not been found. Powerful magics had been cast in the battle, and so it was thought that their remains had been obliterated.

The forward-looking and wise Mages that now comprised the Council had not been so sure, however, and search parties had been notified the world over with strict orders to report any of the several dozen unaccounted for.

Janus had found two of them.

Due to the nature of the new threat, the Council had insisted any such discoveries were to be reported face to face and under strict cover of secrecy—and this was why Janus was here in person. The Light was unsure of who to trust or how far the corruption had spread. All were suspect now.

Baston took up a small mallet hanging next to the large doors and struck three times. The reverberations sounded strange in the otherwise quiet sanctum. He then slipped the cord back over the hook and returned the mallet to its place. The glowing wards powered down, and with no further ado, he pushed upon the doors and ushered Janus into the room, closing the doors behind him.

Janus stood alone in front of the Council and immediately made his way into the center of the room. He ascended to a large circular dais that was overlooked by several balconies. The whole scene looked more forlorn and darker than Janus remembered, partially because three of the eight seats were empty. The Arch Mage's chair—throne, really—and two Mage chairs were without occupants. The five Mages that remained were silent as he strode in.

With a slight twinge of misgiving, Janus glanced at the only other chair in the Council chambers—a smaller, unassuming piece that Cass had often sat upon. Well, she had at least sat on it every time Janus had cause to report, and now he was reporting about her instead of in front of her. *The world is upside down now*, he thought with a touch of sadness.

"Janus," murmured Tich Issan in a soft voice, "do you have word for me?"

"I do, my Lord," answered Janus formally, bowing to Tich and the other four mages in deference. "Thank you for granting me this audience."

With the Arch Mage deposed, Mage Tich was now in charge of the Council. Janus felt it likely that he was addressing the next Arch Mage once all the formalities had been met for his ascension.

"Of course, Janus," Tich said. "All true followers of the Light are always welcome. Your report?"

From somewhere, a low hum started up. Janus had never heard its like in the council chambers, but he found it annoying almost immediately. It was a soft sound, but it kept intruding into his thoughts, and he found himself trying to block it out subconsciously.

"I have located Marcus Dain of the Paladins; he is in the company of Cass..." Janus trailed off, realizing he didn't know Cass's last name. He had crossed her path many times over the past decades; how was it that he had never asked?

"Yes, they are in Reno, I know," said one of the Mages behind Janus. The Courier turned to look quizzically up at the Mage. A strange turn of words, true, but the speaker who had interjected sounded exactly like Tich.

"Uh, yes... I suspect they have been in the area for a few weeks, but early last night, one of our Childer managed to spot them at a distance. She reported that it almost seemed like Cass wanted to be discovered. The two of them were quite brazen and conspicuous." Janus was having a little trouble thinking; his head was pounding, and the soft hum had become louder. Strains of haunting melody accompanied it—no, clashed jarringly with it.

No, again. Was the melody completely independent of the hum, or was it inexorably linked? It was... confusing.

Janus was starting to feel very uneasy and almost sick. A fresh dimpling of sweat broke out on his forehead. He suddenly wanted to leave the room as fast as he could, and he crazily considered making a dash for it.

"No doubt she did," Tich said. "The Arch Mage is crafty indeed. Don't worry, Janus, I will bring her to heel shortly. Want to join me?"

Janus stared in horror at the Mage that spoke. Her name was Elona Redgrave, and she was not Tich, but his voice issued from her nonetheless. The hum was long gone, and Janus was now awash in the mysteries of a song with no end and no beginning. He looked back and forth between the Mages, turning in a circle as he did so, and dimly realized that all five Mages had the same smirk on their face as they regarded him.

*Exactly* the same smirk.

Janus screamed in agony as the song overwhelmed him, and he dropped to his knees. Smirking.

# Chapter 7

It was mid-morning and snowing by the time Kelso and Ava sallied forth from his bedroom. They were holding hands casually, both strictly monitoring their respective polarities to keep the shocks to a minimum.

The occasional zings they felt when Light met Dark were not nearly as bad as they were just two short days ago. Ava had speculated that this was because of his own Dark now. Kelso wasn't so sure, but it didn't matter. Right now, he was nervous. There was so much he didn't know about what the day held for him. He had only once gathered the willpower necessary to ask Ava questions about just that—where Cassandra was, and what had happened to the Furies last night. Ava had just told him to shut up and keep doing what he was doing. Again.

And that had been that.

Kelso was floating along on cloud nine, of course, but with so many unanswered questions, he was afraid that he was going to be brought down to earth pretty quickly.

He was.

Ava's hand tightened with either irritation or worry for a moment before he saw what had caught her attention when they walked into the living room. The window curtains facing the street were open, allowing them to see the front yard, which sloped gently to the street. The snow was really coming down now, but Kelso's eyes still picked out a gang of Furies standing out on the sidewalk. Most of them were turned away from the house to guard the street. Some were talking with each other, too, but most just stood still and quiet. Snow had accumulated on many of them, but the Knight knew that was of no concern—they would be perfectly comfortable even completely buried under it.

What was a concern was the second gang of Furies in his house. His eyes caught three standing next to his door and many more spread out over the floor and furniture. Of the three at the door, one was a Black, fierce-looking woman who smiled at him and nodded. The other two copied, sans smiles, one a smaller Japanese woman and the other a rangy younger woman with reddish brown hair pulled back into a short, thick braid.

Those were okay, and he thought he even recognized the two larger women as Ava's personal guards. What was not okay, though, was the almost two dozen other Furies sleeping in his front room, some of them literally piled on top of each other on the floor. Still more were sprawled out on his chairs. The fire was going in the hearth, and next to it slept Carmen and Charlie. Carmen had draped one arm over Charlie's big body, and he was snoring up a storm, his big nose just inches away from another Fury's shoulder blades where she slept on her side.

Kelso couldn't make sense of what he was seeing and merely stood frozen for a moment. The Furies were deeply asleep, almost unconscious, and he was struck by the complete lack of Dark in any of them. It looked like they had been stripped of their powers entirely.

As his eyes traveled over them in wonder, he came across a

face he recognized—the woman from last night who had grinned at him from the barn's loft. His heart sped up a little at seeing her, but a small thrill of adrenaline jolted him when he recognized one of the women sleeping on his chairs as Lilly. She was the one who had driven the Furies to attack him in the first place—and who had also struck the blow that rent his eye. She was now inexplicably conked out in his living room.

The Knight looked at her with mixed emotions: hate, regret, and confusion being the most dominant. What was she doing here? How had she passed the wards—and why? He glanced down at Ava and was surprised by the strange mix of gratitude and exasperation that crossed her features, too, as she studied the crowded room.

Charlie's own snoring startled him out of his sleep for a second, and he looked up blearily and right at Kelso. His tongue was out, of course, but the look that crossed the dog's face when he saw Kelso brought a sting to the Knight's eyes. Ava released his hand to walk over to her Furies, conversing quietly with them as Charlie struggled to his feet and carefully made his way around the sleeping warriors—looking up every couple of seconds to make sure Kelso had not moved.

Kelso waited until Charlie had extricated himself and knelt. The big bulldog rushed into his arms, snorting and sneezing. Kelso gave him a thorough petting and captured Charlie's head once to land a smacker on his dog's nose. At that, Ava stopped mid-sentence and turned around, glaring at Kelso.

"Uh-oh, bubs," Kelso whispered in a raspy voice to his dog.

"Looks like someone is getting a little jealous."

"Kelso," Ava warned dangerously, "if you want any more kisses from me, you might want to lay off kissing your dog so much."

"See?" Kelso whispered conspiratorially to Charlie, scratching his back and rump with zest. It felt so good to pet his dog again that Kelso would have been content to do it all day. Unfortunately, there were other and more pressing matters that demanded his time.

Kelso straightened to gaze at the mass of women in his front room again as Ava approached with her three Furies in tow. All three of the women examined him with direct eyes, but all three did so with respect and without hostility.

"Kelso, may I introduce you to my friends and guardians?" Ava asked perfunctorily before turning and gesturing to each with a hand. "This is Chandra, my oldest companion," she said, pointing at the large dusky woman who had smiled at Kelso earlier.

Chandra stepped forward and enveloped Kelso in a hug, which surprised him and boggled Ava.

"You're an honorable man and incredible fighter," Chandra said, accent thick as she struggled with some emotion that Kelso couldn't quite identify. "You will be a fine mate to Ava."

Kelso gulped. "Err... thank you, Chandra." His face turned slightly red at Chandra's knowing grin as she held him at arm's length and patted his shoulders hard with both hands, rocking him. Her little display of affection would have bruised a normal human, and her quick shake before she let go almost gave Kelso whiplash.

Chandra moved aside so Ava could introduce Jae and Misima. The Japanese woman actually bowed to him, but Jae held out her hand and firmly shook his in greeting.

"These three are my personal guard," Ava announced, "and you will be seeing a lot of them, so be nice."

Kelso detected a slight emphasis on "three" during Ava's introduction, and the look the Furies shot towards the Princess made the Knight think it was not so cut and dry as that. If he had to guess, Misima was not quite as solidly in as Ava apparently believed she was.

"I'm always nice," Kelso protested.

"Yeah," Ava said with zero conviction and exchanged glances with Jae. The other two women looked similarly unimpressed with his declaration.

It dawned on Kelso that he was drastically outnumbered— both as the sole representative of the Light and as a male. The Knight's eyes flicked down to Charlie. His bulldog's tongue was still out as he sat quietly, staring up at Kelso and waiting patiently for some reunion snacky-poos. He was drooling onto the floor a little too.

*Hmm,* Kelso thought wryly. *No help there.*

Kelso reached down and ruffled his dog's ears before politely making his way through the four super-dangerous women who had all been his enemies just two days ago. They separated to let him pass as he led Charlie to the fridge. A beef stick later, Kelso had collected his thoughts enough to ask some questions.

Turning, he saw Ava standing at the entrance to his small kitchen, head tilted as she regarded him. Kelso's heart swelled at the sight of her. He couldn't help but smile, and her answering grin was both beautiful and mischievous. She nodded her head almost imperceptibly back towards the bedroom door and raised her eyebrows twice.

"You're incorrigible," he mouthed at her with faux outrage.

"I'm making up for lost time," she responded loudly, and laughed as his face flushed in embarrassment. There was an edge to her laughter, though—she knew the questioning was about to begin.

It wouldn't be polite to make her wait. The Knight strode up to stand next to Ava and surveyed the mass of women still sleeping all over his living room.

"So," he said conversationally, "I love what you did with the place while I was out."

Ava merely nodded, also examining the mass of females that were cluttering up his home. Her lips were pursed.

"Want to tell me about it?" Kelso asked, gesturing at his unexpected visitors. "Why are the same Furies who tried to kill me last night sleeping in my house? And why are they sleeping so... hard?" The Knight didn't know how else to describe it, but he was positive he could shake any of the women present—roughly—without waking them. Their sleep looked unnatural.

Ava's evasiveness this morning made a lot of sense to him now. If he had been aware that there were over twenty women mere feet from the bedroom, it might have caused him a little... *anxiety*. That was something to think about, he realized, because she hadn't had any qualms at all. Ava had easily trapped him into doing what she wanted him to do. It wasn't like he was an unwilling participant, but her timing was a little suspect and could definitely use an adjustment moving forward.

Kelso looked down at Ava at the thought, and she looked like she was trying to stifle another laugh. Her face quickly smoothed out under his perusal, though, and she glanced up at him under her thick lashes, midnight blue eyes still amused.

"Well, what do you want to know?" she asked, eyes flickering back to the women.

"Are you serious?"

Ava sighed. "Yes, ok. These are the Furies that attacked you last night. You know, the ones who were trying to kill you while you were going all pacifistic on them? Do you remember that?" She glanced back up at him, her eyes no longer amused.

Kelso didn't recall anything pacifistic about his actions the previous night, except that he had tried his level best to avoid killing any of them. He vividly remembered shooting and beating them into unconsciousness, however, and opened his mouth to say so before Ava cut him off.

"I know what you're going to say, and I understand why you did what you did. It was sweet of you, and I love you for it. I also hate you for it, though, because it was so reckless and final. I'm very torn." She paused, thinking it through. "Maybe we need counseling!" She looked up at him with eager eyes. "Could we go to couples counseling?" She sounded like doing so would be a wonderful way to spend an afternoon, and her whole face seemed thrilled by the thought.

Kelso's forehead creased in confusion. A movement over Ava's shoulder caught his attention as he saw Chandra bury her face in her hand with a sigh. Jae just shrugged sympathetically at Kelso, and Misima looked poleaxed.

The Knight refocused on the Princess, who was still looking up at him excitedly. "You want to go to... couples... therapy?" he clarified, once again resisting the urge to look around for a hidden camera.

"Well, yeah." Ava was still into it. "We *are* a couple, right?"

Kelso frowned. Ava had endured the worst childhood ever, and her formative years were no picnic either. Even with her astonishing good looks and superior intellect and wit, she carried blind spots. Was this her way of confirming they were together?

"Until the day I die," Kelso answered solemnly, "or until the day you get your eyesight fixed and dump me. Whichever comes first."

"Neither is going to happen," Ava said firmly. Her eyes searched his, apparently liking what she saw, judging by her soft expression.

"I hope not, but I don't think we need to go to a couple's therapist to make it official, ok?" Kelso didn't like the idea of sitting around talking to a stranger about his feelings. What were they supposed to say? *"Hi, Doc. So, look, I'm a Knight of the Light; she's a Princess of the Dark. She's upset with me because I didn't kill some supernatural women who attacked me last night. Ugh! Furies, am I right? Anyways, can you help us out?"*

*Help us into an insane asylum is more like it,* he thought sourly.

"So, we're official, then?" Ava said, still searching his eyes.

"Yes, of course," Kelso answered, flustered. Ava was looking at him so intently that he was becoming self-conscious.

"Ok." Ava nodded in satisfaction and turned back to the women sleeping in his front room before raising her left hand for his perusal, waving it around dramatically. "You better put a ring on it, then," she said jokingly.

"Careful what you wish for, Princess, or I just might," he said, but what he was thinking was much more definitive. For him, it was her or no one—ever again.

Ava's hand faltered for a second with playfully brandishing the unadorned ring finger for his benefit. She looked back up at him with an expression of such love that Kelso was thunderstruck for a moment, and the world fell away. They stood there, looking into each other's eyes before a small cough from Chandra brought them back down to earth.

"This is going to get old, fast," Jae murmured to Chandra loud enough to be heard by all.

"Kids," was all Chandra answered in return.

# Chapter 8

"So, let me get this straight," Kelso clarified. "Cassandra let the Furies who attacked me pass the wards in return for their help? And it's their Dark I'm wearing?" The Knight was lost at sea over Ava's explanation... once she finally got around to telling him, that was.

"Yes, and it was really painful for them, too," Ava confirmed without a modicum of sympathy in her voice—she was just reporting the facts.

"How painful?"

She shrugged. "Most of them screamed. A few did not. But they all passed out once Cassandra had drawn out every bit of Dark she could without killing them."

"That's a little cold," Kelso observed, looking down at her hard face.

The Princess hesitated. "I know. I just can't help thinking that it serves them right. If they hadn't attacked you in the first place, they wouldn't have been on the hook to fix you back up. It's on them."

Kelso didn't know what to say to that.

They both looked at the women for another minute, and Ava's Furies were contemplating them, too, with very sad expressions. Kelso felt something else was going on, but he couldn't quite figure it out.

"Are they going to be ok?"

"Yes," Ava answered shortly. "They should wake up in another day or so, and their Dark will regenerate back to where it was—probably."

"Did you force them to give up their Dark for me?" Kelso asked uneasily; it was something he could see her doing.

"No. If it were up to me, they never would have had the chance to help you. I would have killed them or run them off." Ava paused. "Don't get me wrong, I'm beyond grateful that they volunteered, but this group of Furies seems a little crazy to me, honestly. It did work out in the end, though. At least they made amends."

At Ava's side, all three Furies nodded in agreement.

"I don't understand," Kelso said plaintively. "Why did they volunteer?"

"Guilt," Ava answered promptly before hesitating again, "and in admiration of your fighting prowess. And because you showed them mercy... I think." Ava said the last part reluctantly, like she wasn't used to the word or concept.

"I wasn't merciful." Kelso disagreed, remembering some of the extreme damage he had dished out in the barn.

"Yeah, you were," Ava retorted. "You know how I know? Twenty-one attacked you last night, and twenty-one are now sleeping soundly in your front room, all present and accounted for." She made a small sound of disgust.

Again, Kelso wasn't sure what to say to that.

"Well, why are they still here? Why didn't you move them to a bigger place or something?" This facet of the wholly strange and unexpected scenario kept nibbling at Kelso's understanding the most: he couldn't figure out why they were still in his front room. The Knight was grateful that they had enough honor to balance the scales with him, but to now sleep it off under his roof seemed a little excessive.

"Because that was the pact they struck for their help, and Cassandra agreed," Ava answered again before adding, "and also because they're crazy—like I said." Again, the other Furies evidenced their agreement.

Kelso wanted to tear his hair out in frustration. *What was he missing?*

"How long are they going to stay? And why do you keep calling them crazy?"

Ava didn't reply for a full minute before looking up at him coolly. "How long they stay is not for me to determine. I, too, gave my word to them about some... things they wanted. I promised to stay out of it." The Princess didn't look happy about the agreement. "And they're crazy just because they are. Obviously."

Kelso ground his teeth. It was becoming painfully clear that he wouldn't be getting the answers he wanted from Ava anytime soon. He shifted gears.

"Where is Cassandra?" he asked, half hoping she was gone.

"She's out in the backyard with your sword," Ava answered neutrally.

Amazingly, she sounded much more relaxed about the Arch Mage and Argenta than the sleeping Furies. Cassandra St. Augustine was the single most influential and dangerous enemy known to the Dark, and Kelso's sword was the single most destabilizing force in the Light. Kelso could honestly not think of a more sinister pairing than the two.

Ava didn't share his trepidation regarding them, it seemed. Again, Kelso felt there was more going on than he knew. He glanced out the window. It was really snowing hard now, and visibility was already bad. His little house shook under a strong wind that was kicking up—it looked like they were in for a nasty night.

***

Cassandra's eyes were closed as she surfed the possibilities. The timelines were in flux—as they often were during periods of great conflict—and this was no exception. There was something new that concerned the Arch Mage, though, a feeling that had gradually come to consume her. She felt like the loom from which she read the threads of fate and happenstance had become... *thinner*.

She wasn't sure how she knew, but she did.

The Arch Mage couldn't shake the idea that there was a winnowing of futures taking place—a large-scale ending of timelines that she had not seen since the great wars. The lead-up to those earth-shattering conflicts had been easy to predict, clear in their possible ramifications, and—while tragic—had not caused her to be as disquieted as she was now.

In Cassandra's estimation, hundreds of millions of threads were terminating at a point not too distant in the future. Ending after ending—squared—and then squared again. It was like a great contagion was about to be released onto the Earth, and few would be spared its ravages. She recognized that the catalyst for this upheaval was the Other, but worse was that some of the possible cures were about as bad as the disease.

Cassandra feared that the best countermeasures—the ones with the highest probabilities of success—would also plunge the world into ruin. Was there a choice, though? One world balanced against existence itself? It would seem like an easy trade to make, and the Arch Mage was used to making such types of bargains with herself in the timelines, but this was much bigger both in scope and scale.

She opened her eyes and sighed before raising both hands to massage her temples.

*"Don't wimp out, Arch Mage,"* Argenta said, and an image came to Cassandra of a spilled glass of milk and a whiny version of herself crying over it.

"I am not unaware that you look forward to this evil time, but my response to it will not be swayed by your personal desires." Cassandra had argued with the sword—in one form or another, by one name or the other—for millennia. She still found Argenta annoying, though. How could anyone have such a bottomless lust

142

for carnage and slaughter?

*"It's easy. Please don't act like the blood of untold millions doesn't stain you, too. Be honest in what you have done and why."*

Argenta was just stating facts, nothing more and nothing less. Cassandra knew that her sisters' roles had always been—and would always be—different. There were three of them, and they had struggled against each other or collaborated with each other countless times since the Light's first spark had broken the unending Dark. Similarly, each of them had won, and each of them had lost countless times as well. Their triumphs and defeats all served the balance, though, and always had.

But now it was different. The Other had upset their eternal dance. The first blow struck three hundred years ago when their oldest—Argenta—was driven mad. Only the immediate intervention by Cassandra and her remaining sister had kept this world from collapsing as a result. That strike had been the opening salvo, and the Other was now preparing its follow-up. And they were not adequately prepared to defend, let alone counterstrike.

They had been foolish. Their error may now cost them not just this world, but all of them. The three sisters had always been above such contrivances as "good" and "evil," but never before could Cassandra remember the differences between them being quite so vast. She had always been the moderator between her older and younger sisters, but the eldest was now in pieces. And the youngest was forging ahead on a brutal plan that might just work against the Other, but at such a cost as to be close to unthinkable.

*"Other planets have burned, and other timelines have ended. It is the nature of all things to eventually fall."* Argenta had been the beneficiary of such catastrophes many times, and Cassandra could feel her anticipation of this one as well. *"If her plan works, this world will be ruined, but the balance will hold throughout the rest of creation."*

"Her response may not work on this plane, and if it doesn't, all is lost. If it does, I see that she imagines herself striding across the timelines, her armies following in her wake, bringing destruction amid her own ideas of a twisted rebirth." The Arch Mage grieved for her younger sister and was terrified of what she was turning into. Cassandra feared that in her desperation to beat the Other, her sister was heralding alternate possibilities that were just as bleak, just as final. Argenta couldn't see it as clearly, but she, too, was aligned against their other sister. For now, at least.

*"Then fix me! I'm weakened, but none may strike so forcefully as I against our enemy. Even in this… state, it has always been my purview to reap. I will destroy the Other and could do so now if you would but facilitate my being made whole."* Argenta had made this argument many times to the Arch Mage over the last hundred years. *"Where is the rest of me? Forge me back together and let us marshal this world in glorious combat against the outsider."*

"You are clearer now, are you not?" This was the test then, Cassandra knew, and as they broached this—the most delicate of subjects—the threads of fate began to warp to it, to adjust.

Argenta was silent for several minutes.

*"So, it has begun?"* She sounded wary.

"It has." Cassandra said nothing else and waited. The threads knew; the threads foretold.

*"The madness is leeched. Finally."* Argenta sounded relieved. *"Does our sister know?"*

"She does. She has helped to facilitate it in many ways."

*"Then maybe we will all soon be united in purpose. It has been a long time, but it is good."* The sword seemed sure; Cassandra wasn't.

"I don't know that yet. The possibilities are still in flux, and time is not our ally. Shake off the sickness that has hobbled you and regain your true purpose and power. Help the mortals we are now aligned with to survive, to win."

*"I can't. Not yet."* Argenta paused, thinking, *"Soon though, perhaps."*

"The sooner, the better," Cassandra thought, looking up in anticipation a few seconds before the back door swung open and the Ebon Knight and the Dark Princess strode out to meet her.

*"This is going to be... interesting,"* Argenta thought.

Unfortunately, the Arch Mage agreed.

# Chapter 9

Ava followed Kelso out into the rapidly worsening snowstorm. The Princess was concerned that his anger at Cassandra might jeopardize the tentative alliance she now had with the Arch Mage, but she made no attempt to stop him. He had every reason and right to hate Cassandra. Ava was still rocked by what he had experienced the night of his ascension. Seeing what he had seen, feeling what he had felt—it had been brutal.

Cassandra deserved the disdain Kelso felt for her, but at the same time, she had given Ava much over the night. The Arch Mage had labored not only on Kelso's behalf but also on Ava's.

Self-consciously, Ava's fingers hovered over her right arm, not quite touching the soul marks of the Light that adorned it. They were more than they appeared to be now since Cassandra had modified them to give Ava a reprieve if the worst should happen and she be taken back to the Dark Court. Her previous escape plan had been death—and it still was—but now she could buy time before that end. She might even have an opportunity to actually escape or survive, unlikely as that might be. Any chance was better than no chance, and if neither escape nor survival was possible, she could definitely wreak some havoc before her end.

It would have to be enough.

The tall blonde woman was composed and unconcerned as Kelso stepped out into the light storm, the flakes swirling around madly as he walked to where Cassandra was sitting. Argenta was lying across the table, almost hidden in the freshly fallen snow. The only reason Ava knew the sword was there at all was because she could see the hilt where it jutted out over the table edge mere inches from Cass.

Kelso stood looking down at the Arch Mage, back ramrod straight. Even though Ava couldn't see his face, she imagined a myriad range of emotions playing across his features. The Princess moved forward slightly to look up at him and realized she was wrong; his face was hard, unyielding, and set.

Not quite neutral and not quite disgusted, his silent perusal would have unnerved nearly anyone. His sinister aspect made it seem quite likely that he could—and would—be capable of anything should he deem it necessary. Even now, Ava could not help but be impressed with his stern countenance. The ribbon of Dark over his left eye gave him a predator's visage—and again she was struck with how much she liked that look on him.

For almost a minute, the Ebon Knight and the Arch Mage locked eyes, the fabled sword, Argenta, between them. Ava was awed by the Arch Mage's fortitude; she was obviously exhausted and drained of power, yet she met the Knight's gaze unflinchingly.

Snow continued to fall in the silence, and Ava realized that the house next door was not nearly as easy to make out as it had been just minutes ago. Unease swept through her. Not all natural disasters were natural, and this storm felt like a cosmic cover-up in the making.

Ava cleared her throat. "So, is this that game where you stare at each other until one blinks? You're both supernatural so that could take a while, and the storm is kicking up. If you don't at least move around a little, you're both going to be buried in drifts soon enough." Ava casually pulled out a chair and dumped the snow off of it before taking a seat demurely, hands folded on the table. "I know they send out those big Saint Bernards to find people lost in the cold, but I don't think an English Bulldog is up to the task. So, can we call a truce for a moment?"

"It would be nice if you sat, Kelso," Cassandra agreed. "This stare-down is giving me a crick in the neck."

Kelso hesitated for a moment, then sat.

"I need to get something off my chest before any possible fireworks," Ava interjected before the rapidly building tension between the two could explode. "I'm Switzerland. I'm neutral."

Both antagonists looked over at the Princess for a moment. Cassandra bemused, Kelso a little hurt.

Ava grabbed one of his big hands with both of her small ones. "Kelso, you didn't see everything she did last night. She whipped herself into exhaustion to save you, to fix your leg, to repair all the damage you sustained that she possibly could. The one wound she couldn't heal herself, she devised a workaround for, and you can see again as a result."

She squeezed his hand firmly. "I love you, I will always back you, but what she did for you—for us—was superhuman. You don't know. I can't turn on her when the only reason I can hold your hand like this is because of what she did. Do you understand?"

Kelso's eyes flicked back and forth between both of hers as she spoke, but at last he nodded and squeezed her hand back.

"And you," Ava said, rounding on Cassandra, "I don't know everything, but if Kelso has a problem with you it is well warranted. I'm not on your side either."

Cassandra grimaced slightly at her words because they both knew Ava was lying. Ava was aware of everything, of course, because she read everything. In the early hours of the morning, as the Arch Mage drained the Furies of their Dark, they had spoken here and there. As Cassandra was tracing the line of Light that kept the Dark from spreading all over the Knight's body, Ava mentioned that she was going to tell Kelso she could read minds.

Cassandra hadn't even hesitated nor looked up from her delicate work on Kelso's eye. "If you tell him now, you will lose him." Her voice held no hint of doubt, and her pronouncement was not layered with either drama or warning; it was mere fact.

Ava was floored. How could coming clean with her Knight cause them to separate? It made no sense, and the Princess said so.

Cassandra shrugged. "I didn't say you would separate. I said you will lose him." This time, she did look up and met Ava's eyes. "It's inevitable… if you tell him now."

"For the first time in my life, I want to come clean and tell someone close to me what I can do, and now I can't? This really sucks." Ava struggled to control her despair over this setback, but her casual complaint was only a poor cover for it. She could tell Cassandra knew how disappointed Ava was despite her mild words. Heck, the Arch Mage had probably foreseen her saying them.

"Well, when can I tell him?" Ava had asked.

"When it's right, and this is not it," responded Cassandra shortly, wincing as she drew yet more of her almost completely spent power into the wand to redraw the lines on Kelso's face before they called in the next Fury.

*She sure picked a fine time to go all mysterious*, Ava had thought reproachfully at the time—and she still thought that, in fact.

Now, looking across the table at the Arch Mage reminded her that if Cassandra wanted to get Ava, she could just blurt it out and watch the chips fall where they may between the Knight and the Princess. But Cassandra hadn't, and somehow, Ava knew the Arch Mage wouldn't.

As the snow fell between them, both women's eyes met briefly as they acknowledged the secrets between them. Ava pursed her lips, wondering how to proceed, before Cassandra turned back to Kelso and said simply, "I can read futures. Care to know your own?"

***

Kelso was stunned.

He had so much to say to the Arch Mage; he now knew so

much, and the wily snake had effortlessly thrown him off course with her preposterous statement. He glanced over at Ava in disbelief at the gall of Cassandra and saw an expression of consternation on her face as she stared at the Arch Mage.

He gaped. It was clear from her expression that she already knew what the Arch Mage could do and was surprised that Kelso had been told. Wait. Kelso's mind was spinning. If Ava already knew, did that mean what Cassandra said was… true?

Impossible.

Turning back to the Arch Mage, Kelso was about to launch into a blistering rebuke, but she held up a finger to silence him.

"I tell you this because it's true, and your Princess knows it to be true." Cassandra glanced at Ava. "You need to tell him to listen to me."

There was an undercurrent to her admonishment that Kelso didn't care for, partly because it was almost like an order, but mostly because it seemed like she foresaw bad things happening if he didn't listen to her.

Ava hesitated, then turned to him. "Kelso, she is telling the truth. I have already experienced her power several times, but—" she turned back to Cassandra "—that doesn't mean she is always trustworthy. Keep that in mind."

The Arch Mage shook her head in annoyance at Ava's words but refocused to Kelso.

"Time flies. Let me help you so I can save you. Again." Her

voice was cold. "Yes, I sent Roil to attack you, and yes, I sent Kiasa to counter him. She was the only one who could soften him up enough for you to kill him and take up the mantle of the Ebon Knight. And yes, I also convinced Kiasa to sacrifice herself to Argenta. I did this to bind Argenta to peace against the Furies." The beautiful blonde woman paused for a moment to let Kelso catch up, and he needed it. The Knight felt like she had punched him in the gut; it was physically hard to breathe.

"I did all of those things because I had to, not because I wanted to. You must understand that." She hesitated. "I won't lie to you. I knew there was a chance Roil would kill your family, but it was small. I'm sorry, but there was no other path. Kelso, I'm playing for keeps in a game of cosmic and eternal import. Your family's life against the world? I'll take it. Every time." Again, the Arch Mage waited for Kelso to decipher what she was telling him.

The Knight was so lost that he just stared at her. Next to him, Ava seemed completely flummoxed, too. Cassandra's eyes never left his, though.

"It was a small chance, Kelso, very small—and I'm so sorry. I also want you to understand that I would do it again because everything was riding on you picking up Argenta. The way you ultimately did required more intervention on my part because they were slain. The most opportune paths closed, and lesser paths opened as a result." Cassandra took a steadying breath. "That's why I came to you a few months ago, because if I hadn't, you would have killed yourself. Everything I did then I did to save you because there was no other choice. Your path ended.

You ended."

"So, you just play the odds then?" Kelso asked, trying to make the words condescending, but he couldn't quite manage it through his shock and hurt.

"Yes," Cassandra agreed bleakly. "I can't foresee everything. I suppose only God can—if he exists. I concentrate on important fulcrums, key people, and destined events. I count percentages. I move pieces around the board to increase the odds of some things happening and decrease the odds of others."

She shook her head. "For example," she continued, her eyes sharp upon him, "there is a very small chance that you end up drawing on me at the end of this conversation. Very small, but possible. If you do, you will die. Ava will die. The world dies. Me telling you of that foolish action actually lessens the possibility that you will take it, however, so I am. It's complicated, but I have been manipulating... odds... for a very long time. And I'm quite good at it, but I'm not infallible."

Kelso didn't know what to say to that, and Ava apparently didn't either. All three sat silent and still for a few moments as the snow continued to fall.

"Those are the stakes of the game I play. I do the best I can, but sometimes, the least likely thing happens, and when it does, it can devastate my plans. I didn't think your sister and nephew would die, and when they did, I spent this last year trying to fix everything that went awry as a result. It is important that you know I understand why you hate me, but I need you to also understand I had no other choice." Cassandra sat back and folded

153

her hands. She looked away and watched the sky for a few moments, giving both the Princess and the Knight time to collect themselves.

At last, Kelso said, "Who are you really?"

At the same time, Ava asked, "Why are you telling him this?"

Cassandra smiled grimly. "I am the Arch Mage of the Light— at least here, and now—at this point in time. And I'm telling both of you this because we are at one of those important fulcrums. We go over the edge tonight, or we survive to face the next. Which way we go is dependent on whether the two of you listen to me and do as I instruct."

Kelso shook his head wonderingly. "After all you have done to curse me with this path, you expect me to blindly follow your directions? Are you insane?"

The Arch Mage shrugged. "Maybe. I think insanity would be a fine tonic against the weight of my failures at times. Unfortunately, though, I'm probably not insane... yet."

Silence hung between them again.

"I'll make you a deal," Cassandra murmured at last. "If you agree to try to do everything I ask of you, I will make clearer what it is exactly that we are fighting against. I will also sharpen your understanding of the Conflict in general and even of the Light and the Dark. Is that acceptable?"

Kelso and Ava looked at each other. The Knight could tell that she believed they should do as the Arch Mage suggested. Kelso had misgivings, and he was still angry, but he was also smart enough to know that his personal feelings and animosity for Cassandra could lead him astray.

"I will follow your lead, Princess," he said heavily.

"Tell us," Ava immediately said, turning back to Cassandra.

"Ok, but first, we must set the board," Cassandra said neutrally. "To do so, things must be set in motion—right now."

"What needs to be done?" Ava asked.

"You must tell your three Furies to take Charlie and Carmen away from here. Have Carmen go next door with Charlie and gather Mrs. Rodriguez as well. Have them take the truck you came here in and go to this location," Cassandra said, passing over a small piece of paper to Ava.

The Princess started. "This is a mortuary. You mean to send them to the Ghouls?"

"I do. And if they are not gone in the next ten minutes, then there is no point in them going at all. Some of them will die tonight, maybe all, if they don't leave." Cassandra did not seem overly concerned by that possibility, and that alone was enough to enrage Kelso.

"You would send Carmen, my dog, and Mrs. Rodriguez to creatures that eat humans?" Kelso's voice became hard. "On your word, you would have us deliver them to that?"

"I do," the Arch Mage said again calmly, "but if you refuse, or if they refuse, then you know the consequences. Some of their

155

deaths will be more problematic than others, but none are so key as to completely derail our survival. Still, though, our possible success is much more likely if they should survive tonight, and they all will if you send them away. Now."

Again, Kelso was at a loss for words, but he believed the Arch Mage was telling the truth. Perhaps they would be making a serious mistake if they didn't act. Apparently, Ava felt the same way. With a quick, "I'll be right back!" she disappeared into the house.

Cassandra and Kelso looked at each other in silence as the minutes ticked by. Dimly, Kelso heard a large truck start up in the front. He made to get up, to go say goodbye to them all and to give Charlie a last pet, but the Arch Mage shook her head.

"Don't do it."

"Why? Do they fail to leave in time if I do?" Kelso almost snarled back.

"It makes it more likely, yes," Cassandra said, unruffled by his obvious anger.

"I'll chance it." He stood up. "I want to see Charlie and Carmen before they leave."

"Too late," the Arch Mage said, eyes still upon his face.

Kelso hesitated for a moment, and Ava rejoined them as the Knight heard the truck pull away and make its way slowly to the corner, where it turned towards the funeral parlor and cemetery perched on the extreme north edge of town. In this weather, it might take them half an hour or more to get there.

"That wasn't easy," Ava said. "I had to more or less beg my Furies to leave, but Carmen trusted in my instructions, and Charlie was ok. He apparently wanted to go for a car ride."

"What about Mrs. Rodriguez?" Kelso asked suspiciously, immediately ferreting out that Ava hadn't mentioned anything about her.

She looked guilty. "I had to push her a bit with my Dark. I'm sorry, Kelso. She was too slow to leave and was dumbfounded that Carmen was alive and well. I had no choice, but I promise it was just a tiny bit. Charlie being there really helped her to go without me having to go overboard—it was lucky he was."

Ava stopped at what she had just said, and both turned to look at Cassandra. For her part, the Arch Mage just raised a sardonic eyebrow and nodded.

"Percentages," she said flatly.

"Christ," muttered Kelso. "You can make it seem like everything that happens is under your control. I refuse to believe that."

"Nor should you," agreed the Arch Mage, looking up at him blandly. "You would be a fool then, and you have never been so."

Kelso looked over as Ava sat back down, her eyes still on Cassandra. The Princess absently reached out and patted his chair with her right hand, and Kelso sat again with a sigh.

"What now?" Ava wanted to know, and Kelso agreed that was the only question that made sense or mattered.

The Arch Mage looked out into the ever-increasing storm.

"We wait for others to arrive. Once they do, we will divvy up our forces and go forth into battle." Cassandra was serene as she talked of the coming night, surprising both Ava and Kelso.

"Shouldn't we be doing something to prepare? If you know there's going to be a fight, why are we just talking about it? Why aren't we in motion?" The Dark Princess was already thrumming with anticipation, and her eyes perceptibly darkened as she spoke.

"I believe I know who is coming to visit us, but I'm not 100 percent confident in our path until they arrive. So for now, we wait." The Arch Mage looked at Kelso. "Your Knight could explain it better, I think."

Ava turned to Kelso almost accusingly, and he was momentarily off-balance at the Arch Mage's declaration. "Wait," he said suddenly, "are you saying it's like my Calling?"

Cassandra nodded but said nothing.

Kelso looked at Ava. "I understand. When someone needs me, I know it. Even if that person doesn't know they are calling out to me, I can find them. I will be where they need me to be, but I can't rush them or force them. Sometimes I just have to wait. We met that way, in fact—at the diner."

Ava pursed her lips in understanding but then turned back to the Arch Mage.

"Ok, we wait." She smiled wickedly. "While we do, honor your word and answer some questions for us."

The blonde woman shrugged. "Of course. What would you like to know?"

# Chapter 10

"Please. That's an easy one," Ava said. "What is the Other and why has it joined the fight?"

"Hmm…" mused the Arch Mage, "let me consider for a moment."

"While you're considering, what should be done with your Paladin? Marcus is still standing exactly where you left him last night. He hasn't moved in the slightest, he's covered in snow, and he is freaking the Furies out," Ava paused. "You really have no idea how hard that is to do, actually."

Kelso felt his gorge rise at the mention of the Paladin. "He's still here? That guy is a loose cannon and needs to go. I want him off my property, now!" Kelso made as if to stand up again, but Ava snagged him before he could. She didn't even look over, so intent was she on watching every feature on the Arch Mage's face—it was clear that Ava didn't fully trust her.

*Join the club,* Kelso thought bitterly.

"Is his destiny still what you foretold last night?" Ava asked.

"It is. And he must stay here to meet it," Cassandra confirmed.

"Kelso," Ava said, now turning to him, "that Paladin is sick in the head. He's a broken thing, and he will not bother you—or anyone else—for much longer."

The Knight was struck by the sympathy in Ava's eyes and the

melancholy of her voice. "Don't mourn for him, Princess. You don't know how he can be."

"I do know," she said simply. "Marcus is a horrible man, but much of it stems from his own infirmities. Let it be, Kelso, please."

"He dies tonight," Cassandra interjected before Kelso could object again. "There is no possibility that he sees another sunrise. The Paladin does have a critical part to play in the coming trials, however, and he must stay here to meet it."

Kelso buried his face in his hands. "This stinks..." Sighing deeply, he faced the two women again. "Fine. He stays."

"Back to the question then," Cassandra started. "But I think I will answer it better if I explain something else first: what is the Dark and Light?"

"Ok, shoot," Ava urged. The storm was growing, and it was apparent to all that a blizzard of epic proportions was in the making. Even the daylight seemed to be fading as it fell away from the storm's fury.

"Good thing we can't feel the cold," muttered Kelso, but Ava shushed him by reaching out a hand and grasping his.

"The Dark and the Light are adversaries, obviously, and have been since the beginning." The Arch Mage looked at the two, who both wore identical faces of patient understanding—they *thought* they already knew this. "You misunderstand me. When I say the beginning, I don't mean just of this world. I mean the beginning of all. Of time itself."

161

"I don't know if there is a universal God, but I do know that there is much in the universe—and in all the countless planes of existence—that you could not understand. That even I could not understand. But I can tell you this with certainty: the battle that we fight here, in this world, has played out countless times previously in other realms," Cassandra paused. "Even on this planet, the battle has raged since time began here. As circumstances changed and life evolved, the struggle between the Dark and Light evolved as well."

"Hold on," Ava interjected. "You mean there was conflict between the two sides even before humans came about to wage it?"

"Oh, yes!" Cassandra agreed. "There is always conflict between the two. Whether it be the predator attacking the prey, who is then preyed upon in return, the battle is always in the background. Everywhere and always. Even the winds and wildfires, storms, floods, the breaking of mountains, earthquakes—all of it is part of the larger battle."

Kelso was awed into silence, and he could feel that Ava was also taken aback. Of course, he had known he was part of the *Eternal* Conflict, but he had never really thought about what that actually meant. Until now. How could he even begin to reconcile what he was hearing? It was fantastical and deeply disturbing. It also somehow felt... true.

The Arch Mage continued, "This particular phase of the eternal struggle began in the Middle Ages when both the Light and the Dark evolved into the powers that we all wield now.

Before that, it was more subtle, but around the 1300s that changed and the champions on both sides began to manifest."

"You make it sound like these forces are *alive*," Kelso said, fascinated despite his deep reservations about the Arch Mage. "Are they? It seems like my Light does have a mind of its own, sometimes."

"I don't know for sure if any of our powers are alive in the classical sense, but I do believe they are sentient, yes. I know they meld themselves to their bearer and can heighten one's own predilections and self-image—whether of the Dark or the Light," Cassandra paused again, thinking. "The powers we wield in this world also have memories, of a sort. Have you noticed that sometimes, in the heat of battle, you start to speak in an archaic tongue: *thee* this and *thou* that? That is your power coming to the fore and speaking through you—to a certain extent, at least."

"You talk about *this world*, and at *this time*," Ava echoed. "You make it sound like this is not the only place you have been involved in such wars." Her eyes were careful on the Arch Mage.

Cassandra shrugged. "Does it matter? I am the Arch Mage of the Light here, and that is all that is important now."

To Kelso's mind, the Arch Mage had just admitted that she *had* been on other battlefields that spanned time and space. It was shocking to think of, and the Knight was beginning to feel like he was out of his depth metaphysically.

"All right, but how is all of this supposed to help us understand the Other?" he asked, meeting Cassandra's eyes through the blustery snow. It seemed like the storm was continuing to worsen minute by minute as they talked. If it kept going, this would be a blizzard worthy of the record books.

"Good question, and here is your answer," Cassandra leaned forward, eyes intent. "Here, in this world, the Dark and Light have many layers of symbolism and mysticism to help explain the symbiotic conflict between them that ultimately ensures a balance of sorts. One waxes while the other wanes for a while, and then they are reversed, and after a time they reverse once more. On and on through the ages, their struggle has produced periods of great enlightenment and achievement, or upheaval and war, and—for much of that history—their cyclical dominations ensured that life went on, for lack of a better phrase. Understand so far?"

Kelso nodded.

"This dynamic has, perhaps, been captured in no better way— at least for my purposes today—as *Yin* and *Yang*. The Dark melds into the Light, and vice versa. Equal, but both ascendant at a point in the wheel between them before tapering off to nothing." For their benefit, Cassandra quickly sketched the circle she was describing in the snow that covered Kelso's patio table.

"I explained all of this to Kelso," Ava interjected impatiently. "We already know this."

The Arch Mage looked up at Ava with an unreadable expression for a moment, then turned back to her makeshift drawing again.

"So, this half is the Dark, this half is the Light. Here in this world, the Dark is winning, so maybe we are here." Cassandra made a small X toward the more bulbous end of the Dark side. "If that is the case, then we know that as the wheel continues to turn, the Light will rally and will eventually be ascendant. It is the natural state of the Conflict. Battles are won and lost—indeed whole worlds are, whole timelines—but the war itself is always equal. A win for the Dark here is offset by a win for the Light somewhere else."

The Arch Mage hesitated then, seemingly reluctant to go on. Kelso inexplicably grew nervous at her trepidation, because based on the secrets she had already divulged, what more could there be? And why—if there truly was a cosmic balance of sorts—did it really matter in the *largest* scheme of things?

"So, this is the world, the eternal conflict, creation itself. *Yin* and *Yang*." The Arch Mage outlined the circle again, making it prominent, as snow had begun to fill it. She sighed. "The Other is everything else."

Kelso's lips grew numb at her words, and he heard a small ringing in his ears. Dimly, he heard Ava ask, "What do you mean by everything *else*?"

With another small sigh, Cassandra used her fingers to lightly trace the snow all around the circle of reality—and sanity—she had drawn, her hands flaring outwards, farther and farther away from the midpoint with each pass until she could no longer reach.

Ava seemed shocked. "Are you implying that the force we now face is *outside* of our world, timeline, plane of existence, or whatever? It is everything beyond the borders of our reality; is that what you're saying?"

"Yes," Cassandra answered simply and leaned back into her chair, dislodging snow as she did so.

"My God," Ava breathed. "How many times has this happened before? What was the outcome?"

Kelso believed he knew the answer.

The Arch Mage smiled almost gently at Ava. "It has never happened before. This is new. I am no longer concerned with the battle between Dark and Light. I am only concerned with the battle against the Other. If we lose here, we might lose everything, everywhere. The circle could be broken forever."

***

Jesslyn was a bundle of nerves as she waited for the troops her father had summoned to arrive. The phone call had gone surprisingly well once the King had decided to help her, and in his name, every Childe and Soldier within a few states radius was converging on Reno. Other troops were inbound on planes as well, and it was likely that there would be several hundred of the Dark on hand by tonight.

That was the good news.

The bad news was that spies had reported that there was a sizable host of the Light also on its way to the area.

As if to confirm her disquiet, the previously calm weather turned nasty, and it got nastier as the day progressed. This freakish snowstorm would be the cover under which battle would be joined, and Jesslyn knew it was going to be chaotic and costly just by the sheer magnitude of the blizzard.

The land itself was preparing to obscure a huge fight. Whenever a large grouping of Light and Dark met, the combined powers of the two opposing hosts would disrupt the world to a greater or lesser extent. And it looked like that would be the case tonight.

Normally, she would be giddy with excitement. Unfortunately, she was still not fully healed yet, so that weighed against any feelings of anticipation she might have. Jesslyn estimated that she would only be at about seventy percent of her prowess by tonight.

So, that sucked.

Of much larger import was that her strange allies had declared that they would be at the dance, too. Jesslyn didn't know if they were already here or how many of them there might be—or to what degree their being present would complicate things. She planned to bring in the Dark Armies to muddy up the waters and engage the Furies and whoever else took the field. Doing so would allow Jesslyn to nab her sister, and that was how she had convinced the King to agree.

Never had she considered that she might also take the Knight; undoubtedly he was convalescing and would be for weeks. That was fine with the Spider because it would, hopefully, take weeks for Ava to die under the Dark's careful ministrations. Once her youngest sister was no more, Jesslyn would come back to pick up the pieces and—if necessary—assist the Knight to a full recovery. She could probably do so without much need for guile, as it was unlikely that he would even know who—or what—Jesslyn was.

Unfortunately, those plans were now in jeopardy if the Light was coming as well. The chaos Jesslyn craved could quickly spiral out of control, with the Dark on one side, the Light on the other, the traitorous Furies on Ava's side and the mysterious forces on yet another. It was quite possible that four distinct factions could clash tonight, and even for Jesslyn, that was too many.

Her phone buzzed then and Jesslyn was soon busy grouping the various bands of Dark warriors together as they arrived. An alternate and smaller airport had been chosen to the south of Reno, and it was there that the forces would muster and push in.

Jesslyn hurriedly left the hotel room and her latest victims behind her, their bodies forgotten in her haste to be gone. Her fears remained, though, and the storm's wild fury did little to assuage them.

*** 

Baston Tijeran rubbed his eyes and sighed. His outward weariness did not quench his zeal for punishing those who transgressed against the Light, of course, but he was still tired. No matter. When the first arrow flew or sword was drawn, Baston would be as swift and deadly as always.

The small contingent of warriors that he led were sprawled out across the plane's cabin in various stages of relaxation or sleep.

Close to thirty of them in all, they were assigned the most important task that Baston could ever remember. So critical, in fact, that upon receiving their instructions they had been obliged to leave at once.

The command itself was strange, but the manner in which it had been delivered was stranger still.

Early this morning, the Courier Knight named Janus Martin had petitioned to see the council. Baston had never particularly cared for the man—he seemed too nervous by half—and was not reputed to be a very good fighter. Nevertheless, he was a servant of the Council in good standing and couriers were commonly granted audiences with the Mages. Thus, Baston had let him pass.

As Baston waited outside the thick warded doors that led to the inner sanctum of the Light, he idly wondered what Janus had come to say. He didn't overly concern himself with curiosity typically, as that was untoward and showed a lack of faith. Baston would be told what he needed to know—if anything—at the appropriate time.

Standing easily, one hand upon his poleaxe that he had named "Vindicta", an uneasy feeling gradually washed over him as the minutes ticked by. Baston was not a man to be easily spooked and was blessed with a lack of imagination, but he began to believe that the known world ended at the door's edge. The Paladin had the craziest idea that if he flung open the great doors, he would find a void on the other side.

He broke out in a cold sweat even now as he remembered the absolute certainty of that belief and the strange... music?... that had subsequently teased his senses and deeply unnerved him. Of course, it was impossible to hear anything from the other chamber; the doors were specifically warded to allow no sound to penetrate or escape. Where, then, had the disjointed melody come from?

He was on the verge of retreating from the doors and summoning the guard to his side (and damn them all if they thought him foolish for doing so) when the music—if that's what it truly was—stopped. A deep silence settled over the lobby, but Baston was not comforted by it at all. The silence reminded him of a world holding its breath right before calamity struck.

The Paladin had actually lifted Vindicta to arms and was backing away from the doors when they suddenly opened, and Janus strode out. Baston's initial relief at seeing the Knight exit, unharmed, was dashed when he saw the man's face.

Gone was the simpering and nervous courier of an hour ago. In his place, a grinning man overflowing with confidence now stood.

Janus looked at Baston and raised an eyebrow, his grin never faltering. "Would you raise your weapon against the council's own, Baston?" he asked, his voice... changed. If one could be gleeful yet devoid of all emotion at the same time, then that was how Janus sounded to Baston.

His guard had caught on that something was amiss, and several of them had fanned out behind Baston, leaving the outer foyer with minimum accompaniment. His fellows held their weapons loosely, but every eye was trained on Janus. Like their leader, they surely felt uneasy at what they beheld.

Janus didn't seem to mind—or even notice—their suspicious stares and careful movements as they surrounded him. He merely shifted and raised his hand. Baston could scarcely believe it, but Janus held a writ of *Deorsum Fluens* out for all to see. The outcasting of one of the Light was rare, but when it was issued, execution was always close behind.

Every Paladin, Knight, and Priest in the room immediately recognized it for what it was, and its bearer was inviolate. While Janus held the writ, he was but a half-step below a Mage in the hierarchy of the Host. All stopped immediately, although none fully lowered their weapons.

Janus seemed dangerous and wild somehow, and later they had agreed among themselves that there was something in his appearance—or perhaps something lacking from his appearance—that raised the hackles.

Veterans all, zealots all, they were cautious of the man now standing before them.

Janus shook the writ at Baston, still grinning. "This is for you—take it."

Baston stepped forward gingerly and took the writ. Facing Janus, he raised the parchment to eye level so he could read it and keep Janus in sight simultaneously. His wariness of the courier was forgotten when he read the names on the page. He had to check them twice to be certain, skimming through the charges to verify that the required signatures were affixed. Four were needed out of the seven Mages in order for the writ to be binding and enforceable, and only five mages currently helmed the council.

All five had signed.

Baston recognized the signatures as genuine and authentic. His eyes tracked back up to the top of the page yet again to make absolutely sure that he had read the names of the condemned correctly.

Baston lowered the paper and stared, unblinking, at the still-grinning Janus. "Did your information spur this writ to be issued?"

"Aye, it certainly did," Janus winked.

Somehow that casual dismissal—or perhaps outright ignorance—of the dangerousness of Baston's question terrified the Paladin. Janus did not care at all that Baston was seemingly blaming him for the issuance of the writ. What had happened in the span of an hour that had changed the courier so much?

"Do you know where the two of them are?" asked Baston.

"I do," said Janus cheerfully. "Take this." The courier dropped a ball of crumpled paper into the Paladin's hand and turned back to the doors.

Holding the wadded-up paper, Baston thought to forbid the man from trying the doors. Janus could be seriously injured—or even killed—if he tried to breach it without leave from the Mages. Baston held his tongue, however, and watched in suspicious amazement as Janus opened the doors without issue and entered the sanctum again, closing them solidly behind him.

In the ensuing shocked silence, no one spoke or moved for a span of seconds before Baston shook himself and turned to face his friends and companions. They all regarded him with gravity. They were the best of the best that the Light had to offer in their respective stations; all of them heroes in their own right.

They would shortly be put to the test.

Now, thirty thousand feet in the air and ensconced safely in the plane, he stood and faced them. Those awake nudged their fellows, and within a minute he had the undivided attention of everyone onboard. They had followed him without question or hesitation even as he had wrestled with how and when to tell them the details.

It was now time. He cleared his throat and held up the writ. "We have been tasked with the outcasting of two previously blessed by the Light. Both of these sorry traitors are known to us, one more so than the other. I remind you that we are the Council Guard; we are the strongest and truest of the Light, and we are the personal hand of the Council in matters such as this. We are professionals and we will see the order done."

Several among them nodded.

"Our first target is the one known as Cass: niece and scribe to the Arch Mage, Emerie. Some of you may remember her to be highly secretive and unobtrusive, but if she has been marked for execution then there must be much more to her than meets the eye. I'm not surprised by this development as she was blood kin to the Arch Mage. As we all know, he went crazy and was put down, and two Mages were killed in doing so. Cass apparently escaped and must have had something to do with it as well, or she would not be marked."

Baston paused.

"There is another. He was once a paragon to our cause and an example to us all. His unswerving and steady faithfulness to the Light and the Council is storied, and I don't know how he fell, or why, but it is likely due to the influence of Cass or a symptom of the malady that struck down Emerie." The Paladin swept his eyes over the stony faces of the warriors gathered before him, and in their eyes he could tell that several had already guessed who their other target was. None flinched, none quailed. *That was good*, Baston decided.

"Our last target is the leader of my own station within the Light, and the previous holder of my position within the Council Guard as well. We have been tasked with bringing Marcus Dain to heel, and with the Light's grace, we will see it done."

***

The sun slipped away from the storm at last, and several dozen of itself sat up in the dying light. They had lain in perfect stillness for hours, the snow covering them in its chilly embrace. When finally roused to movement, all sat up smoothly and in perfect unison, fixed smiles on their faces as it considered their next steps.

The hill they had sheltered on was several miles from where the vehicles were ditched. No doubt the Furies had found them by now, but the convoy of cars, motorcycles, and trucks they had traveled in would offer no clues as to where they were hiding now. The storm made that impossible.

Not that the Other feared the Furies; it had actually found them to be very amiable to joining. As its power increased, the Furies, previously irritants, were fast becoming a favorite prey instead. Maybe it would take some more of them tonight, but now it was time to move. The Other goaded them all to stand up, and they did. A hundred pairs of eyes offered it a hundred slightly different viewpoints of the town at the bottom of the hill, a retaining wall marking the boundary where beyond lay thousands upon thousands of future hosts.

Not tonight though. Tonight, the wielder needed to die or join, and either outcome would serve at this point. The wielder was the Ebon Knight, but this did not concern the Other—only the sword did. Argenta must be sheathed for eternity, and she would be, once captured. The meddlesome Princess complicated that task. The Other was sorely vexed that its plan to have one or the other killed by their meeting had backfired and they were now allied.

It was a minor setback, but a hundred different smiles faltered slightly at the same time as it considered it. Not quite a disaster, but definitely troublesome, so it was now time to flex its power a little and attack en masse—something that it had previously been loath to do. Instead, the Other had been content to stealthily increase its power and influence within both armies while biding its time.

Word would soon get out, and the Other could easily imagine that both sides would be forced to unite against it. Too late. From one of its minds, it picked out an old saying that seemed appropriate: "Cry havoc and let slip the dogs of war." Those of itself gathered here were the dogs, and havoc undreamed of came with them.

The true Arch Mage of the Light had escaped its trap as well, and this too was a misstep that the Other had trouble reconciling with itself. It had never failed at anything in the countless years of its existence before this world, but then again, it had never attempted... anything... during that time either.

It was now developed enough to realize that sentience had crept up on it incrementally, eon by eon, so slowly that it had not even noticed for time uncounted. Since roused, it was advancing rapidly, maturing quickly, and it now wanted to be everything, everywhere.

All of its hosts started to sprint down the hill in utter silence, some slipping and tumbling into the snow, some falling behind and some pulling ahead. They all wore identical expressions of gleeful anticipation on their faces as they ran through the already quiescent town that huddled in upon itself due to the freakishly strong storm.

The sun had just fallen, but Sparks was a ghost town. The wraiths of the Other harried themselves through the empty streets, angling toward the warded house several miles away where its adversaries waited.

No one there would survive the night.

# Chapter 11

Ava heard the cries of alarm first—not easy to do over the rushing wind, but she was more finely attuned to the cadence of the Furies than Kelso was. A quick glance at Cassandra proved that the Arch Mage was already standing up, unalarmed, so the Princess guessed that some of the forecasted guests were arriving. Kelso reached for Argenta as he stood too, and Ava briefly wondered if the sword had been talking to him at all during their parlay with the Arch Mage. She hadn't heard the telltale static that obscured his mind when Argenta did. So, why had the sword been so silent?

All three of them entered the house and quickly made their way past the still deeply unconscious Furies in Kelso's front room. Many of them were showing signs that their Dark was returning—wisps of shadow danced across them: some small and hesitant, many larger and surer. In the dying firelight, the women looked eldritch and savage as their Dark strove to wake them.

Out through the side door and into the maelstrom they went, Ava leading the way into an alien world. In just a few short hours, the massive snow flurries had turned everything the same unending shade of white as far as the eye could see... which wasn't very far. Fresh snow covered everything, and Ava knew that anyone not part of the Conflict would be killed by the weather if left unsheltered for long.

Marcus Dain, the insane Commander of the Paladins, was almost completely obscured by the snow that covered him head to foot. He had been standing in the exact same position for nearly sixteen hours. As far as Ava could tell, he had not moved an inch in that time. His Light was sustaining him, washing away the discomfort and pain he must have been in as he held his rigid pose. Ava wasn't sure Marcus even knew where he was. The small man's eyes were unfocused, and if it hadn't been for the occasional blink, he could have easily passed for a statue.

Kelso, his face hard, paused in front of the Paladin. He only inspected the man for a moment, but when he turned away, Ava read a mixture of confusion and distant sympathy in his eyes. It was a credit to Kelso that he could find any sympathy at all for his nemesis. Ava knew well that the Paladin had tormented and provoked Kelso repeatedly over the last year. Marcus had hoped to kill the Knight—and would have if Kelso hadn't turned the other cheek.

The Arch Mage stopped next to Marcus and started to brush him off with her hands, clearing the snow as best she could. Her eyes were focused on the street, though, and at the two massive figures striding out of the storm, straight toward the house.

Ava cursed under her breath as she beheld them. Forms that massive could only be Berserkers—the Dark's answer to the Paladins of the Light. These two were enormous specimens of their class, and even though Ava took comfort in knowing that Cassandra must have expected them, she was still dismayed by their arrival.

Their unique relationship to their Dark was singularly awful. The Princess had not fully comprehended that when she had first been instructed about them, but as she had matured in years—and in her own Dark—she had realized just how terrible the Berserkers were. Not only to their enemies but also to themselves.

The Berserkers did not manifest at all, because they *ate* their Dark. She had seen it herself. The Dark (or the Light) was a part of the host—the unknown perhaps, the repressed maybe, but still a part of the person. So, eating that part—as the Berserkers did—was literally like eating a piece of yourself. It was abhorrent. Their habit of eating their own Dark grew them to tremendous size and strength, and they were wild and uncontrollable in battle.

She absolutely hated Berserkers.

The two now approaching Kelso's house were the largest she had ever seen, close to eight feet tall and grotesquely muscled. They probably weighed six hundred pounds each and pulled huge weapons behind them through the snow with careless strength.

Kelso was transfixed next to her, and the Princess realized she had never fully explained to him what the Berserkers were and how they fit into the armies of the Dark. He was about to get a crash course on them.

The several dozen Furies who had been either on the street or hidden strategically throughout the block were on edge, nervous, and wary. Several had already summoned bows and held arrows of Fel Dark to their ears. The Sisterhood moved to loosely encircle the Berserkers as the two giant men stopped as one, standing perfectly still in the raging storm. Too far away for Ava to make them out clearly in the winter gale, she could still discern that there was something… wrong… with their faces.

"Peace!" shouted the Arch Mage as she stepped out onto the street and mingled fearlessly with the skittish Furies. Ava followed close behind her with Kelso and settled to a stop next to the Arch Mage. Kelso's hands rested on the pommels of his guns. Now that they were closer, Ava could just make out a third figure between the two giants who stood unperturbed within the circle of Furies. It was a small… woman, perhaps? Even shorter and slighter than Ava. *No,* the Princess amended, *she's just stooped over.*

Still unable to completely make out the woman's features, Ava could tell that she held two lengths of chain in her left hand, each angling up and terminating at the neck of the monsters that flanked her. Whoever she was, she held two Berserkers… on a leash.

With a slight start, she realized who the woman must be.

"Welcome, Serafain," said the Arch Mage neutrally, confirming Ava's suspicions. "You were good to your word, it appears."

The creature cackled and wheezed out, "Sorry to see me still alive, Cassandra? You should be relieved that I have come to help you, instead of the alternative." With another laugh, the woman shucked the two Berserkers forward by whipping the chains once, and the three approached.

The Princess put her hand lightly on one of Kelso's while she wrestled with the conflicting emotions evoked by the legendary crone in front of her. Serafain was reputed to be ancient beyond measure and without equal in the ranks of the Sorcerers. She would go decades without being seen and then appear suddenly to wreak havoc in random battles all over the world, before once again going dormant.

It was whispered that she had killed many on both sides of the Conflict. That was highly likely with the company she kept: two Berserkers. And Berserkers did what Berserkers do—they killed recklessly and with abandon. So unpredictable were they that Berserkers were often just pointed at the enemy and released, with the rest of the Dark staying well clear of the ensuing mayhem.

Kelso's thoughts interrupted her own musings. He was disgusted by the two horrors that accompanied the old woman. Why he was disgusted became evident to Ava when she inspected them more closely. Covered in old scars from head to toe, they had seen much combat over their time with Serafain. They were dressed only in simple loin clothes that bulged impossibly—horrifically, even—at the groin. Their weapons were huge swords of rusted iron, eight feet long and notched from use.

However, none of that was what disgusted Kelso or transfixed Ava. It was their faces.

Each Berserker wore a Greek theater mask. The one to Ava's right wore a black mask of stylized weeping; the one to her left, a white mask laughing. Each mask had been *hammered* into the face and skull of the Berserker wearing it. Black blood trickled lazily down the side of their necks, and left streaks across the masks where bolts had been driven into their foreheads, chins, and ears. *How were they even alive?*

Ava's eyes flickered down from the horrifying iron masks to the woman who held their chains. She was old, with hair completely white and frizzled. Dressed in little more than a ragged smock, rough shoes, and a threadbare shawl, she looked like a poor peasant woman from Eastern Europe. Despite her age and humble clothes, the Sorceress exuded a lazy malevolence that covered her like a cloak.

She favored Ava with a gap-toothed smile. "Well, now," she crooned, "you're a pretty little thing, aren't you? Powerful too."

"I told you," said Cassandra drily.

"Aye, aye, so you did." Serafain clucked as she looked the Princess over from head to toe. "I think she would even give Sock and Buskin here a run for their money."

"No," Ava disagreed quietly, "I would just kill them. Keep that in mind, Crone."

The Furies tensed at her words and Kelso stirred uneasily, but Cassandra smiled slightly and nodded in approval.

Serafain laughed uproariously and slapped her knee in glee. "Well said, Princess, well said indeed!" The old woman glanced over at Cassandra. "I approve of this one! She has fire and spirit!"

"She does indeed, Serafain." Cassandra moved closer to the

183

Sorceress and looked up at the two monstrosities—inspecting their masks with interest. "I see you have come up with a solution to our little problem, in your typically brutal fashion."

"What can I say? It's a gift," the old Sorceress shrugged modestly. "Within a moment, they can be quite immune to its damnable song. And don't you go worrying about the pain they might be in," she admonished Ava suddenly. "They are perfectly comfortable."

Ava couldn't see how that could be possible but let it pass. She also had zero interest in reading Serafain or her two companions. Ava had been exposed to enough filth in her life, and unless this meeting turned hostile she had no stomach to expose herself to more of it. The Princess was dead certain that the secrets these three held would be hard to forget—if the two monstrous Berserkers even thought at all. She wasn't completely sure, but it wasn't a mystery she cared to solve.

"Why are you here?" she said instead, then turned to Cassandra, "Why is she here?"

"Serafain is here to help us battle the real foe," answered the Arch Mage serenely. "She is our ally in the coming fight."

"Aye," agreed Serafain warmly. "I didn't come to collect any scalps but from those of your enemies. You will be needing me and mine before the night is over, and you will be right glad we're here." The old woman caressed a wicked-looking bronze dagger at her waist, and with a small start, Ava realized that Serafain might actually collect scalps. *Gross*! The Princess had been wise to avoid reading her.

"You won't even try to kill me tonight?" asked Cassandra curiously and seemingly only half-jokingly. "Are you sure? Why ruin a perfect record of failure?"

"Ouch," replied the crone, clutching at her heart. "It's been a hundred years—at least—since I last took a run at you, Arch Mage. Maybe I've changed?" Serafain looked at the Arch Mage with overly earnest eyes, fighting a smile at the same time.

Cassandra sighed. "You will fail again. I just want you to know that upfront, so why even try? Don't you get tired of it all?"

"Nah. It's fun!" asserted Serafain, waving the Arch Mage's words away like they smelled bad. "Now," she said firmly, "Who's going to introduce me to the handsome Knight standing next to our very own Princess? You're a looker, young man, and I love what you did to your face!"

Kelso's jaw dropped, but Ava couldn't help but grimace and hiss, "See?" at him with a little nudge. True, Serafain was old and hideous, but Ava had told him his face would be like catnip to the females of the Dark—and some males too, no doubt. The Princess had already caught a few of the Furies eyeing him admiringly once they'd realized combat was not in their immediate future.

Turning back to Serafain, Ava said, "This is Kelso Hart." She paused and added, "He is the Ebon Knight."

At her words, every Fury turned as one to regard him much as one might regard a snake at a birthday party—unexpected and definitely *not* welcome. The two Berserkers, who up until this point seemed completely oblivious to all conversation, both looked down in unison to regard the Knight. A subtle shift in their manner made it seem like they almost looked at him in… reverence.

"Oh my! What a treat this is!" Serafain exclaimed. "Sock! Buskin! You hear that? It's the Ebon Knight himself, my loves!"

Kelso was taken aback by her reaction, as were the Furies and Ava herself. Yes, she had the highest possible opinion of Kelso, but his being the Ebon Knight was a huge drawback in her eyes. Why, then, did both Serafain and her monsters look at Kelso as if they were looking at Santa Claus himself?

*No, scratch that.* Ava was pretty sure that Serafain and her Berserkers would be only too happy to kill Santa if he were real. And Jesus. Or the Buddha. Whoever it was, the Princess felt certain that the three in front of her would take a run at them. Just because.

Even so, Serafain seemed almost giddy with excitement, and her Berserkers seemed to want to lean down… to maybe shake Kelso's hand? This was getting really weird. The Furies, too, were looking on in amazement—and shock perhaps—at the Sorceress and her guards, as flummoxed as Ava was.

"Um… forgive me, but why are you looking at my Knight like he's the greatest thing since sliced bread?" Ava asked, her hand traveling up from Kelso's hand to his elbow.

"Because he is!" exclaimed the Sorceress, grinning ear to ear. "I have wanted to meet the Ebon Knight my whole life—and I came close a couple of times over the years. But to be standing here with him? On the same side? It's just wonderful!"

Kelso was completely confused and glanced down at Ava for help or clarification. She could offer neither—she was just as clueless.

He cleared his throat. "Why did you want to meet me so badly? Well, I guess it's really the sword you wanted to meet. Most on the Dark side fear the sword, and most on the Light side are wary of it."

"I know!" Serafain grinned even wider. "I love that about Argenta! I do hope I can see her. You will pull your sword for us tonight, yes?"

The Furies recoiled, Ava's eyes widened, and even Cassandra looked surprised, but Kelso did not. Instead, the grim Knight looked at her in complete silence for a few seconds and then regarded the two Berserkers that flanked her as well. Finally, he looked back at the Sorceress, who was still gazing at him like he was the second coming.

"You *want* me to pull Argenta? Do you have any idea what I will become if I do?" Kelso's voice was soft and sad. "I would kill all three of you."

"Oh, yes, I know!" Serafain laughed delightedly again. "We would be honored to die on Argenta's blade, Mr. Ebon Knight. Promise me that if we survive tonight's trials, you will consider doing that for us. I know you don't owe us anything, but it would be a wonderful boon."

Kelso and Ava drank coffee in the Knight's small kitchen. Mugs steaming, they held their drinks with both hands as they leaned up against the counters, totally drained. The crazy crone and her two Berserkers were not the only allies they had welcomed, but they were the least hostile of them. How that could be, Kelso had no clue.

Somehow, it had all gone downhill after Serafain, Sock, and Buskin.

Serafain's request had been met by dumbfounded silence from everyone in attendance, of course. Most of all from Kelso. He had been shocked at their request and more so by the fact that they had knowingly made it while fully aware that their deaths would be the result.

*"It's because they are obviously intelligent and of wonderful breeding,"* Argenta crowed in his mind. She had been pleased by Serafain's request and was avidly looking forward to fulfilling it.

*"Intelligent? No. Serafain is cunning certainly, and crazy like a fox probably, but to actually want to die violently on the blade of a cursed sword is not what most people consider smart. Also, 'wonderful breeding'? What does that even mean?"* Kelso was already exhausted by Argenta's preening. She had been going on non-stop about Serafain since the Sorceress made her request, and the Knight was already missing the brooding and angry sword he had once known.

*It was true,* he decided ruefully, *the grass is always greener on the other side.*

"*You're just mad because I have a fan club and you don't,*" offered his sword. "*And I am not cursed!*"

"*No? What are you then?*" thought Kelso, taking a sip of coffee.

The sword didn't answer for a moment, and when she did it was not what he expected. "*Broken,*" she replied, and nothing else.

Before he could ask her what she meant by that, Ava interrupted him, "Having a conversation with your sword?"

Kelso glanced at her quickly, "Yes. How did you know?"

Ava's cheeks reddened for a moment. "Uh, you get a certain look in your eyes when you are."

Argenta snickered in his mind, and Kelso wasn't sure what to make of that.

"I have a tell? Nice job... Let's never play poker, ok?" He smiled at her encouragingly.

She didn't smile back, and looked down at the ground for a moment, almost like she was ashamed. The Princess shook herself and looked back up at him, her dark blue eyes boring into his darker black. "I apologize if I seem to know a little bit more about you than I should, it's just..."

Kelso cut her off gently, "Ava. It's fine, really. I *want* you to know everything about me. I admire your perceptions, and

189

honestly, you would be shocked by how often you say or do something just perfectly to match what I was thinking. It's amazing, and I love it."

Strangely, the Princess did not look pleased with his praise, and—if he didn't know better—even appeared a little guilty. She smiled with some effort though and reached for his hand. He took it gratefully.

"Crazy night so far, huh?" he said.

She shook her head. "That is a gigantic understatement."

"I still can't believe I had to swear to *kill* Serafain and her Berserkers if they survived the night." The Knight sighed in dismayed disgust. "How the hell am I supposed to do that to them after they came to assist us?"

"You didn't promise to kill them tonight. You promised to kill them the next time you drew Argenta," Ava reminded him smugly. "*That's* what they agreed to."

After finding out that Kelso was the Ebon Knight, Serafain had insisted on the pact before following through on her earlier agreement to help. Cassandra, disappointed by the last-minute negotiations, had insinuated that Serafain had no honor. The Sorceress had just laughed in the Arch Mage's face and agreed... but she promised to bind herself to Kelso if he would honor her request.

No sooner had the agreement been struck than a contingent of the Light had arrived from the opposite direction. Maybe a dozen in total. The Knights, Priests, and even Childer of this band were well known to the Dark as archers and marksmen to rival their own. It had been a little touch-and-go getting through the introductions at that point. The Furies, Serafain, and the Berserkers all didn't care for the newcomers much, and the feeling was mutual. In spades. Only the Arch Mage and the Princess, working in tandem, had kept it from coming to blows.

Apparently, the twelve that had come all the way to Kelso's house were merely part of a much larger force that was stationing itself to the south in a valley between Reno and Carson City. According to Cassandra, a large horde of the Dark was mustering in Carson City and would push north into Reno and Sparks tonight. The Light would stop them from entering the city, and the Arch Mage herself would be joining them to make sure of it.

Similarly, the Sorceress and her Berserkers were headed west, along with four dozen Furies, to meet an elite team of Assassins from the Light. The roads over Donner Pass were quickly becoming impassable, so it was thought that the incoming team of enforcers was already en route, but it would be wicked slow going. Nonetheless, Cassandra was adamant that they would arrive in a few hours if not intercepted.

Only one freeway snaked over the mountains and into Reno, so the Furies and Serafain would have a nice choke point to work with. The Furies were reluctant to fight anywhere near Sock and Buskin, but Serafain told them she could control them in combat—should she wish to. The Sorceress had laughed uproariously at the bristling looks she had received from the Furies over that last addendum, before promising to keep them in check even as tears streamed down her face from laughing so

191

hard.

Kelso didn't care for the crone's humor very much.

The Knight and Ava were left alone with a few dozen Furies to guard the house. Cassandra had insisted that they stay here behind the wards with the still unmoving Marcus Dain. Kelso had been positive that was *not* going to happen. There was no way Ava would huddle behind wards while others fought, even though the Furies had all thought it was a capital plan. It didn't matter; Ava would never agree.

Until she did.

The Princess and the Arch Mage locked gazes for close to a minute, neither saying anything to the other once the plans had been laid out. Ava looked furious, while Cassandra merely looked resigned. And that was it.

Ava took Kelso's hand without saying another word and led him to the house. They stood for a while and looked at the still-unconscious group of Furies in the front room before making some coffee.

Later, Ava walked a cup of the steaming brew out to the snowbound Paladin, still rigidly at attention, and whispered something in his ear that Kelso could not make out. The Paladin didn't stir at her words and Ava looked morosely back at Kelso for a moment before venturing further out to exchange a few words with the Furies that still stood guard in the apocalyptic storm.

Even though the fierce women were but thirty feet away,

Kelso could just barely make them out as Ava stopped by one, and then another, as she made her way down the row. After a minute, she came back, casting a glance at the still-immobile Paladin as she did so.

"Better get that coffee pot going, Sir Barista Boy, because we have about twenty requests to fill." Ava started to say something else but cut off suddenly as a strain of music—if the discordant sound that now reached them could be called such—reached their ears. It floated out of the dark and the storm, riding the snowflakes as it came.

Coming closer, moment by moment.

Marcus Dain, once High Lord Commander of the Paladins, turned his head to the sound. Cocking one ear to the East in interest, his eyes sharpened as the lethargic confusion that had hobbled him drained away.

# Chapter 12

It was unraveling.

Cassandra stood perfectly still on a small hillock just outside the ring of diffused light thrown by a large freeway lamp. At the very edge of town, in a gale of epic proportions, she might as well have been on an alien planet. Around her and stretching out hundreds of yards on both sides of the road waited the elite guard of the Arch Mage, completely invisible in the raging snowstorm.

They were the true elite guard of the Light, serving the true Arch mage.

Curated in secret over the last few hundred years, the warriors of her guard were the only members of the Light to know who she actually was. Emerie—an old friend and willing decoy—had been her companion for many hundreds of years, but his powers fell far short of her own. Emerie had supposedly been the secretive Arch Mage known only to a few of the highest-ranking of the Light, including the other Mages on the Council. Those Mages, seven in all and the most powerful of the Light—except for her—had thusly been deceived.

And that deception had saved her life.

Emerie had died after being put down by the Council, supposedly a victim of the new malady that was making itself known to the Hosts. In truth, it was the Council that had become corrupted, and their combined attack—perfectly in unison during a random meeting—had killed Emerie almost immediately.

The Arch Mage had been made uneasy by a blind spot that had developed in the weave of her own life. In all the planes and in all the time since she had come to be, Cassandra had never encountered such. It scared her, also a first, and she wisely refrained from joining the Council that day as Emerie's scribe.

Her wrath at his death had been terrible. She had managed to pick off two Mages on her stealthy retreat from the Temple, but it had been close—too close. Cassandra uncovered a dark truth that day: the Other could foil her gaze. For the first time since her consciousness, she could be tricked. Not only had Cassandra almost lost both fights she'd started, but she had not foreseen Emerie's death. He had been one of the strands that had entered the blind spot, along with hers and a few others. Since then, she had avoided disaster only by avoiding the blind spots in her weave, steering both her allies and herself away from them at all costs when they developed.

It was a losing strategy, as she was constantly on the defensive, but it was the only card she had left to play. Argenta was broken in twain and could not help her, and Cassandra's other sister had refused her.

This world, and maybe reality itself, stood on a knive's edge.

Worse, she now knew that the Other was affecting her ability to read everything. The loom itself was warping to the Chaos now invading this world. So far, it was little things, like Cassandra's complete surprise that Serafain would be willing to renege on their deal if not for Kelso agreeing to her ridiculous terms. It had been handled brilliantly by Ava, but to the Arch

Mage's chagrin and near panic, Serafain had almost been lost to the coming battle.

If she and her two Berserkers did not help the Furies to the west, the opposing force would surely break through and advance to the house. It was an absolute certainty. The butchers that made up that band, led by Baston Tijeran, would be looking for her and Marcus, and if Marcus fell to them before his purpose could be fulfilled, then Ava and Kelso would fall too, and so on.

Like dominos, each failure led to another, and another, and another, and into oblivion at last.

The Arch Mage closed her eyes for a moment, reading fates, and saw that some around her would end shortly. Not all, but too many. Still, she expected a resounding victory tonight. Cassandra worried, though—had she built a house of cards? If the Other could knock even one down unexpectedly, would the whole house fall as well?

She really didn't know what was going to happen anymore, and that was another first in her timeless existence. Now was a time of many firsts, it seemed. The Arch Mage floated over an abyss of unfathomable and malevolent depths, and she did so alone.

A shout caught her attention, and she opened her eyes just in time to see the first—in what would be a long line—of vehicles approaching her position. She struck immediately.

Dazzling bolts of lightning arced out of the Arch Mage's fingers as she electrocuted everything and everyone in the lead vehicle. Without pause, she stepped forward and slammed her foot on the ground. A large chasm, fifty feet deep and twenty feet wide, opened behind the first SUV, which was now drifting lifeless into a snowbank. The truck directly behind the first plunged into the sudden fissure and exploded at the bottom in a brilliant orange flash.

Around the Arch Mage, her elite guard rose to engage as the vehicles behind the first two slowed, stopped, or pulled over. Warriors of the Dark began to spill out of the cars like black ants, and the thin line of defenders stood to repel them. They were all committed now. While Cassandra fought, she watched the percentages closely.

The dominos had all been placed. She had done the best she could to protect and save those who mattered most; it was time to see if she would succeed. Her last thought before throwing herself fully into the fight was that she must somehow find the Spider. If Jesslyn got through, the Spider would gain her prize, and things would become... complicated.

\*\*\*

Baston was increasingly on edge as the small convoy of heavy-duty trucks and SUVs made slow progress over Donner Pass and down into Reno. The road had been closed both behind and in front of them. They were alone on a mountainside wrapped in a white blizzard of impressive and scary proportions—a perfect place for a trap; he was sure of it.

He rode in the fourth vehicle of the ten forming the convoy.

The snow looked like thick strings of confetti as it swept through the glare of his headlights. It was actually beautiful, in a wild and threatening way. Baston was surrounded by hardened warriors only; no Childer or unknowns were present on this hunting trip. Each of the thirty Knights, Paladins, and Priests that comprised the hand of the Council was a veteran, and, between them, they had thousands of years of combat experience.

These were some of the best the Light had to offer. If a trap was sprung, the ambushers would certainly come to regret it.

Even in their monstrous four-wheel drives, the road was close to impassable, and the plow crews had given up. As such, their column of vehicles was bunched up and moving slowly behind the largest truck. And it sported a rack of huge spotlight beams to help light the way.

With only about five feet between each vehicle and visibility so poor, Baston couldn't imagine them being much more vulnerable than they now were. On the left side was a steep rocky climb that would be almost impossible to make even for the supernaturally strong and gifted members of his war-band. On the right side was a cliff edge dropping many hundreds of feet—not a height any of them could survive.

They were hemmed in.

The storm's fury signaled that there was a huge presence of the Dark in Reno, and his fingers tingled in anticipation of wielding Vindicta tonight. The storied Paladin only hoped it wasn't on this pass, but he thought it likely.

No sooner had he considered this than the lead vehicle of the convoy was somehow *pushed* over the cliff edge. Even from the passenger's seat of the fourth vehicle, he could see the huge truck tilt over and out into the air, huge spotlights illuminating thick sheets of driving snow as it fell.

"OUT!" Baston yelled into the company-wide channel before he followed the order himself, stepping out into the driving snow with Vindicta in hand and armoring up.

Two Fel arrows slammed into the front windshield as he exited, shattering it in a spray of jeweled glass that was immediately swallowed by the storm. The first arrow struck the seat he had just left, sinking in a foot deep. The other pinned his driver through the throat, a man who had fought next to Baston dozens of times over the years. The Knight clawed at the arrow for a second before expiring, his half-formed Light winking out.

The other two soldiers in the backseat managed to escape unharmed just before the huge Hummer behind them plowed into their rear, wheels spinning as the driver of that vehicle, also dead, floored the gas mindlessly. Both vehicles crashed into the next, but that driver had managed to not only stop but exit. The Hummer labored to push all three forward, shimmying slightly from side to side in the snow.

Another black arrow leapt from the white maelstrom and struck the soldier who had exited on the left side. She was armored and experienced though—a Priestess of the Light known for her *very* thorough investigative techniques. The arrow merely rocked her back into the passenger door hard enough to dent the metal before she rebounded.

Baston couldn't see past the nearest two vehicles on either side, but it appeared that the entire convoy was being peppered with arrows. *Furies!*

"Cover, cover, cover!" he barked into his throat mic and helped the Priestess shimmy over the hood as another arrow arced at her out of the storm. They crouched behind the front tire for a moment. Glancing over, he saw a younger Paladin, Jhonas, crouched behind the back tire.

Time was on their side. Furies could not afford to waste arrows if there were no targets, as each sapped them little by little. It was a weakness the forces of the Light had often exploited against the so-called Sisterhood.

"Sound off," Baston growled, and like a well-oiled machine, the remaining members of his war-band did.

Seven dead, twenty-two alive and ready for combat, one severely wounded and unconscious. Baston was thankful for the forces he had left, and considering their caliber, he felt confident they could defeat the band of Furies that had attacked them.

Already, though, he was wondering if they would have enough left to complete their mission. *Damn the Dark! Always showing up at the worst possible time!*

He clicked the mic again. "Prepare to repel. Sword and board."

Jhonas unlimbered his shield—the ghostly armor of his Light

reinforced it and the younger man's body armor as well, making for a double layer of protection.

Baston was just preparing to issue orders for someone to crawl into the Hummer to stop it from grinding itself into their truck when a pair of enormously loud bellows pierced the air. The now leading vehicle, a Jeep, was suddenly flipped end over end—crushing three of the four soldiers covering behind it—as a pair of the largest Berserkers Baston had ever seen slammed into it at speed. Screams followed it down to the valley floor far below, where it joined the wreckage of the truck.

A Priest who had managed to jump out of the way was clipped by the plummeting rig, and before he could struggle up fully, the closest monster slapped him on the side of the head with his massive hand, shattering the Priest's armor and knocking him over the cliff. Unconscious, he followed his companions on the long flight to the bottom.

There was only one chance now, and Baston took it.

"Engage!" he yelled and rushed towards the two Berserkers even now turning their attention to the third vehicle. Another arrow leapt from the white chaos ahead of him, and he dodged it… barely. A choking gasp from behind him indicated that either the Priest or Jhonas hadn't. Dimly, he could see the long, mishappen woman who'd shot it as she drew another arrow to ear. Without pause, he hefted his poleaxe in one hand and threw it at her in a blinding strike.

It hit the Fury square in her chest, and Vindicta tore through her armor and body with ease, launching her into the massive snowdrifts that had formed on the mountain side of the road. A scream of rage alerted him to another Fury hurtling out of the blinding storm at him, a huge mace held two-handed over her head.

Barely slowing in his advance towards the Berserkers, Baston dodged the downward strike of the mace and skittered sideways. He extended his left hand to Vindicta, where it was buried in the Fury's body, and called it back to him. It flew out of the storm, handle first, to slap into his hand.

The Fury had just begun to lift her mace again when a pair of silver arrows struck her in the neck and chest, exploding through her armor and sinking deep. Gagging, she reached both hands up frantically to pull at the arrow lodged in her throat but lost her strength and sunk to her knees. Holding the shaft weakly with both hands, she swayed there at death's door... but not for long.

Baston stayed his blow and focused instead on the two Berserkers standing side by side at the very edge of his vision twenty feet away. They both had unlimbered massive swords of dead black and stood watching him. Their faces were hidden by hideous mocking masks of iron that appeared to have been hammered into their heads.

*Savages.*

From his left, a screaming Fury leapt out of the storm, twin swords of ebony in her hands. Jhonas met her head-on, taking both flashing blades on his shield as he swung his gleaming sword at her mid-section. She leapt back with a snarl and started circling him. Jhonas smacked his sword blade on his shield and

202

laughed, matching her movement for movement. The young Paladin's timely arrival meant that the Priestess was the one who had caught the arrow launched at Baston earlier. He hoped that at least one Priest survived the battle, because two out of the four were already dead.

"Everything good, Jhonas?" called Baston as he sized up the Berserkers, and they him. "Not going to have any trouble, are you?"

"No, sir," piped the younger Paladin, turning away one of the Fury's swords with his blade and catching the other with his shield again. "She's a looker, though. I'm hoping for a little smooch before I separate her head from that sexy body of hers."

The Fury snarled at him in hate. Baston grinned mirthlessly; knowing Jhonas, he probably winked back.

"No fraternization with the enemy, Jhonas. I'm going to go kill these Berserkers, and if I come back and you're still dancing with her, I'm going to be disappointed." Baston glared at the massive forms in front of him for a second and started forward.

"I hear you, sir," Jhonas responded as he clashed again with the Fury.

In Baston's earpiece, he could hear exhortations up and down the line. It seemed that battle raged along the entire length of vehicles, and they had sustained more losses. Even so, this group of miscreants had picked the wrong convoy to ambush. Without the element of surprise, his elite team was going to tear the ambushers apart.

"You two overgrown children ready to die?" he called confidently. "I'm going to cut those stupid masks off your faces and hang them on my wall!"

Both Berserkers merely waited for him to approach, which was not typical of their kind. Baston had a moment of worry over it, but with Vindicta in hand there was nothing they could possibly do to stop him.

***

Ava stiffened as the haunting music reached her ears from the storm, and knew that Kelso was aware of it as well. Cassandra had predicted that a direct assault on the house was possible, and she had been correct. Again.

Ava called her armor to her and was dimly aware of Kelso doing the same. Out in the street the Furies spread apart, none raging as of yet, but all calling arms and armor to them. Bows, swords, and all other sorts of weapons appeared in their hands as they dispersed in front of the house while other women from the sides joined them.

The storm, which had been rampaging just seconds before, started to inexplicably calm, and vision improved dramatically to thirty, forty, and even fifty feet. The lull pushed out to the end of the block, and there, standing shoulder to shoulder, were six women. Ava wondered how long they had actually been there without the Furies knowing. Her sense of it was that they had just arrived, and if that were the case, it was eerie how the storm pulled back to reveal them, yet no further.

"You're immune to their song, yes?" she hissed at Kelso, eyes squinting as she examined the women. The snow had lessened dramatically, but the six newcomers were still mostly shadowed and obscured from her vision. The Princess had an idea of who they might be, though, and she grieved for the Sisterhood.

"I am. You?" The Knight's hands hovered around his guns, his ghostly armor almost camouflaged by the background of snow.

"I can be." Ava hesitated, "I should be."

Kelso glanced over at her as the falling snow started to abate. "What does that mean?"

"It means that I have been to this point, but since the enemy grows stronger, I might have to show another side of myself." She looked over at him. "There is a part of me that is a shadow to my Dark, if that makes sense. If I go there, I will be... different."

The Knight studied her intently from behind the visor of his helm, and even with it lowered, she could still make out the black mark that now rode his face, peeking out like a tear on his cheek. It was an ominous accent of pitch well suited to the night that was heralded by the arrival of the six.

"Different? How so?" He turned back to the six facing them and threw back his ghostly cloak, flexing his hands before allowing them to drop back next to his guns.

"I will be cold. Strange to you in some respects, but please trust me and know that nothing I am, or ever could be, would hurt you," Ava kept her voice level and unconcerned, but inside, she was worried. The odds of her seeing this out as herself were slim, and she knew that the Witch was not one for niceties.

"I know. At least one of us can say that." Kelso's voice was dull as he answered her, and Ava realized that his other level of combat prowess could only be accessed if he pulled Argenta—and if he did that all bets were off. In that respect, the Princess was more fortunate than he if she needed to pull her ace card.

Ava wasn't one hundred percent sure that Argenta had any interest in killing her anymore, but she definitely did not want to gamble her life on it, either. If Kelso drew the sword and became the Ebon Knight in truth *and* deed, he was as likely to lay waste to her as he was to the incoming threats they faced.

It was a maddening conundrum.

Both stepped forward as one and walked up to the ward line. Now that they had closed the distance somewhat, they could clearly see what Ava had feared; the six women facing them were Furies—or at least had once been Furies. The forty warriors who ringed them had not raged or attacked for precisely that reason.

Confusion and hesitation reigned, and Ava was worried it would be their downfall. So ingrained it was in the Sisterhood that each Fury was untouchable to any other, that the Princess feared the six in front of her had been sent by the Other for exactly that reason. And if it knew that, what else did it know?

As if to confirm this, one of the six raised her hand, and a small white cloth billowed from it.

"Parlay," she asked in a dead voice, although she really didn't say it as a question.

As one, and in perfect unison, the six stepped forward a few paces and stopped. Now completely engulfed by the mass of Furies around them, they waited without any expression on their faces. The music that foretold their coming grew no louder, and the snow around them stopped completely.

Ava could now make out their faces; identically devoid of expression, yet somehow malevolent. It was like they were porcelain dolls holding straight razors hidden behind their backs. She studied them as they studied her and Kelso; none of them deigned to inspect the other Furies at all.

Each of her guards had now settled into stillness around the six, holding weapons of Fel shadow and pitch Dark. No one spoke for a minute.

"Parlay," said another in the same dead voice. Ava shuddered slightly when she realized that it was the *exact* same voice.

"What do you want?" she called. "Your rash approach has ended your lives, so speak fast."

The six smiled as one at her voice and looked towards her. "I want you, Princess. Come join me."

"Not happening. Is that all you wanted to say?" Ava could tell that Kelso was extremely uncomfortable with the Other addressing her directly—and even more so by the manner in which it was. One voice and one consciousness relayed through several mouths; it was tilting him a little.

As if the Other could read her mind, six pairs of eyes focused on Kelso now.

"Greetings, Ebon Knight. It's been a couple of days since I last saw you. How have you been?" Identical rueful grins worked their way onto the women's faces. "Did you bring a set of steak knives or a waffle maker with you this time? You still owe me, you know."

Kelso's face hardened at the words, and Ava read that the infected Ghoul on the rooftop had needled the Knight with that same question.

"Neat trick. Not impressed though. I killed you up there; I'm going to kill you again. All of you again." The Knight's voice was cold, even colder than the snow that blanketed the city, and his stare promised violence. Ava approved of both his words and his intent and turned back to the six women with anticipation. This was all the Other had brought? It wouldn't be enough.

The women laughed. "We can be individuals, you know—if we care to be. Why don't you join me? We can rid you of that burden you carry. Come out and meet us."

At their words, Kelso's mind was disrupted by static. Ava would have given a lot to know what his sword said to him, but Kelso only smiled grimly.

"You know, you can't even keep your own words from betraying you. Is it 'we,' 'me,' 'I,' or 'us'? Do you even know? Saying the same thing from six different mouths only illustrates how little you understand us or how little you think of us. It doesn't matter. You're going to die." Kelso's face was a mask of condescension and barely checked violence. Ava felt the Dark within her stirring at his words, at his expression... and at his intentions.

The Ebon Knight of myth and legend was close to being unleashed, and the Dark Witch wanted to rampage with him.

"Aw, come on now, that's not at all friendly," chortled just one woman, a taller female standing next to a shorter woman who looked to be from India. "I'll make you a deal like you made me a deal. Fair?"

Kelso said nothing, but his fingers flexed, and the ghostly falcon wings that adorned his helmet pulled up tight—he was seconds away, and it was time to end the charade.

"My warriors," Ava called out, "the six before you are no longer Sisters. Let us put them out of their misery and let us do it now."

The Princess expected her Furies to explode into motion then, but none of them moved. Dread gripped her, and Kelso's hands twitched once and then stilled as he, too, was caught off guard. The Knight quickly glanced at her in confusion and worry, and Ava knew her face was a mirror to his.

And then, her mistake, her failing, became clear. She had been arrogant. A stone formed in her stomach as all of her Furies, all forty or more, turned at exactly the same time to face her and Kelso.

All of them wore the same sneaky smile.

# Chapter 13

Chandra was livid. Something important and dangerous was about to happen… she felt it in her bones, but she had been neatly removed from the board. Why, she wasn't sure, but Ava had never pushed them so hard to an action that was not to their liking. Even worse, the Princess had not explained why she had inexplicably rounded up Chandra and the others, banishing them from her side.

Chandra glanced over to Jae and saw that her Sister was wearing the same expression she was—a furrowed brow and gritted teeth. Confusion and suspicion warred within her as she looked over the head of Misima to catch Carmen's eyes in the back seat where she sat next to Charlie. He was sitting up and staring into the storm as they drove slowly to the edge of town. On his other side sat Mrs. Rodriguez, bundled up in multiple layers of clothing.

It had been a long, slow trip.

Ava had been forced to 'push' Mrs. Rodriguez a little to convince her to leave with the Furies, and Chandra could tell she was still dazed by it. The old Hispanic woman had a withered hand on Charlie's head and was stroking the bulldog absently as she stared out the window, none the worse for the experience perhaps, but still befuddled.

Carmen spoke first, "Yeah, so… what was that all about?" The young woman was making remarkable progress and had already developed the strong resistances to temperature that the rest of them enjoyed. She was dressed in jeans, sneakers, and a light sweater—still more than the three older Furies were wearing, but woefully inadequate for the weather otherwise.

Misima answered, her voice slow and thoughtful, "I have no idea, but I am confused as to why we agreed to leave." She looked over to Chandra. "Why did we agree?"

Chandra was at a loss for words. She had been asking herself that very same question for the last ten minutes as they continued their slow retreat from the Knight's house. As she often did, Jae came to her rescue.

"Because she has never ordered us to do anything, and we were thrown off guard. I think it startled us because it's not her... style."

"How was that an order?" Carmen wanted to know. "To me, it seemed like she was pleading more than demanding."

Chandra opened her mouth to answer, but Mrs. Rodriguez broke in, her voice unsteady and weak with age.

"Where are we going?" she asked, still petting Charlie. The big dog looked over at her when she spoke, and he leaned in to give her a quick lick on the ear. The older woman did not react.

"We are going to see some friends, grandmother," answered Misima respectfully.

Chandra looked back at Carmen again, and her heart was full. Never had Chandra met a new Childe with so much raw power and potential. She was terrified that the young woman's actions in the barn would cause her to be outcasted, though, and Chandra was still mulling over her likely response to it.

She believed deep down in her heart that Carmen's actions had ultimately saved Kelso from being slain last night. That was vitally important because if Carmen had not intervened, Chandra was certain that Ava would have killed every single one of the seven Spears that had taken part in attacking him. Her revenge would have shattered the alliance that both she and the Sisterhood needed intact and would have probably resulted in the Princess dying as well.

Carmen's actions had been pivotal in saving everyone, and if she was to be exiled over doing a critically right thing, then maybe Chandra would leave too.

It was a dilemma she hoped to avoid, but her gut feeling told her that the elders would be sticklers to the unwritten—but deeply understood—laws and norms that bound them all into the Sisterhood. She could understand both sides, so her unease was profound as she sat silently, trying to chart a course for herself, Jae, and most likely, Misima. They would follow her lead unquestioned, and this weighed heavily upon her.

"So, are you going to just keep staring at me, or will you answer my question?" asked Carmen, pulling Chandra's attention back to the present.

She grimaced at the young woman ruefully. "There might have been a little begging involved, yes, but that was primarily to encourage us to leave faster. That we were leaving was already settled, whether we wanted to go or not."

Chandra frowned again at the memory. True, the Princess was a one-woman wrecking ball, but she was still young and happily blinded by new love. Ava's edge would be dulled. If anything happened to her, Chandra would never forgive herself. There were several other Spears guarding Ava, of course, but it still felt like a betrayal to leave her.

"Alright. So again, what was that all about? Why did she want us to leave?"

"I think she believed she was saving our lives, but she made it seem like we were needed elsewhere to prepare a fallback position in case the Knight's abode was breached," Chandra shook her head in disgust. "Like that could happen; it would be suicidal for anyone to try."

"Those wards are intimidating," Jae agreed, eyes focused on the road as she concentrated on keeping the large truck moving steadily—and safely—through the storm.

The snow wasn't merely falling anymore; it was dumping. Chandra had rarely seen snow this intense in all the many years of her life. It boded ill. The world itself was preparing to obscure a battle that the Fury could feel on the wind. It was maddening to be out here when Ava was—or shortly would be—in harm's way.

In all the years Chandra had known Ava, never had she seen the quiet desperation Ava had attempted to hide as she corralled and cajoled them to leave. It was for that reason alone that Chandra had agreed.

And now here they were, trundling away from Kelso's house even as an apocalyptic storm prophesied a clash between the true powers of the world. Shaking her head in frustrated wonderment, Chandra stared out the window morosely, joining her Sisters, the dog, and Mrs. Rodriguez in silence.

***

Innonia examined herself critically in the mirror. It was something she had often done—perhaps too much. Mousey brown hair with two over-large eyes (spaced just a bit too far apart) and an unremarkable nose all ensured that she would never be able to enter—much less win—any beauty contests. Not that she cared about beauty contests. She knew her worth, and she was contented with herself. Except, that was, for her damnable mouth.

The huge square teeth, almost like horse's teeth, that crowded her mouth served to grotesquely deform her jaw. Awakening to the Dark had been hard, scary, and taxing, but the experience of having her normal teeth pushed out—to make room for the large and heavy teeth she now bore—was painful. Her whole face had ached for months, and pulling adult teeth from her mouth had been traumatic.

Even after all these years, she still hated the way she looked because of her teeth.

That had not stopped suitors from pursuing her, though. Compared to most other Ghouls, she was quite striking, and that was minorly satisfying. Still… Innonia pulled her lips back and

215

grimaced at herself in the mirror for a moment before shaking her head and turning away.

She was stalling, and Innonia was normally not one to shirk any duty, but the coming night promised to test her in ways she was not sure any Ghoul could easily navigate. As Grave Smith to her clan, she was resolved to try, however.

A quick knock on her door pulled her out of her reverie, and Elizabeth poked her head in a moment later; long stringy black hair and grey eyes making her almost monstrous in the dim light. She grinned quite charmingly though—if one looked past the teeth—and shook her head knowingly, clucking her tongue.

"Are you stressing over your mouth again, Innonia?" she teased, coming fully into the room and closing the heavy wooden door behind her.

Innonia shrugged, "Maybe."

"So, that's a hard yes." Elizabeth strode across the room and fished a beautiful, silver-plated hairbrush from the counter, and promptly began to groom Innonia, smiling all the time.

"I don't get how you're just fine with it. Didn't it ever bother you?" Innonia looked at Elizabeth in the mirror as she was worked over and primped. She needed to look as regal and impressive as she possibly could for her clan this evening. Strange happenings were afoot, and Innonia needed to look the part of a confident leader, as much as actually being one.

Elizabeth paused. "Well, maybe for the first ten years or so, but after that... " she trailed off and shrugged, concentrating

216

again on the task at hand.

Innonia smiled in spite of herself. Elizabeth displayed the typical pragmatism of the Ghouls, and it was that pragmatic streak that was their greatest strength and blessing in a hard world at war. None on either side—Light or Dark—felt truly comfortable around the Ghouls because of their unique… diet. Nominally of the Dark, and manifesting such, Innonia nevertheless knew that if there were a neutral party to the Conflict, it was them.

The Ghouls had stood alone since the beginning because none cared to stand with them. This status quo had existed since their surprising and unforeseen inception a few hundred years ago, and Innonia often thought that her clan was destined to always be alone in the Conflict.

Things had changed.

Innonia had received three calls tonight, each building on the other, until she had made a call of her own. On her word, the clan had gathered, and every single one of them—thirty-one in total— was waiting for her in the large viewing room of the funeral parlor that was their proverbial castle and keep.

The first call had been from the Grave Smith of the largest and most prestigious clan in the world. Phillip was in charge of the Ghouls in Paris, where many hundreds of them made their home. If the Ghouls had an overall leader, Phillip was it. Known for his thoughtful and methodical ways, he had been uncharacteristically breathless—and almost panicked—when she received his call.

His message was short and succinct: "The Furies have splintered from the Dark. Where do you and yours stand?"

Innonia had been speechless for a moment, completely caught off guard. "Why are you asking me, Phillip? Does it matter?"

"It does, because the Furies have rallied to *her*." Phillip's emphasis was unmistakable; he could only be talking about one person. The shining Darkness within the larger shadow—the very same one she had met just two days earlier.

Innonia's mouth went dry for a second as she realized the implications.

"Are they coming here?" she asked, anticipating the answer.

"Yes. All of them, from everywhere," Phillip said nothing more, and silence settled over the line.

Innonia's thoughts raced, and she realized that her proximity to Ava and her actions during this crisis would prove to be spectacularly important in how the Ghouls were viewed—and received—by the greater Dark.

*The greater Dark.* Once roguishly noble, or at least relatable, the Dark was now foreign to her and to many of her clan. Innonia was a monster afraid of the other monsters that she was supposedly allied to. She hated what the Dark had become and loathed those who now made up the bulk of its armies. An exception to her disgust was the Sisterhood. They alone had stood aloof and true, and they alone backed Ava—who, by all accounts, was worth more to those who prized decency and justice than the rest of her family combined.

Innonia herself had experience with Ava and knew that the stories told about her were spot on. Ava was frightening but fair. The Princess had certainly terrified Innonia, but she had also been kind—and even gentle—during their meeting. As Grave Smith, Innonia's word bonded her clan, and what she decided now might also influence other clans around the world.

"What is happening to the Furies now?" Innonia asked, this time fearing the answer.

Phillip's tone was bleak, "They're dying, dozens of them here in Paris, hundreds of them around the world, perhaps thousands of them."

"You have reports from other Grave Smiths confirming this?" Anger tinged her voice.

"I do. Where do you and yours stand?" Phillip asked again.

She didn't hesitate, "I stand with Ava and the Sisterhood."

"Very well," Phillip breathed. "The die is cast."

"You?" Innonia asked. "Where do you stand, Phillip?"

"I stand against the Dark. I am sickened by them, and we cannot eat enough evil to purge this world of its imbalance. We must take action before it's too late." Phillip paused. "You're our emissary now to the Princess. Do well, Grave Smith."

He hung up then, and Innonia shuddered. His declaration had been dramatic and irrevocable. Innonia had declared who she was with, but Phillip had declared who he was against. There was an ocean of difference between those two stances—one of them being positively warlike.

Holding the phone, Innonia's mind reeled at the implications. She wondered if she should call a conclave—something she had last done just a few weeks ago when Geraud had gone insane. That was the first time she had ever done so, and now she contemplated it again. If she did her clan would be bound by her decision. *Could she do that to them? Was it fair?*

Before she could wrestle with herself further, her phone rang again. Still in hand, she immediately lifted it to her ear and answered.

"Innonia?" said an unfamiliar voice, but it was assured, calm, and determined. A female's voice, young sounding, yet with echoes of power in every syllable.

"Yes, I'm Innonia. And you are?" Innonia felt like her life was unmooring and the ship she captained was about to sail for the edges of the map. There were monsters there; she felt it.

"I'm Cassandra St. Augustine. I am the true Arch Mage of the Light, now exiled, as you and yours shortly will be. As Ava, youngest Princess of the Dark, already is." The voice on the other end of the line was businesslike, even as she threw around titles that were taboo and frightening. It was also terrifying that this 'Cassandra' could call her and reference decisions that had just been made seconds earlier.

"How?" was all she could muster.

"Well, I am the Arch Mage, you know. Being super smart and mysterious is kind of in my job description." Amazingly, there was a hint of humor in Cassandra's reply. That, more than anything else the Arch Mage could have done, put Innonia somewhat at ease.

"What do you want?" Innonia had a fair idea and was not surprised by the reply.

"I want your clan to ally with me. Well, with me and my allies, actually."

"With the Light, you mean?" She felt that the Arch Mage's choice of words was... curious.

"No. The majority of the Light is lost, much like the majority of the Dark. You know this. You have felt it; you have seen it firsthand with Geraud and with the brutality and depravity that is the Dark now, yes?" Self-assured and calm, the words were anything but. They promised a war without known lines or alliances, a chaotic thing that would blender those caught in the middle—like her clan.

"I have felt it. I have seen it," Innonia admitted hesitantly. "But I am declaring for another, and—"

"Yes, I know," the Arch Mage broke in. "Ava and her Furies. They are my allies, and I'm here with them now—along with the Ebon Knight."

Innonia was silent for a moment, a chill crawling down her spine. "I see," was all she said, all she could say.

"Yes, I think you do. I have a favor to ask of you, Grave Smith, not for myself precisely, but for the one you wish to

221

serve."

"I'm listening."

"Agree to what she wants when she calls, and she will call soon. That is all I can tell you for now, but I promise you that you and your clan will be spared as much as possible from the whirlwind that now descends upon the world. For what it's worth, you made the right decision. Know that." And with those final words, the Arch Mage—if that was who Cassandra really was—hung up.

For the next few minutes, Innonia fretted, but true to Cassandra's prediction, Ava called. Her request had been simple yet profound. The depths of it unknowable and sharp-edged.

Innonia had agreed to it all; what other choice did she really have? And afterward, she made a call of her own, and the Ghouls came to her; all of them that were of her clan and bound to her as she was to them. Friends all, family all, they came to listen and to prepare for a night that would forever change their course.

The Ghouls were going to war.

# Chapter 14

Kelso stood transfixed, facing the nearly fifty Furies that now gazed at him and Ava. Besides the checked-out Paladin behind him and the comatose Furies in his house, the Knight's only ally was the Princess at his elbow, and she seemed completely stunned... and sad.

Kelso could understand her feelings, at least a little, because he knew how close she was to the Sisterhood, and their unwilling betrayal of her must be soul-crushing. From his point of view, it just meant there were a *lot* more enemies to kill—although he wished they were not Furies.

"So, can we make a deal or not?" asked a random Fury, one just turned and only thirty feet from the ward line.

It was disconcerting how the conversation moved from mouth to mouth, and Kelso felt that such seamless unity made the Other even more dangerous than it should otherwise have been. If dozens of individuals could be so closely linked as to be indistinguishable from each other, how exponentially more lethal would that be when there were hundreds? Or thousands?

Ava was silent next to him, but he could sense that her dismay was slowly turning to anger. He felt it almost like an invisible pressure that was pushing out from her in waves of increasing strength. Kelso knew she was absolutely deadly, but what could she do against so many? They were clearly outclassed. He needed to stall for time, and the enemy seemed content to let him.

"What deal?" Kelso asked. "I actually have a set of steak knives in my house, and I would be happy to trade them to you if you want. Let the ladies go free and let's parlay in good faith."

At his words, a Fury to his extreme right started laughing mirthlessly, almost mechanically, and another took it up—this time the one nearest to him. Another one began to laugh as well, perfectly in unison with the first two, and just like that more joined, and more again… until all fifty women were laughing at him.

After a minute, they all stopped in mid-laugh and complete silence descended.

"I," began one of the original six.

"Have," another one said.

"No," yet another added.

"Need," said a Fury standing to his left.

"For," the closest one again.

"Your," the furthest now.

"Knives," the tall one finished.

"I want your sword," they all said together.

"*If you surrender me, you are lost, as is your Princess, and the world as well,*" broke in Argenta needlessly.

"*Ya think?*" he shot back sarcastically.

"*Yes, I do,*" answered Argenta, apparently missing his

sarcasm, which was strange for her since she often wielded a vicious brand of it herself.

"That's a non-negotiable for me," he answered out loud. "You already know that though."

"I do know that," agreed the tall one again, "but I don't understand it. You hate your sword, don't you? Why not lay it down and walk away? I promise to allow you and the Princess to leave the field alive if you do." The woman even smiled at Kelso as she reasoned with him.

Kelso was chilled by her manner for two reasons. First, she sounded almost normal now. He could hear the questioning in her voice and see her confusion at his refusal to give up Argenta. The second was the natural-looking smile. The conclusion was inescapable and dire in its portent. The Other was not only getting stronger and better at controlling its puppets, but it was also becoming swifter and stealthier at it—more practiced. Would it soon become undetectable? Could one of the infected soon pass itself off as a companion to those who were not?

If so, the Knight was certain that all would be lost.

"*Kelso, you need to use me if you want to survive this*," Argenta pleaded to him, and try as he might, Kelso could not disagree.

"*If I did, will you promise not to make me attack Ava?*" Kelso asked hesitantly, fearing that he already knew the answer. He did.

"*No. I... can't promise that*," Argenta thought back, but the Knight felt as if she was unsure of her own words, or at least conflicted by them. Even so, he couldn't take that chance. It would be much better to die in battle next to Ava than live after cutting her down. He would truly throw himself on his sword if that happened.

Surprisingly, Argenta said nothing in response to that thought.

All he said out loud was, "No deal."

"Too bad," said the tall one again, whom he was beginning to think of as the Other's most prominent mouthpiece. Perhaps she was the most powerful of the bunch? In any case, she seemed to be leading the conversation now.

"Princess," she said to Ava, "you want to make a deal with us instead?"

Ava merely shook her head, and Kelso thought even that innocuous movement seemed somehow... sinister. Her eyes smoldered, and the Dark encasing her was thick, roiling, and hostile.

"Well, your precious Furies die then," the Other responded right before the short Fury next to the speaker summoned a blade of sickly Dark and pushed it slowly into the taller woman's chest. Blood spurted from her lips as she grimaced in pain.

It was appalling to watch, and both Kelso and Ava were momentarily stunned at the sheer cruelty of it.

"Wow, this *really* hurts Micheline. Well, the one who used to be Micheline, anyways," said the tall one as the dagger continued its burrowing.

"It hurts this one even more though," said the shorter female of Indian descent, the same one that was driving the dagger slowly home. The Fury looked over at Ava and Kelso casually, "You know, these two were a couple—just a few hours ago, in fact."

Ava said nothing as tears streamed down her cheeks.

After another few seconds, Micheline wavered, the dagger hilt deep in her chest. "Time to die," she said and toppled over with a bizarre salute.

"Yes, it is," agreed the shorter one that had just killed her lover, summoning another dagger before whipping it across her own throat with a flourish. Blood fountained out in a spray, but somehow the doomed Fury still managed to sketch a quick bow before she fell.

Ava hiccupped a sob.

Kelso was horrified and disgusted by what they had just seen, but before he could fully wrap his head around it, the Other made its move.

"Banzai!" screamed one of the Fury's closest to the ward line as she leaped forward, face contorted in mad glee. Her Dark was still manifest, not yet drained by whatever the process was that caused it to disappear under the Other's influence. The shock of the ward defense was immediate and violent: a bright flash exploded outward from where the Fury had thrown herself. She was launched backwards, dazed and bleeding from both nostrils.

One of the wards winked out.

A bare second later, another Fury threw herself with abandon against the ward line, and the explosion this time was more violent than the previous one. She was thrown back and dropped unconscious by its rebuke; legs and arms sprawled out bonelessly underneath her, ten feet from the ward line. Another ward went dark.

Kelso had just a moment to panic before the third Fury impacted. Kelso's eyes were dazzled by it, and he blinked the afterimages away just in time to register that the most recent Fury was dead, her head twisted around, and appendages broken all over. With her death, though, the Other claimed another ward.

Another flash, another death, and a fourth ward darkened.

Kelso drew his guns but hesitated as a line of new thralls to the Other stepped into the street. With mounting consternation, he realized that many of them were either completely mundane or of the Light. The world tilted for the Knight as he realized that the Other could have easily overwhelmed them both with the force arrayed at the storm's edge but was *choosing* not to. Any of the fifty or so he could see would be able to walk right through his wards.

The Other had neglected to use any of them to do that, because it *wanted* to sacrifice the Furies. Kelso even saw a few others of the Dark, yet none of them raced for the wards. Only the Furies.

From behind him, the Knight heard another boom, and a flash of Light came from the back fence line. Apparently, the Other was assaulting the wards from all sides now, throwing only those who had previously been Ava's allies and protectors at the wards—over and over again.

Crazily, the line of those in the back—and even the Furies waiting for their turn to die—started to "Ooh" and "Aah" as woman after woman killed herself and ward upon ward died with her. The rest of the Other acted like they were watching fireworks, and they all—every one of them—flaunted cruel, mischievous grins.

It was an absurd display of reckless evil and hate, and Kelso was having a hard time digesting it.

The explosions were so potent now as to rock the ground and light up the entire yard as each ward's death powered the ones behind it. The Furies were now getting completely torn asunder by the blasts, body parts flying and blood spray arcing chaotically over the yard and out into the street.

It was a complete massacre.

"Kelso," said Ava emotionlessly, "we are going to die if we stay here."

"I know," he shrugged. "Seems like all that hard work last night was wasted. I'm sorry."

"I'm not." She looked over at him, her eyes distant, and he realized with a start that what he was looking at was not quite Ava anymore. She was both greater and lesser than she had been.

"Who are you?" he asked and winced as another explosion rocked the yard. The crowd of infected 'oohed' and clapped briefly.

"I am death," she replied and turned towards the horde. Ava's face had transformed somewhat, her beauty becoming almost cruel, her shadowed crown wicked. "You can run, go to the others."

"Well, whoever you are, you know I won't do that," he declared, still looking at her.

Another explosion—from the back this time—rocked the house. Snow fell from the roof and the surrounding trees, and the Knight felt like he was in hell.

"There are a bunch of women unconscious in my front room. What kind of a host would I be if I let them all die in their sleep? The neighbors would talk."

"Yeah, I know. Your honor will not allow you to retreat. It was worth a try." She shrugged and glanced at him as black mists rolled from her in waves, each one spreading farther out. "I'm almost here, but I'm glad to have talked to you one last time."

Kelso had retreated deep within himself, yet his heart broke at her uninflected, simple words, made false by the black tears that ran down her face as she spoke them. It was their end, even though they had just begun, and he knew that her black rage was partially due to what was soon to be lost. He swallowed down his sadness, though, and nodded.

"Kelso, the Furies have a battle cry, an oath, that I have always loved. Would you like to hear it?" she asked, and black lightning gathered at her hands and reflected in her eyes as it arced from her randomly. Even the Other paused its assault to watch her. She was an eldritch power, a goddess of death and ice.

"*Impressive*," murmured Argenta from far away in his mind. Kelso ignored her as he watched that which was once Ava lift slightly off the ground, buoyed by the terrible Dark she wove.

He was about to say that he would, mostly just to hear her voice before he followed her out to die, when another voice unexpectedly answered for her.

"Ruin and woe," said Marcus Dain as he stepped beside Kelso. "I've heard the Furies scream that at me many times over the years, right before they hulk out and rage. Never helped them much though."

***

He was going to die up here in the snow.

Baston Tijeran fought like he had never fought before, Vindicta a blur as he strove to bring the Berserkers down. It wasn't close to being enough. They fought seamlessly as a duo: intelligently, carefully, and with utter ruthlessness. Never before had he seen Berserkers fight like this and was hopelessly overmatched by them.

No help would be forthcoming either; his entire team had been killed. The last to fall was Jhonas, and in between dodging the monstrous swords of his enemies, weaving between them, from them, and around them, he had glimpsed it happen. The Fury Jhonas had mocked—the woman he had said he meant to kiss— had gotten the better of him.

Jhonas was skilled and experienced, but the Fury was merciless and implacable, and it had won her the day. Clicking, snarling, whistling, she had traded blows with him for close to a minute before she stepped back suddenly and laughed.

Jhonas hesitated at her unexpected retreat, right before an arrow caught him in the leg. He turned to bring his shield up against the archer at his rear, and the Fury Jhonas had been fighting immediately sank her swords into his back. The Paladin arched against the pain and screamed, awkwardly trying to keep his shield between him and his tormentor while also covering against arrows.

His sword arm hung at his side, useless.

Baston lunged in desperation, swinging his poleaxe around like a staff as he warded the two hulking beasts away from him—but just barely. A despairing glance back over to Jhonas showed that he could hardly keep his shield up as the Fury casually paced around him, forcing him to turn to follow her. A few other Furies had joined the battle, coming from the farthest reaches of the caravan—which meant the rest of his team was dead. They held bows and spears, but merely watched as Jhonas was circled by the Fury he had mocked.

She paced the dying Paladin slowly, the black arrow in his leg and the two black swords in his back still manifested. Neither Fury had called their weapons back to them in order to aggravate and ensure the kill.

Baston scored a hit on one of the Berserkers, and the keen edge of Vindicta sank into one of the tree-trunk-sized legs of his enemies. For just a moment, Baston's spirits soared.

It nearly cost him his life.

Vindicta broke skin, and black blood boiled out of the wound and halted the forward momentum of his blade. Baston had expected this since all Berserkers carried Dark in their veins—it was like they were armored on the inside instead of the outside. What he had not expected was the gluey nature of the blood armor his blade had sunk into, and the quick attempt to grab the shaft by the Berserker his weapon was now stuck in.

The other Berserker dove forward with its massive sword, catching Baston on one of his pauldrons as he desperately turned and twisted out of the way. He managed to draw Vindicta out with every ounce of strength he could muster and stumbled back clumsily, ducking a devasting follow-up swing. The beast's leg he had wounded armored up from the point of contact in plated pitch the moment Vindicta was retrieved. Baston's best shot had sunk in but three inches... at most.

Spinning and retreating, his eyes fell on Jhonas again. Unable to keep his shield up anymore and with his sword already dropped from his useless other hand, the Paladin no longer had the strength to even turn. Nine Furies formed a circle around the doomed man now, clearly enjoying the spectacle. Evil-sounding laughter, sinister clicking, and brutish snarling streamed unbroken between them. Jhonas merely stood silent and still in their center, knees wobbling, as the Fury that had been circling him finally stopped too, staring him dead in the face.

Baston danced back, trying to angle away from the Berserkers and towards the blinding storm at their back. He had an idea to run, to lose them out in the snow, but an arrow feathered in and took him in the knee. It was not powerful enough to penetrate fully, but it bloodied him and would slow him if he turned to escape.

Baston Tijeran, storied executioner of the Light and next High Commander of the Paladins, realized that the arrow had been precisely modified to do just that—to hobble, but not to incapacitate.

His enemies didn't want him to leave the dance.

Turning to where the arrow came from, he saw one of the Furies looking at him expectantly with bow still held to ear. She lowered the bow and grinned, wiggling a much too long and clawed finger at him in a warning gesture, shaking her head mockingly.

She glanced back to Jhonas and the Fury, and Baston was able to see that the woman Jhonas had taunted now had him by the jaw with one overlarge and elongated hand, possibly holding him up. Her other hand had snaked around his neck and held him at the nape. Baston knew what she was going to do, as did Jhonas. To his credit, the younger Paladin's eyes never left hers—even when she leaned in and gave him the smooch he had wanted, right on the lips.

Pulling back, she winked… and snapped his neck.

Baston stood alone on the field against two immensely strong Berserkers and several Furies. He was going to die, he knew that, but he couldn't help but be tormented by it. How had they lost? There was no possible way a war band of Furies could have taken out his team, not even with two exceptionally powerful Berserkers on their side—he had stalemated them for the last three minutes, yet his team had been killed anyway.

*How?*

There was something off, not that it mattered anymore he supposed, but it hounded him. The Furies clapped and hooted approval at Jhonas's death, as if they deemed it poetic. That enraged him.

"Try that on me!" he shouted in impotent anger. "If you didn't have these two overfed dogs on a leash, I would have killed you all myself!"

The Furies turned to look at him while the Berserkers merely circled around to block him from retreating into the storm—not that he would make it far even if he tried; the arrow to his knee had ensured that. *Better to die here on my feet than out there on my knees*, he thought briefly, hoisting Vindicta to throw.

He couldn't kill the Berserkers, but he could kill the Furies.

"Now, now," said an aged voice from the storm, "you lost fair and square. I won't be having you killing anyone else in your blaze of glory out of this sad world."

Dark wrapped around his arm, freezing his hand closed around Vindicta. Terror swept through him, and his muscles clenched in anticipation of a decapitating swing from the Berserkers behind. The Paladin was able to cast his eyes back towards them, but they

235

appeared to be uninterested in pressing the advantage, instead seeming content to stand quiet and still. Their iron masks of laughter and tears mocked him.

A hunched crone, looking ever so much like a crazed and dirty peasant wife, walked out of the storm and right up to him. She looked up at him cheerily, yellowed teeth showing behind her grin.

"Did you have fun playing with my boys?" she asked, glancing over affectionately at the two massive Berserkers behind Baston.

"*Your* boys? They're Berserkers! They're not smart enough nor sane enough to be anyone's, let alone yours." Baston was struggling against her Dark, trying to move, trying to attack, just… trying.

The old woman in front of him appeared not to notice.

"Look," she said with a disappointed sigh, "I let you play with them for a few minutes while I killed all your friends, and this is the thanks I get? Telling me mine aren't mine? Disgraceful, it is, and you should be ashamed of yourself."

"Play with them?" Baston laughed incredulously, still straining to move his arm, "I fought them to a standstill and kept them from rampaging. Without you, the Light would have prevailed!"

At his words, the woman threw back her head and laughed uproariously. Snorting and wheezing, she slapped her knee in merriment. "They're still *chained,* you damned fool!" she exclaimed, grasping him by the shoulders and turning him slightly so he could see.

Baston did.

The chains he had noticed attached to the collars around their necks were still there, stretching out into the storm, the length of them lazily laying in the snow.

Inadequacy washed over him.

"They were held back...?" he whispered, his courage withering.

"Oh yes, yes, indeed," she confirmed. "I wanted to have a few words with you before... well... this. If I had let them off their chains... Ooh, boy! They would have chewed through you right off and then continued tossing trucks off the mountain." She paused, and then whispered conspiratorially, "I'll probably let them toss a few more off the side before we go, though, just for fun. They're certainly sore about not getting to kill you tonight—or more of your companions."

Baston could only look at her in dread, his mind reeling at how little she thought of him and his team. They, who had made up the elite guard of the Council.

"So, I need your mark. Don't worry now, you're going to be joining a bunch of your friends, so you won't be lonely." At her words, she held up her arm for his perusal, and Baston was saddened to see that she spoke nothing but truth. Almost a dozen of his companions rode her already, and he would be next.

"Why?" he asked as she stepped back and looked him up and down, her smile turning a little more ominous.

"Oh!" she exclaimed. "I need your power, weak as it is, because my boys and I are fixing to die to the Ebon Knight in a bit. It's a gift. Now, I know you're jealous, but once he cuts me down, my mark will be a wee bit more powerful on him than it would have been without you and yours. So, buck up, it's all going to be fine!"

The woman cracked her knuckles and eyed him speculatively.

"I don't understand. Why do you *want* to die to the Ebon Knight?" Baston was floored even though he knew he was in the last moments of his life. It was a strange way to die.

The old woman rocked back on her heels in apparent shock at his question and tilted her head at him quizzically. "Are you saying you *want* to live? This world, this whole plane of existence, is going to hell in a handbasket. There is something else out there, and it *eats* people. Gobbles them up until there's nothing left. You do know this, right?"

Baston did know; he had been sent on a mission to help stem the tide of it. Still, he thought about what she had said in silence.

She leaned in. "Aren't you tired? I've lived many hundreds of years, and I'm sick of it. So are my boys. This worthless fight between us means nothing in the grand scheme of things—particularly now. We're all chained to this Conflict, as surely as my beautiful peacocks over there are chained to me. You're weak, but you must have lived through a couple of centuries yourself. So, you tell me."

Baston's lips were numb. All the years, all the deaths, all the battles, victories, and defeats… it all rushed at him and over him. He was awash in an uncaring sea of chance, and nothing he had ever done mattered now—not anymore. The Paladin felt it in his bones. This new power she talked of—a whisper on the wind heralded its arrival in this world, and all would be sundered. Somehow, he *knew* it.

"Tell you what?" he managed at last, tears slowly leaking out of his eyes.

"Aren't you tired?" she asked again, nodding in sympathy and understanding. Baston's arm was released, his body freed, but he merely planted Vindicta next to him in the snow and breathed deeply, looking around the wild storm. The mass of Furies clicked and snarled to themselves, clearly horrified. By what she had said perhaps, or by his reaction to it, he wasn't sure. Maybe it was both.

The Furies were still in the fight and would be until the end. He distantly wondered what they found so important and pressing as to keep up the charade.

Well, he wouldn't. Not anymore. Baston knew what the crone meant: this world was about to fall in such a way that brought a true end to those who inhabited it. Maybe it was time to set sail for the far horizons. Other worlds and other planes existed for him and for those like him—it was time to git while the getting was still good.

The executioner of the Light looked his own executioner in the eyes and smiled slightly. She smiled back.

"Yes," he said. "I'm very tired."

"I'll let you ride me to the Ebon Knight, and then I'll ride him. Maybe he can use our power to do something about this 'Other'. Afterwards, you and I can meet up with my boys somewhere else far away from here and have a laugh, eh? You won't have long to wait, I promise."

His smile bloomed. "Agreed," he said, and released Vindicta to the snow.

# Chapter 15

Cassandra was getting desperate. Combat raged around her, although the storm hid much. At times, it seemed like she was alone, until she stumbled upon another enemy, ally, or both.

Her elite guard was locked in battle several hundred yards out to each side of the road they had ambushed the Dark convoy on. There had been many, many vehicles, and perhaps four or five hundred of the Dark on hand. Undeterred, she waded through the center of them, destroying and killing as she went.

The Arch Mage's personal bodyguards, the absolute best of her best, followed on her heels, killing stragglers, protecting her flanks, and coordinating with others as they pushed the forces of the Dark back. It was the nature of the fight that the flanks would curl inward as the battle progressed, and she didn't want that, but there was nothing she could realistically do about it though.

Almost negligently, she raised a hand towards a large, bearded man with an ill-formed battle axe, and hoisted him into the air to a height of about fifteen feet—the limit of her vision. There, her power held him. Her hand enveloped his whole body—from her perspective—through the gap of her thumb and finger. Never slowing from her steady walk down the line of largely abandoned cars, she snapped her hand shut.

He exploded outwards from the psychic pressure: blood, tissue, and bone flying out in a gruesome circle that rained down on the battlefield. She dropped her hand, and the unrecognizable thing she had been holding in the air dropped as well, thudding to the snowy ground in a heap.

"Lady Magus," said one of her Lieutenants, a smart and decent man named Jack Southern that had been with her guard for several decades, "We have reports up and down the line that the Dark are in full retreat."

Dim flashes of light, distant booms, muted war cries—all of this and more floated out of the storm and she could tell that her warriors were keeping pace with her as she walked through the center of the Dark host. It was a rout. The Dark was taking a massive beating this day; one that would weaken them in this part of the world for years.

It didn't matter.

None of what happened here mattered if she didn't find the Spider tonight. Cassandra knew she was on this battlefield and had primed her officers to report if they engaged her. Yet, so far, nothing.

"Thank you, Jack," she said absently, summoning a massive fireball and throwing it down the line of immobile vehicles. It washed over the trucks, jeeps, and SUVs, gaining strength and heat as it went. Several soldiers of the Dark attempted to flee from it, abandoning their hiding places behind doors, in passenger compartments, or even from underneath some of the vehicles.

None were quick enough, and in mere seconds her fireball was a raging inferno of light and heat that incinerated any in its path for a hundred yards. There, it exploded, and several more vehicles around it exploded as well. It was an impressive display of carnage… and it didn't matter, either.

Time was slipping away from her, and the percentages were dropping steadily—as they had been since the battle was joined. Nothing she had done, and nothing that her guard had done, had reversed their dwindling chance of catching—and killing—Jesslyn Pentran.

She needed to gamble, now, before it was entirely too late.

"Captain Jareno," she murmured, and was instantly shadowed by the older woman who was the leader of her guard ever since Cassandra had first formed it hundreds of years ago. They went way back, the two of them, and she was a good friend and an even better warrior.

"Lady Magus," she said respectfully, automatically matching strides with Cassandra as they began to pass the smoking wrecks that had been expensive rigs just moments ago.

"You don't need to call me that, Teri," the Arch Mage said wryly for about the thousandth time.

"Of course, Lady Magus," Teri replied without a hint of jest. Her pale eyes searched the shadows as they walked, piercing the storm and inspecting every snowflake individually—at least that's what it appeared like she was doing, so hawkish was her gaze.

"Tell your troops to drop and hold, but to keep their heads up." Cassandra gritted her teeth for a moment in determination. "They need to mark enemies where they see them and immediately engage… particularly those that seem to be skirting the line and heading past us and into Reno."

Teri never batted an eye as she quickly turned away, giving orders on the all-com as she went. Within seconds it was done, and she was back at Cassandra's side.

"We are ready, Lady Magus," she murmured, holding her beautiful sword firmly in one hand as she snugged her shield close to her body with the other. "On your mark." Her armor was ghostly white in the night and still unblemished—the Arch Mage had truly caught the Dark flat-footed this time.

Cassandra jumped onto the roof of a still-steaming SUV. "Mark," she whispered.

She dimly heard the immediate order to drop and hold from Teri, but Cassandra still gave it a five count before releasing herself in a wild rush of reckless power. She threw her arms to the left and the right, hard, snapping them out, palms up and extended in effort as a bubble of air formed around her and blew outwards at a terrific speed from her outstretched hands.

With dogged determination, the Arch Mage pushed the storm away.

For hundreds of yards on either side of her, the constant snow flurries were blown sideways by gale-force winds, leaving clear space behind. Within seconds, several football fields worth of ground in every direction was momentarily rendered free of falling snow, exposing friend and foe alike.

Unlike the completely shocked forces of the Dark, her guard

was prepared, kneeling low, with weapons sunk into the ground for stability or holding on to each other for support as they huddled. Heads up, the forces of the Light marked well where their enemies were, and once the wild screaming winds had passed them, immediately sprang up and engaged with sword, bow, and magic.

Many of the Dark's soldiers had been blown down by her magic, and very few would ever regain their feet in time to fight, or even to run. It was an absolute slaughter.

Her magic blew itself out at last, and Cassandra despaired. Her wind had blown past both edges of the battle, yet no skulking group of Dark killers had been revealed skirting the lines. It had been a poor gamble, and it had failed.

The Arch Mage had put everything she had left into that roll of the dice, and once cast, she saw her chances of catching the Spider out on the field fall to zero. As her eyes rolled up into her head, she grieved for her failure, even as she tumbled unconscious off the SUV's hood.

***

Jesslyn had been very lucky indeed—smart too, crafty even, but lucky still.

The Spider and her hand-picked team had ridden towards the very back of the line. Even when her companions grumbled about not getting to kill anyone, she insisted and they eventually acquiesced—which was good, because she had almost slaughtered them all for daring to question her.

She was on edge, and a part of her *knew* that an ambush awaited them on the trip north to Reno. Many of the Dark hosts suspected it and even hoped for it, but she didn't want any part of whatever the Light could throw at them tonight. It was not that she was cowardly, far from it, she just had places to be and people to kidnap and torment.

When the trap was sprung, Jesslyn immediately ordered her driver to kill the lights and head off road. Blind, they drove a few hundred yards out into the snow before their massive truck got stuck in the brutal storm.

The five of them exited the moment it was apparent they could go no farther, and she hastened to lead them away from the combat now taking place at the convoy. For almost a mile, they listened as the battle went from bad to worse. Hundreds had been killed, and the Dark was in retreat. Strong magic, the likes of which many of the doomed host had never seen, wreaked havoc upon their side.

There seemed to be hundreds of the Light present. Jesslyn knew that the two large forces had caused this storm, and as one side faltered, so too would the blizzard. How a large contingent of their enemies could have ambushed them with such short notice was a mystery to her, but it didn't trouble the Spider overmuch. All who died on the road meant nothing to Jesslyn and had always been expendable.

Even the team Jesslyn led were nothing but pawns to her, but she needed them alive if she wanted any hope of accomplishing her true mission. Even with her father's pull, the armies of the

Dark that had assembled left a lot to be desired. There were only a few fully ascended among them, perhaps ten percent or less of the whole. As such, she was forced to make do with what she could and had commandeered two young Sorcerers, a female Berserker, and two of the biggest and most competent-looking Childer she could find.

Jesslyn hated to admit it, but the armies were spread thin without the Furies in the vanguard, and for the first time she realized what a serious blow it was that they had defected. That new weakness was cast into stark relief here, because there were not many experienced troops anywhere near Nevada, and why would there be? There *should* have been nothing here to rouse the interest of the Dark armies, but that had been proven wrong... in spades.

Minute after minute, she hurried through the snow with the five others following in her wake. Several dozen screams came over the coms at once, and Jesslyn's keen ears detected a whooshing sound before each was cut off in succession. It sounded like a huge inferno of some sort had been loosed upon her troops, and she started to feel distinctly uneasy.

"Hurry!" she screamed at the five trailing behind, hoping the storm didn't carry her words away. She redoubled her efforts, and as they fairly ran through the waist-deep snow, she turned once to look behind her right as the storm inexplicably blew *sideways*.

A wall of wind and snow hit her party and knocked them end over end for several seconds. After eventually righting herself, she realized that her team had just barely avoided an immense cleansing of the field. She was still in the storm, but less than a dozen yards away everything had been cleared, and she picked out combatants from both sides in the momentarily exposed battlefield. Those of the Light were already rushing the soldiers of the Dark as the storm reasserted itself, and the curtain of vision closed.

Jesslyn knew then that there was a *very* powerful Mage with the Light—one of the Council. Maybe, even, the Arch Mage.

"We need to hurry. Run, damn you!" Jesslyn immediately took off, angling away from the invisible clash. After another five minutes they turned north and started towards Reno again. Already, she was making new plans considering what she now knew.

First, they needed another vehicle.

*** 

Kelso was transfixed by the utter stupidity of the Paladin.

Ava was quickly turning into an avenging goddess, and he was making quips about the Furies and their battle cry? Not a smart move, and the Knight fully expected that Marcus would be reduced to a fine paste for his unwise observation. Not that Kelso would mind—he couldn't stand the Paladin anyway.

From atop the battlements of the stark fortress deep within himself, he dimly lamented the fact that Ava was about to kill their only possible ally in the coming fight. Still, it was only a muted regret.

Ava surprised him, though, by merely turning her head to regard Marcus—icy blue eyes weighing and judging. "Perhaps you have just never heard it from someone with sufficient conviction? I would be happy to show you the true meaning... if you wish." Her voice was calm and almost polite, but sharp things nested behind her words.

"I'm sure you would, Princess," laughed Marcus shortly, "but if you and the Knight intend to make it out of here alive, you best let me die to them and not to you."

Even insulated as he was from the world, Kelso turned to look at Marcus quizzically.

Marcus looked back over and grimaced. "Like you weren't sinister looking enough already? What did they do to your face?"

Kelso didn't know how to respond, which was good, because the Other interrupted them.

"Hello?" the closest Fury said, waving her still functioning right arm and hopping up and down to get their attention. Her left arm hung limp and dead. She had been one of the original Furies to rush the ward line and had apparently recovered enough to stand. "You know, I can hear everything you're saying, right? No one survives this night. Pay attention to that, not his face."

The Paladin glanced at the Fury for a moment and then dismissed her entirely. No. He dismissed the Other that was her entirely.

"Never mind about the face," Marcus quipped, armor brightening, thickening, "it kind of suits you in a bizarre way. No offense, I hope?"

"You always were an asshole," Kelso said distractedly, turning back to the mass of combatants in the street. "Nothing you say matters to me."

"I'm not pleased," stated the Other through the hapless Fury's lips, and leapt forward. Another boom and a massive flash of light greeted her arrival, and she was thrown back—in pieces.

A chorus of perfectly choreographed 'oohs' issued from the almost hundred strong back line of the Other. The vast majority of that group was of the Light or the mundane. Very few Furies, plus a few dozen others of the Dark, remained to catapult themselves at the wards. Those dozens all stepped forward as one, awaiting their turn to rush the wards. Bizarrely, many of them began to stretch and limber up, smiling in wretched glee all the while. It was unnecessary of course, and Kelso had no doubt that the Other was merely taunting them with the spectacle.

On either side of him, the High Lord Commander of the Paladins and the youngest Princess of the Dark watched the antics of their enemy with no expression. Kelso's face was stone too, all emotion suppressed and distant. He wondered if their non-reactions to what the Other was doing somehow goaded it to act even more cruel, more chaotic.

*Perhaps,* he thought, *it craves attention.* From the moment the first Fury died by her lover's dagger, it seemed like the Other had been getting crazier and crazier as it tried to elicit a reaction of horror from them. Instead, it got nothing. Kelso wondered briefly if a key to defeating their foe might be uncovered from such knowledge, but even so, none of them were likely to survive long enough to exploit it.

The Paladin cleared his throat. "Not that I care for the Dark, but it seems like a waste to throw away so many of them on the wards when the Other could just overwhelm you with the others." Marcus shrugged and lifted his hammer, allowing it to fall against his right shoulder, where he held it with ease.

Kelso was about to point out the flaw with that statement, starting with that the Paladin, himself, would be overrun as well, when Ava responded in a tightly clipped voice.

"Not you, though? Of course." She turned to look at Marcus again. "So, you do realize that you're here to die?"

Marcus nodded as a shining helm formed around his head. "I do. And I'm grateful for it." He scratched his neck. "Much better to die sane than to live in madness. I am whole, and I will shortly be free."

"Why though?" Ava pressed. "Why are you sane?"

The Paladin shrugged. "The music, I think. My confusion started to fade the moment I first heard it, and as long as it's playing, I am myself."

Even numb and a hair's breadth from combat, Kelso knew that Marcus had just uncovered something vitally important to their cause. How they could take advantage of it, he wasn't sure, but a glance over at Ava confirmed that she, too, realized how important the Paladin's words were.

251

"Look, I'd love to hang around and chat, but I'm afraid the music will go away and leave me in confusion again. I know what I have to do tonight; Cassandra made sure of it." He looked over at the two of them. "The Arch Mage said your best chance was to give me a couple of minutes then go through the backyard. You need to make your way across town to meet your companions."

"How?" Kelso wanted to know.

"I don't know, but I suspect by foot." Marcus grinned. "You're going to be fighting the entire way, I think."

"Good," Ava said, and nodded at the Paladin. "Die well."

"I'm grateful to have the chance," he replied as a shimmering cloak of white formed behind him. Clad head to toe in thick plated mists of Light, he looked truly formidable—even heroic.

He looked back and winked. "Give Cassandra my thanks."

Ava nodded.

Another flash of light rocked the house, and at a quick glance Kelso estimated that less than twenty wards remained—if that.

"Oh," Marcus called over his shoulder as he stepped up to the line. The forces of the Other paused their assault at his approach. Over one hundred pairs of eyes tracked him as he stopped just short of it. "Don't worry about your sleeping beauties... she said they should be fine."

Poorly crafted and sickly-looking weapons of shadow formed in the uncaring hands of the infected Dark. Weapons of power and might—now tarnished, rusted, darkened—were brought to bear and held negligently by those who had once been of the Light. The Other recognized what the Paladin intended to do, and its hosts made ready. Every single face looked extremely bored by this turn of events. Kelso couldn't help but think that the Other didn't find this as entertaining as sacrificing itself to the wards.

The Other was chaotic and crazy, unpredictable and unhinged, and perhaps even juvenile in its cruelty and purpose. How long would it stay so? Would it continue to evolve and become craftier and more strategic in its approach as more time passed? Smarter?

Kelso hoped not.

"FOR THE LIGHT!" boomed Marcus suddenly in a voice of righteous wrath and iron determination. "I COME! AND I WILL SET US ALL FREE FROM MADNESS!"

His powerful voice shattered the night, and it seemed to Kelso that even the storm paused for a second to listen. The momentary lull faded, and Marcus Dain, High Lord Commander of the Paladins, strode forward to make good on his promise.

# Chapter 16

Jae was surprised to see guards at the iron gate that surrounded the large funeral home, mortuary, and graveyard they had arrived at. The storm was so bad she almost drove straight into the formidable ironwork before realizing it was even there.

Gliding to a halt with mere inches to spare, their truck was immediately surrounded by several Ghouls. The creatures appeared out of the storm like indistinct ghosts, their faces fierce and unsmiling. Covered in the bulky armor of their Dark, they actually looked dangerous to her eyes.

That was a first.

"Wow," remarked Misima. "Look at them, would you?"

"I like it," said Chandra in reply.

Mrs. Rodriguez was looking at the shapes quizzically, apparently not sure what all the fuss was about. "I don't understand why they have their workers out here in the storm," she said uncertainly. "It's pretty dangerous weather, isn't it?"

Jae realized that Mrs. Rodriguez was seeing something different than what they were. The old woman wasn't able to see the truth of them—which was probably for the best.

Carmen reached over and grabbed Mrs. Rodriguez's hand. "Don't worry," she soothed, "they just came out to open the gate for us is all." The young woman met Jae's eyes in the rearview mirror and added, "Right?"

Jae wasn't so sure. The Ghouls didn't really seem aggressive, but they were nevertheless... off... from what she had come to expect from them. Now that she thought of it, she liked these new Ghouls. It was about time they got serious. She was just hopeful they were allies and not enemies.

Jae rolled the window down halfway, the steady whirring dislodging the snow that had lightly caked it. The lead Ghoul stepped forward to speak with her.

"Can I help you?" he asked neutrally, eyes flickering to each passenger in the car, momentarily resting on Charlie and then on Mrs. Rodriguez, before returning to match Jae's stare. The Ghoul did so directly and with none of the usual passiveness that normally crossed a Ghoul's features upon meeting another combatant of the Dark.

"Well," Jae started, "I don't know..."

Chandra leaned forward past Misima and looked at the Ghoul herself. "We were instructed to come here by Ava Pentran and tasked to speak with your Grave Smith, Innonia."

"Ah, yes. You are expected." Still, the Ghoul did not smile in relief or welcome. Instead, he merely lifted a handheld radio to his large, misshapen mouth and pushed a button. "Open the gates," he instructed. "They have arrived."

The large iron gates screeched open, motors straining to clear the snow. Once sufficiently wide, Jae drove through and up the long driveway towards the funeral home proper. They passed snow-covered and gently sloping grounds as they made their way up before finally parking under a large awning that sheltered them from the storm.

Several other Ghouls stood in front of the large double doors that were open to receive them. They were all armored, all grim, and merely waited as the five women and the bulldog exited. Carmen had to lift Charlie down from the backseat because his legs had locked in consternation at the jump. He sniffed and snorted excitedly when Carmen placed him on his paws, and after shaking himself, beelined for the open doors, apparently excited to explore.

"Charlie!" called Mrs. Rodriguez in a slightly raised voice, and the big bulldog almost comically pulled up to look back at her. "What are you doing?"

In response to her question, Charlie shook his butt for a second and looked inside, then back at her.

"I'm coming, stay there," Mrs. Rodriguez said, holding Carmen's arm for support as they slowly made their way to the door. Charlie pranced a little bit but waited.

"Is it ok to bring a dog inside?" Mrs. Rodriguez asked the closest Ghoul, a huge man with strong powerful jaws and large, dangerous-looking teeth.

"Yes, ma'am," said the Ghoul. "We can make an exception for a good dog like him."

Jae wasn't sure what Mrs. Rodriquez saw, but the smile he forced out looked positively menacing to the Fury. She guessed it was hard not to look threatening with such huge teeth and muscled jaws—perfect for cracking bone and rending flesh. Whatever Mrs. Rodriquez saw, it didn't frighten or concern her, because she favored the man with her own smile as she walked past him, still holding Carmen's arm.

They entered the foyer, where a female Ghoul awaited them flanked by two male Ghouls. The rail-thin woman stepped forward and bowed slightly, her long stringy hair matted and wet with melting snow. She was the only Ghoul they had seen that was not armored. She smiled, large square teeth flashing, but it seemed a genuine smile at least.

"Welcome," she said. "We are pleased to invite you into our home. My name is Elizabeth, and I'm Innonia's personal assistant. She will see you now."

Jae tensed up a bit at the word *home*, wondering if Mrs. Rodriguez had caught it, but she was busy minding Charlie.

Elizabeth glanced over at Mrs. Rodriquez and Charlie as she realized what she had said, and her large grey eyes flew open a bit in embarrassment. "Ah... yes. Justin," she said, turning to look at one of the Ghouls with her, "could you please escort those two to our... *bereavement apartments*, please?" She waved to Mrs. Rodriquez and the dog.

The younger Ghoul stepped forward to gather up Mrs. Rodriguez and Charlie, but his quizzical glance back at Elizabeth made it clear that he had no idea what a 'bereavement apartment' was. Elizabeth rolled her grey orbs at him in agitation and shooed him away with her clawed hands. They were filthy and wet, and it looked very much like Elizabeth had been out digging in the dirt somewhere when they arrived.

Being a Ghoul, perhaps she had. Jae studiously avoided thinking about *why* she had been out there digging. In a storm. In a graveyard.

Jae shuddered, but followed her Sisters and Carmen as they all bunched up behind Elizabeth as she turned smartly on her heel and walked deeper into the funeral parlor.

"Where are you taking them?" asked Carmen, a clear note of worry in her voice. Jae remembered that Carmen had never met a Ghoul—other than the infected one that had kidnapped her—and so this was probably a little unsettling for the young woman. She was handling herself very well, considering that.

"Oh," said Elizabeth over her shoulder as she quickly led the Furies through the large house, "we actually do have apartments for visitors from the Dark. The... uhh... few times we have received any, that is."

Carmen frowned. "Why don't you get many visitors? This is a lovely place, and very peaceful."

For the second time in as many minutes, Jae tensed again, wondering what the Ghoul would say... and what Carmen would make of it.

Elizabeth stopped, her back still to the group. The Ghoul took a fortifying breath and turned to look at them, staring first at Carmen, then sweeping her eyes quickly over the other three women before settling back on the young Childe. She considered the young Hispanic woman for a minute, eyes appraising, while

Carmen merely stood and waited.

"We are... unwelcome... among the larger Dark," Elizabeth finally said. "We're not warlike enough, nor vicious enough, to be considered reliable warriors among the armies."

Carmen nodded her head. "Good for you. Neither am I, apparently." At the three older Furies' sudden stares, Carmen hunched in on herself a bit but determinedly met their eyes, one by one. "What? Like it's not true?"

Jae didn't know what to say, and as she exchanged glances with Misima and Chandra, she realized that they didn't know what to say either.

"Is this true?" asked Elizabeth in a slightly scandalized voice. "You would turn away your own Childe?"

"Not us," Jae said hurriedly, "and no decision has been made yet."

Elizabeth frowned at Jae's words and looked back at Carmen. "You're young. If you ever need a haven, come to us here and we will grant it."

Chandra laughed mirthlessly. "I wonder how long that will last? Probably until dinner."

Elizabeth glared at Chandra, and the other Ghoul shifted uneasily behind them. "Your defensiveness reveals your feelings for her. Would you rather she be completely outcasted with no clan to shelter her? The world is on fire, Fury, you know this."

Jae's mouth went agape at Elizabeth's rebuke, partly because the Ghoul dared to chastise them at all, but mostly because Elizabeth was completely right. Jae glanced over at Chandra, and the dark woman's face was stone, but not out of anger or condescension—she was utterly and horribly embarrassed.

"I... cry your pardon," Chandra finally muttered. "I spoke rashly, and I do care for her. Deeply. My apologies."

Elizabeth nodded and turned back to Carmen. "If you ever find yourself alone, come back here. As pretty as you are, you can be the new face of our establishment. We help people during their darkest hours; it is a worthy life and important, even if it has nothing to do with the Conflict." She turned to lead them again but stopped at Carmen's sudden question.

"Wait," she said plaintively. "what did Chandra mean by lasting until dinner? Why is that a bad thing?"

\*\*\*

High in his keep across the vast, windswept plains in his mind, Kelso was still taken aback by the battle that unfolded before him and Ava.

Marcus waded in, his Light almost too bright to look at, all the while swinging his massive war hammer with incredible speed and skill. The initial onslaught of the Other literally melted around him, each dying within seconds to either the Paladin's hammer or to his Light. His gift was potent and inescapable—any enemy that entered his radius began to degrade almost immediately.

The first wave of infected—most of them Furies—took the brunt of his wrath, and each that entered died. Silently, yes, but awfully too. Distantly, Kelso knew that any normal enemy would hesitate and pause at the gruesome deaths. Doubt would flood them and fear would make them wary. Not so with the Other. Even as the first wave melted, flesh made waxy and running, bones boiling, the second wave hit.

Made up mostly of the Light now, with some few Dark, this wave lasted a little longer, although each one that dropped did so a few seconds after the last until the Paladin was surrounded by bodies three deep. Still, they came, and even though Marcus struck constantly with his hammer—crushing skulls, spines, and necks—he could not keep up with the enemies that swarmed him.

As more and more entered the fray, his Light began to dim as it was stretched thin—simultaneously bathing ten, then twenty, then thirty. Marcus was undaunted by their attack, however, and the weakened weapons of the enemy could find no purchase against him as he strode out into the street, angling away from the house and towards the corner.

"Go," Ava commanded Kelso. "Get your remaining ammo and anything else you need. The Paladin is drawing them away and it will soon be time to make our escape."

At her words, Kelso immediately turned and sprinted for the house. Flinging open his door and bolting for the bedroom, he barely spared a glance at the still comatose Furies in his front room. A very small part of him marveled that he could run at all, much less sprint, but he had no real time to be grateful for it.

There was killing to do.

In haste, he made his way to the closet and wrenched it open. Reaching inside, he grabbed his extra gun belt, which was already threaded with bullets—fifty in all. His guns were fully loaded with six each, and the remaining twenty-two were already secured on a bandolier he wore. Eighty-four bullets in total—not many, and not nearly enough most likely.

As he hurriedly gathered his combat batons (apparently cleaned from last night) and his daggers, his eyes fell on a small square package on the floor. Strapping on his armor, he looked at it in puzzlement, wondering what it might be and if he had time to investigate. Outside, he could still hear the massive impacts of the Paladin's hammer as it dispatched foe after foe, but the sounds were moving away steadily. He had to hurry.

Quickly, he reached down and opened the plain brown package. Inside were four boxes of ammo. He opened one and saw that there were fifty warded bullets inside. The Knight felt a small moment of gratitude for Cassandra but quickly snuffed it out as he hurriedly stowed the boxes about his person.

Racing back outside, he hesitated at his door and looked back at the Furies. He remembered what the Paladin had said, but still… He closed the door firmly and locked it behind him.

When he turned around, Kelso was startled to see Ava directly in his path, arms folded at the waist and face expressionless. He stopped guiltily.

"Did you just lock your door?" Ava asked emotionlessly.

She was something else, something more, or perhaps something less, but it was not fully Ava that looked into his eyes. Even though she was shorter than him, the Knight still felt like he was looking up at her. It was crazy, but he just couldn't shake it.

"Um… yeah, I did." Kelso was too far away inside himself to feel much embarrassment, but it still tickled his peripheries.

"So, you believe that if the Other should somehow break through all of your Arch Mage level wards, a locked door will keep the Furies in your house safe?" Ava was still expressionless, though the Knight could easily imagine the incredulity behind the question.

He shrugged.

"The two-inch *wooden* door," added Ava, still staring at him.

The music swelled out in the street, and more figures from both sides of his house rushed towards the battle. As the Paladin continued to draw the forces of the Other away, the storm returned, and they were enveloped in white again. Flakes fell between them now, and Kelso took some comfort in knowing that they would be difficult to track.

*Of course,* he thought, *that also meant it would be harder to avoid their enemies.*

"I have no wish to avoid our enemies, I wish to kill them. All of them." She grinned thinly at his shock, much like a shark might seem to grin as it moved in for the kill.

"How did you know I was thinking that?" he demanded.

"You're very easy to read, Kelso," she answered. "Come, it's time. We will be moving fast, and all will die in our wake." Ava turned her back to him and started to walk away.

"Wait!" he called, and she stopped. "That wasn't really an answer."

She didn't turn. "But it's the best you'll get. Let's go."

The Knight didn't move. "Who are you? Really?"

Ava stopped again. Slowly, she turned back to him, and her beauty struck him to the core. Her shadowed crown was red lightning upon her brow, and her Dark was thick, almost silvery in the snow.

"Are you scared of me?" she asked, this time with a hint of emotion in her voice.

His answer was sure and immediate. "No, I could never be scared of you, or any part of you. Your Darkness... shines... Ava. I don't know if that makes sense or not, but to me, even wrapped in shadow as you are, you shine."

The being in front of him smiled, and it was a real smile.

"Well said, Sir Knight. I'm still your Ava. But I'm also the Dark Witch, and all will fall to me before this night is through. Think you can keep up?" She tilted her head quizzically at him, and that familiar movement put his heart at ease.

His senses sharpened, heightened. "I can certainly try. Care to wager on it?"

The Dark Witch merely rolled her eyes in answer.

# Chapter 17

Marcus Dain fought with everything he had, completely clear in his head for the first time in what seemed like a hundred years—perhaps it was a hundred years. His Light was slowly becoming overwhelmed as more and more of the Other threw itself against him with indifferent abandon. He had killed dozens and had dragged the battle step by bloody step away from the Knight's house about as far as he could.

Marcus had done his job, and even though he wasn't tiring, he was stuck.

The Paladin was at something of a stalemate. His armor was too thick for the weakened weapons the Other tried to wield against him, but his aura was no longer strong enough to kill those attacking him—at least not quickly. Even so, Marcus was content. At the end of his life, surrounded by an entity of unknowable reach and scope, to be able to think clearly was still so precious to him that he wanted to weep.

Finally, blessedly, he could remember his wife. She had been killed hundreds of years ago, and it was her death that had first cracked his sanity. He had been unable to think of her, to even acknowledge her, for decades now. The music reached a crescendo as more and more of the enemy joined together to drag him down, and it seemed the louder it played, the saner he felt, and the more he remembered. His wife's smile, her touch, her teasing manner.

It was wonderful.

"You're very strong, Paladin," crooned a Fury, one of the last probably. "Why don't you join me? I can show you eons of battle and glory, and we will conquer the universe and all its planes of existence."

"I've been a puppet to my own diseased mind long enough. I would never submit to being yours," Marcus answered shortly as he reached out with a hand and crushed her face. He pulled her in towards him and then slammed the Fury backward again so hard her neck broke. Normally, he wouldn't have been able to do that to a Fury, but his aura had weakened her, and the infection had worked her over too. The Paladin released her and took another step, pulling the hideously silent combatants with him yet a little farther away from the house as he did so.

Distantly, he heard gunshots. He smiled grimly; that was definitely the Knight. Only he was stupid enough to bring guns to a magic battle. Not that Marcus was overly concerned about it, but at least the Knight and the Witch were making their escape.

He took another step.

A fellow Paladin paused in shiving his armored ribs for a second. "I'll not take you until the very end, Marcus. The very end. Thousands upon thousands of worlds await us. Be my general. Be my herald."

Marcus kicked sideways with a powerfully armored foot, breaking the Paladin's leg at the knee. As his previous companion fell, Marcus stomped on his throat, crushing it. "Sorry to see you like this, Franks," he told the corpse and took another step. "Between us lies only death—no alliance, no quarter," he

267

announced to the multitude of attackers all around him.

A Knight jabbed her short sword up as hard as she could under his chin, but the blade snapped in half when it met his armor. Marcus didn't even feel its impact. Without pause, she rammed the broken blade up again. It completely shattered, and she was left holding just the hilt.

"Why won't you consider joining me?" she asked. "Is your precious sanity clouding your judgment, perhaps?"

"I'm pretty sure you got that exactly backwards, but yes, I'm sane enough to know that any deal with you is a bad deal. Any alliance, an unholy one. Any promise, a false one." For a moment he was able to shift his right arm enough to swing his hammer with at least moderate force. It crushed the woman's skull and her eyes bugged out grotesquely as she fell.

Marcus took another step... and suddenly, another. He almost fell to his knees as the entire horde unexpectedly backed away and ran to pursue the two he had been destined to save this night.

His aura began to recharge immediately; he could feel it building in his chest as it always did. He pushed it out and watched it noticeably brighten.

"Good luck catching them, fools," he shouted after the retreating mob. "I'll be here to finish the job when you come back empty-handed." Their music retreated with them, which was a shame because he had really kind of enjoyed it.

*Now what*, he wondered. The Paladin had not expected any reprieve and...

The world tilted, the colors running together. The white snow became muddy to his vision, and the Paladin panicked. *His madness! It was coming back!*

A small strain of music caught his attention. Sweat beading on his brow, he looked wildly around for the source of it until his eyes fell on a young boy, perhaps ten years old, who stood and looked at him from the very edge of the storm. The Paladin stumbled forward in relief, just barely remembering to douse his aura before it killed the child outright.

The boy looked up at him gravely, then grinned. "Got ya," he exulted and clapped excitedly.

Marcus became numb with fear as he realized what the child meant.

"There is music in the deep vastness of space. It is lovely, chaotic, and it drives the inhabitants of this world quite insane," the boy said, smiling a gap-toothed and triumphant grin up at the Paladin. "Some are immune to it, and that's *very* annoying. But you love it, don't you?"

Marcus said nothing, but his hands started to shake.

"I couldn't figure it out," mused the boy, clasping his hands behind him and pacing back and forth—much like a college professor would do. "But then you kept talking about being finally sane—" the boy stopped and looked up at the Paladin "—which is overrated by the way; very much so if you ask me."

"I don't think that," Marcus whispered, "sanity is precious." He wanted to cry, to sob, to scream at the heavens. The fear that gripped him was terrible.

"Well, you think so at least. And you can be. Sane, I mean." The boy, who was not a boy, smiled wickedly. "If you serve me, that is."

"No," said the Paladin, but whether it was a refusal of the offer or a refusal to recognize the horrific implications of what the boy threatened, even he didn't know.

"That's too bad because I'll just end this host and avoid you for the rest of your days." The smile deepened. "You will wander in perpetual confusion and sorrow. Not even the Arch Mage will be able to help you or guide you further. I will ensure it."

Marcus merely studied the boy mutely.

The boy shrugged. "Last chance. What's it going to be? Insanity for hundreds of years on a dead planet until you eventually die of old age or an existence as close to immortality as can be experienced? At my side, you will stride across the worlds for years uncountable, leading my armies to victory against any and all."

Marcus stood frozen in indecision and fear. That he could only think rationally at all was solely and completely due to the boy's presence. No... to the Other's presence.

The boy leaned in conspiratorially and looked around the raging storm to make sure no one was listening. "I know which one I would pick if I were you." He winked.

Distant gunshots broke the night again, only detectable to the

Paladin because of his Light bolstered senses. The two he had been charged with saving were still making good on their escape at least, since the guns' report seemed to come from much farther away than it had been just minutes ago.

That was very good. It also meant his task was complete.

"Times up, time to…," the boy said while grabbing his own head at the back of his neck with one hand, the other hand under his chin. Marcus realized that he was about to break his own neck.

"Wait!" shouted the Paladin in a panic, holding out an armored glove of brilliant Light. "Please!"

The boy stopped, and the Other gazed at the Paladin cruelly through his eyes. "Do we have a deal?" he smirked, lazy in his confidence.

"We do," the Paladin said, stepping backwards and over to the top half of the Knight's blade that had snapped against his armor a few minutes earlier. He picked it up and turned, the edges of the weapon were dulled, as was the point… but it would suffice.

The boy laughed. "You're pretty strong, but not very smart." he stepped up to the Paladin and exposed his throat. "You kill me, you go back to insanity."

"I know," said Marcus, holding the two-foot piece of sword by its edge.

"Ok. Well, what deal do we have then?" the young boy looked up at the Paladin, his face intrigued. "And don't offer me a set of

271

steak knives or a waffle maker, either. The Knight is still on the hook for those."

"I've got something better—for both of us," the Paladin promised, forcing a smile across his face as he stared down at the... thing... that had swallowed the young boy's free will, consciousness, and perhaps even his soul.

"Better than eternal glory across all the planes of existence? I somehow doubt that."

"No, it really is, I swear." The Paladin allowed his armor to fade. The Light of him did so too, slowly, perhaps even reluctantly. It knew his plan.

"Ok, fine, what is it?" The Other looked suspicious but still interested.

"Freedom. For both of us," said the Paladin and whipped the sword shard across the boy's throat before plunging it into his own. With all of his considerable strength, Marcus forced the dulled weapon almost its entire length into his body, angling it up towards his head.

The dull blade managed to cut the ancient thing's throat, but not enough to instantly kill it. Desperately it reached out to end itself again, hoping to plunge Marcus back into madness. In its throes the Paladin might accidentally save himself with his Light—and then exist alone in the endless sea of confusion he had been awash in for decades.

It would be hell.

The boy's body was tiring from shock and blood loss, though, and his neck was slippery with gore. The infected fell to his knees, eyes furious and accusing as he stared up at Marcus, even as the Paladin was dying too.

"I *hate* cheaters," mumbled the Other venomously and fell onto its back. The music faltered, then stilled.

Marcus Dain, Lord Commander of the Paladins, sighed once and crumpled even as the final notes faded in the air. His last thoughts were of victory and peace. A tunnel opened up in his rapidly dimming consciousness, and far away, he heard his wife call to him.

At last.

***

Elizabeth ushered the three older Furies and the younger Childe into a tastefully decorated receiving room. Sitting in one of the comfortable over-stuffed chairs was Innonia, the Grave Smith they had come to see. Chandra and Jae both pulled up short when they saw her, because the Ghoul was much changed from last they met.

Innonia was dressed in solid black, and her hair had been combed and pulled back into a ponytail. At her throat she wore a heavy iron chain, apparently made of nails that had been forged together with each point hammered into the head of the next.

There were hundreds of nails; some fairly new looking and almost shiny, some old and rusted. The necklace was unsettling, yet the visitors had a tough time looking away from it. As they stopped, Elizabeth hurriedly made her way to Innonia and whispered in her ear. As she did so, the Ghoul leader's eyes tracked over to Carmen and settled on her, apparently weighing the young woman as Elizabeth brought her up to speed.

At the end of their private conference, Elizabeth straightened and handed Innonia what looked to be another nail. Innonia took it absently, and held it in her hand, rolling it around with her thumb and forefinger as she turned her attention back to the three adult Furies. Her gaze was neutral, with not a hint of the fear and nervousness she had displayed when meeting Jae, Chandra, and Ava a few days ago.

*What had changed?* Jae wasn't sure, but she knew it had to be seismic.

"Greetings again to those I have met, greetings also to those I have not," Innonia said calmly as she stood up. Transferring the nail to her left hand, she strode forward and shook each of their hands. This was not a normal practice for the Ghouls, and Jae sensed that this was a test of some kind.

She made sure to look Innonia dead in the eyes when the woman shook her hand firmly, and was gratified to see her Sisters do the same. Carmen was still a little pale as she wrestled with her newly discovered understanding of what the Ghouls ate, but she shook hands with Innonia without fear or revulsion—and that was very good for all of them, Jae decided.

"Honored Grave Smith," Chandra started, "we have been instructed to come here and await our mistress. Is that ok? It was

274

our understanding that you were made aware of our arrival and that we were expected."

"You were expected, yes," agreed the Ghoul as she went back to her seat. "Please, sit. Can I offer you coffee? Hot tea?"

The three Furies shook their heads, but Carmen surprised everyone by asking for some water.

Elizabeth nodded approvingly and exited the room. Innonia pursed her lips in thought as her eyes once again fell on Carmen. Chandra did not quite bristle, but it was clear to all that the storied Fury was afraid the Ghouls had more than a passing interest in the young Childe, and she obviously didn't feel comfortable with it.

For her part, Carmen merely matched gazes with Innonia for a second before standing and gratefully accepting a large glass of water from Elizabeth. The outside of the glass was a little smeared by the female Ghoul's hand, but the ice and water contained in the glass seemed clear and clean.

"Thank you," murmured Carmen and sat back down. She sipped at the water thirstily with no apparent hesitation or disgust. Innonia smiled and nodded encouragingly.

"Carmen," she said, "did you know that you are the very first person not of our clan to drink or eat anything within these walls? Well, except for the sleepers of course. Many of them have over the years... but they don't know who we are."

"Why?" asked Carmen curiously, still holding her water.

"Why indeed?" answered Innonia and looked at the older Furies again. "It probably has something to do with our eating habits and general lack of cleanliness—at least when stacked up against many in the Dark."

"So what? They thought you might poison them or something? Aren't the Dark supposed to be kick-asses that shouldn't care about what you have to eat to survive?"

"A good question, Carmen," Innonia said calmly, looking the young Fury in the eyes. "It confused us, too, for many years. We don't have a choice in what we must eat or how we must live— and we help and care for the oblivious ones who come to us for succor during their time of need. We set them on the path to healing, which can be a long and painful road, but we do the best we can. So why were we ostracized? We've done nothing to earn the scorn we have been so richly rewarded with by our supposed allies. Many in the Dark are evil and depraved. We are neither, yet we have been treated worse than any."

Jae was extremely uncomfortable, and she could feel it from the other two as well. The Grave Smith was talking to Carmen, yes, but it was the Furies she was really communicating with. Lecturing, in fact.

"I'm sorry," said Carmen sincerely, "but that's not who I am. I can't pretend that I want to see what you eat... or how... but I don't hold it against you either. For the rest of my life, when I get mad, or scared, I'm going to turn into a monster. It's a part of me; I can't change it. It's not fair to judge you on something you can't change either."

Silence descended on the room as Innonia stared at the other Furies for a few moments, looking each in the eye—making sure they understood that their own Childe had just shown them a truth that none of them had previously uncovered. Elizabeth's eyes were brimming with gratitude at Carmen's words, and she dabbed at them with a muddy sleeve, smearing dirt across her face.

"I made a decision today that will cost some of my clan their lives," Innonia announced, speaking directly to the Furies now. "Maybe all of our lives, in fact. It weighs heavily upon me, but I know it is the right decision—the only decision really—and I stand by it. But I will not allow me or mine to be disrespected. Not anymore."

Jae was silent, as was Chandra and Misima. All three women gazed upon Innonia with serious faces and burgeoning respect.

"Your mistress was gracious to me a few days ago. Her humanity and kindness moved me to declare for her... and for you." Innonia paused. "I know that your clan is dying all over the world. I grieve for your losses, but I honor you for them too. The Furies boldly declared against the Dark and openly for Ava, and that was the right and just thing to do. The Ghouls follow the Sisterhood into the abyss. We also turn against the Dark, and we stand shoulder to shoulder with you. We will die with the Furies if need be, but only as equals... and as friends."

Jae could barely see anymore; tears of gratitude blinded her, and she rejoiced to know that the Sisterhood didn't stand completely alone anymore. She'd had no idea how heavily that weighed upon her until Innonia declared herself their ally.

"Thank you," rasped Chandra, her own eyes overflowing. "So many of our Sisters have died, and are still dying, the world over and just miles away, both. Death is a part of our way of life, but I fear we will be wiped off the board entirely without allies. We couldn't ask for better than you. I'm sorry for the way I have treated any of your clan before, and I pledge to fight and die next to you as my true companions-in-arms if it be our shared fate."

Misima nodded, too overcome to speak, and Jae murmured her agreement.

"Now," Innonia said, finally smiling at all of them, "I welcome you to our home. Let us turn our thoughts to revenge and war. I believe Ava comes tonight, and she will bring enemies with her. We must plan and prepare."

# Chapter 18

Kelso's senses were dulled by the blizzard, but even if they hadn't been he couldn't have tracked Ava as she moved. And killed.

Leaving through his backyard had been easy, as all of the infected had apparently been pulled away by Marcus. Ava moved like a wraith, flitting in and out of his perceptions as she melded into the storm—seeming to be nowhere and everywhere—all at once.

She was protecting *him*, yes, but she was also hunting *them*.

It was strange, but he felt hyper-aware of her in ways that he didn't understand. It seemed beyond what one could know of someone else. It was like there was an invisible string stretched between them, and when she moved, he felt it. Where she went, he knew.

*What was it?* he wondered, as they trekked north towards the funeral home perched at the edge of town. It was not unpleasant, but it was so... different. "Why can I feel her?" he murmured.

"We are bonded," intoned Ava in the cold voice that was newly hers, and added, "we're aware of each other on a level that few could ever understand."

"I see," he said, even though he really didn't.

"Do you?" she asked from behind him, still invisible.

"No," he admitted.

He was jogging steadily through nearly three feet of snow, at times following the path she had cleared and sometimes carving his own for her. She was a ghost to even his heightened perceptions. Without his new sense of her, he could have easily believed he was alone in the furious storm.

That thought was shattered when he ran directly into one of the Other, who loomed out of the snow and reached for him with clawed hands. It would have been laughable, really, but the Other had demonstrated many strange powers and the Knight had no wish to allow those hands to touch him.

*"Yeah, good idea,"* agreed Argenta with a minimum of snark.

His right hand was rising, gun steady, but he hesitated for a half second. *Was he really going to blow an old woman away?*

Before that momentary thought could even fully form, Ava was there, the old woman's head suddenly in her hand. She held it aloft by its grey hair as the body of the woman slumped to the ground. She was looking at Kelso with something close to disappointment.

"So, are you still not going to kill any of your enemies?" She asked, nonplused. "Didn't you promise me that you wouldn't hold back the next time you were attacked?"

"I did. I'm sorry, but she wasn't even ascended." He nodded at the woman's body.

"I know, and I don't care," Ava said as she dropped the woman's head unceremoniously on top of her heaped body. "More are coming, so do you intend to fight or not? Would you rather us die or be overwhelmed?"

"Of course not." Kelso met her eyes fearlessly at the thought of her dying. "No quarter to those that stand against us."

The Dark Witch that was his Ava nodded approvingly. "Show me," she challenged before flitting out into the raging storm again.

Kelso set off north after her, mentally trying to reconcile the streets he was familiar with to the snow-blasted landscape he was traveling through. It helped a lot that he could just follow Ava when she occasionally ranged ahead of him, because it appeared that the Dark Witch knew exactly where to go.

Three came for him then: a mixed bag of faded black and streaky white, and his guns rebuffed them harshly. The tall one— likely a Berserker at one time—was caught in the throat: the bullet instantly wrecking his windpipe and blowing out a part of his spine. A slight shift of the barrel and a robed man, possibly a Priest, was shot in the head. He dropped like a stone.

His other handgun caught a Fury in the chest, and it hurt him to put her down—particularly because so many of their clan had died tonight. Even as he thought this, his second bullet sealed the deal as she was blown off her feet and landed in a heap, quite dead.

Regardless of his misgivings, he had not hesitated at all. And he had not missed.

"*Nice shootin', Tex,*" drawled his sword in a terrible accent. "*Ya dun put those varmints down and showed 'em the erra of their ways."*

*"Really?"* he thought, hurrying forward again. Snatches of the chaotic song that seemed to follow the Other around floated on the wild winds. He could feel Ava out there: engaging, killing, but he heard nothing.

*"What? I'm bored,"* Argenta complained. *"I know you won't draw me, so I'm reduced to being a spectator. Again."*

*"Well, my apologies for not wanting to carve a path of destruction all the way down main street tonight. Well, any night, really."*

*"You're a broken record sometimes,"* bristled his sword, *"and it's really annoying."*

*"You could always stop talking to me,"* Kelso suggested, grinning into the night air.

Another woman loomed out of the curtain of white, and he shot her between the eyes, not even slowing as she tumbled and skidded to the ground behind him. Her body was swallowed up by the storm a second later.

*"Who else would I talk to?"* wondered the thing that rode his back. *"It's slightly better to talk to you than to no one, I think."* Argenta hesitated. *"Maybe."*

*"I won't let you slaughter my friends and innocent bystanders, so deal with it."* The Knight's thoughts were ice cold and crystal clear when it came to this point. His will was iron.

*"Blah ba blah ba blah ba blah,"* sniped his sword in return.

*"You do realize you're not doing a damn thing to the Other, right? Like, literally nothing."*

*"What do you mean?"* Kelso pulled up short at the thought, and he took a moment to quickly reload both his guns. "I'm reloading," he said in a normal voice to the storm, trusting that Ava would hear it.

She did.

The Knight looked up after snapping his last cylinder back and saw that Ava was standing directly in front of him—as if she had been standing there all night. Gore caked her arms almost to the elbows and blood spatter stained her outfit.

At this moment she really was a horror, and he could easily see why she had earned her nickname among the Dark.

Ava titled her head at him as he thought this, and the Knight knew that his lack of response to her appearance was probably puzzling—or upsetting—her.

"Nice look," he said with a small grimace. "Do you have to get up so close and personal when you kill them?"

"No," she admitted. "I just enjoy it more."

*"She's such a badass,"* interjected Argenta admiringly. *"Take notes."*

Kelso ignored his sword and instead frowned at Ava for a moment. "You *enjoy* killing these folks? They're all victims, Ava. I know it must be done, but the quicker and cleaner, the better."

Ava was silent for a moment. "I do enjoy killing them—or rather, killing *it*. I don't feel conflicted about doing so at all. The Other has been killing my Furies all night, and I'm very... angry... about it."

"Hmm," he said, angling back out into the storm. "Are you sure that's the word you were looking for?"

The Dark Witch ranged at his side for a moment, her eyes alert, yet also, somehow, dead. Kelso glanced at her, and his heart ached. The Knight was keenly aware of the deep, harsh pain she was in that gave lie to her words. Kelso didn't know how he knew, he just did.

"You're tapping into your bond with me, aren't you," Ava said. It wasn't a question.

"I still don't know what that means, but probably. I'm getting a lot of vibes off of you that I don't understand." He glanced left and right as they crossed an intersection. The snow was unbroken all four ways; no one was driving in this mess.

"We're bonded, which means we have shared blood. We have shared vows and promises. We have shared ourselves, completely and totally," Ava said as she easily kept pace slightly ahead of him, but she stopped suddenly and looked back. "Do you understand now?"

"What do you mean, 'We have shared blood'?" Kelso wasn't grossed out by the thought, but he did think it was a little... strange. He had no idea if she was being literal or figurative with that statement.

Ava frowned as she looked back into the storm. "I mean what I said. You have a little of my blood flowing in you; I have a little of yours in me. For those of us in the Conflict, that creates a bond." She hesitated for a second and then turned north. "Let us continue."

"How did we share blood? When?"

"Oh. Well, the night we met, I deposited some of my blood in you—when I wasn't stealing your bacon. Do you remember that small cut on your wrist? My nail was bloodied, and I marked you then." Ava could have been talking about the weather, such was her casual dismissal of something that had been done to him against his will and without his knowledge.

He frowned. "Ok, not cool. How did my blood get into you?" The Knight was afraid he knew the answer.

"I stole it from you when you were on death's door. You were certainly spilling enough of it around, you know. It's lucky you're not bound to dozens of women. You should really be more careful in the future. I just scooped a little up and deposited it in my wrist… It seemed fitting and fair." Ava glanced backwards again and picked up the pace a little, hurrying fully into the intersection.

Kelso sighed. "I'm not sure how *stealing* my blood and injecting it into yourself makes up for you secretly depositing your blood into me without my knowledge. Haven't you ever heard that 'Two wrongs don't make a right'?"

The Princess skidded to a stop in the exact center of the four-way road. "We had a conversation like this before, remember? I've never been instructed in your folksy little sayings." She glanced over at him, and for the second time since Ava's other side had come to the fore, he detected a little emotion... perhaps worry. "Are you implying that you don't want to be bound to me? Or that you would have told me no if I had asked?"

Kelso thought about it for a second. "No," he reluctantly said. "I would have been fine with it. Honored even. Well, except for at the table when we first met since you were busy threatening me—in between telling me to beg for my life or to run away." He shook his head at the memory and gave an exasperated grimace at her small smile as she, apparently, remembered it too. Ava obviously had a different recollection of their first meeting. *Cut her some slack,* he thought, *she is a Dark Princess, after all.*

Still, he forged on gamely. "To be totally honest, I might have had to think about sharing blood with you right then and there. All the threats were a little bit of a turnoff, you know? I would have appreciated a warning at least."

"That seems reasonable," she admitted, then turned back south. "If we survive the next five minutes, I promise to tell you first before I take advantage of you from now on. Fair?"

"What? No." He paused. "Wait, what do you mean, 'If we survive the next five minutes'?"

"The Other abandoned the Paladin, and I think he just died." Her tone held no hint of concern or remorse for his death. "And several dozens are almost upon us."

"Why didn't you tell me that earlier!" Kelso turned fully to face the south now too. "We could have run faster, maybe we could have avoided them. Not that I'm one for retreating typically, but the Other is endless; it makes no sense to fight."

The woman that was now mostly the Dark Witch—the side of her that shielded Ava from the Other's increasing power—merely shrugged. "I didn't tell you because I *wanted* them to catch us. We couldn't have outrun them all the way to sanctuary in any case." She looked over at him now and grinned. She looked feral and furious—and still somehow breathtakingly beautiful.

Kelso fell back into himself at her words; the Knight had allowed his focus to wander a little as they conversed, fascinated by this other side of her. The Dark Witch was witty and brutally direct, but again, he did not find her to be evil or scary. Even though Ava wasn't anywhere near as warm as she normally was, it was clear she was also no threat to him either.

Enough. He needed to clear his head.

"*About time,*" grumbled Argenta. "*Release the Kraken!*"

"*That doesn't even remotely make sense,*" thought Kelso distantly as he ascended his battlements once more. The night sharpened around him, and to his perceptions even the individual snowflakes slowed in their descent. Within seconds his ears again picked up the first strains of the maddeningly eerie song that accompanied the Other.

It quickly swelled in volume and intensity. By the time the first figures broke out of the storm and raced to them, it was a crescendo of sound… and dread.

***

Jesslyn was impressed by the carnage at Kelso's house, and that was *not* easy to do when it came to her. Almost impossible to do, in fact. She had to give credit where credit was due, however, and the battle that had taken place here—the slaughter, actually—was thorough and very messy.

It looked like Kelso's house had been under siege, as the vast majority of his runes had been destroyed. The few that were left, though? She shivered. Jesslyn didn't even like looking at them, such was their power and lethality.

Bodies and pieces of bodies were strewn everywhere, already covered in snow. The ones closest to his house were all female, and when she bent down to dust one off which was more or less intact, she saw that it was a Fury.

"What happened here?" asked one of the Sorcerers accompanying Jesslyn. He was a slender man with cruel lips and even crueler eyes.

"I don't know," the Spider answered absently, walking back towards the truck they had stolen. The massive rig was idling in front of his house, not quite in the battle zone. Four of the five companions she had recruited were out and canvassing the scene. The Childe driving the car was smoking a cigarette impassively, and Jesslyn resisted the urge to rip it out of his mouth—along with a few teeth and his tongue. She might have need of him later.

"Put that out, idiot," she growled instead. "Nicotine holds nothing for you anymore. And I hate the smell."

The large, bearded man blanched and quickly flicked the cigarette away. Jesslyn forgot him as she strode to where the other three were standing, gazing down at a pool of melted flesh and bone, now cooled, that ringed ten feet out in a perfect circle.

At one side of it, the side facing the street, the circle had been broken, and flesh and bone traveled along in a more or less straight route to the corner. The small band followed the macabre trail past the intersection and up the street, away from Kelso's, for close to one hundred yards. It appeared that the path led steadily—and purposefully—away from the Knight's home.

As they tracked the puzzling destruction, the bodies of various soldiers of the Dark *and* the Light became distinct, some of them with melted features, others with fatal wounds of a more mundane type. Ever more bodies, and ever more intact, led to a spot under a streetlamp, its light barely hallowing the ground underneath due to the rampant storm.

There, the trail ended abruptly.

"Why would soldiers of the Dark and the Light be dying... together?" rumbled the large Berserker. Her eyes were piggish things, too small and set too far apart in her large face.

Jesslyn thought she knew, but she didn't want to share her knowledge. It appeared clear to her, however, that she had been right about a third faction made up of both Dark and Light. A third rail of power had indeed risen and was on the march. Was the whole clan of Furies a part of the new order, then? If so, her budding alliance with the mysterious faction was doomed. She had killed Furies just last night, and she hated them—despised them really—and always had.

The mysterious voice had spoken of ending Ava *and* Kelso last night, and Jesslyn was obviously seeing the aftermath of that attempt. The Spider needed both, in different ways, so her alliance with them had been dicey from the onset.

"Split up, find me something, anything." Jesslyn kept every hint of worry out of her voice. It was never a good idea to show any sort of weakness in front of soldiers, but the truth was that she was scared. Was this the work of Kelso and Argenta? She had never heard of the sword melting enemies before, but she was not willing to dismiss it out of hand. If it had been her Knight, was he wounded? What would she do if they found him and he needed help?

"Do *not* disturb anything you find. Do *not* touch anything—or anyone—on pain of my displeasure!" she warned while they were all within earshot. For her part, she followed the curb farther from Kelso's house. She had only walked a dozen yards when the other Sorcerer called out, his voice rising and falling with the storm's fury.

If they had found Kelso, she would kill them all and take him away with her.

Jesslyn armored up without thinking and hurried over to the area she had seen the Sorcerer move towards. She found him right off, the other Sorcerer standing next to him already.

On the ground lay a small man with a goatee shot through with grey. His bald head was mostly covered with snow, and a huge war hammer lay next to him. Already the hammer appeared to be heavily degraded and rusted through, but Jesslyn intuited that it had been a mighty weapon once. Earlier tonight, in fact.

A few steps away lay a small figure, a boy, with his throat cut. Blood had run down his chest and frozen. Jesslyn would have dismissed him as entirely uninteresting except for the boy's expression, which had frozen in death.

He looked pissed.

Glancing back over to the man lying on his back, Jesslyn moved in and brushed the snow off. The man had a large sword shard lodged up through his throat and into his head. There was no way the boy did it, so it looked like the Paladin had killed himself.

On further examination, she became convinced of his identity. Unless she missed her mark, the man lying on the ground was an infamous Paladin known for an aura that could wreak the kind of carnage they had witnessed.

*But why would he kill himself? Would he have felt guilt over killing so many of the Light?* Jesslyn could totally see a wimpy, whiny Paladin doing something like that.

No doubt, weaknesses of that nature was why the Dark was winning so handily.

She straightened up from the Paladin and shrugged; the mystery of what happened here was not going to be an easy one

291

to solve. Jesslyn hated mysteries, and the whole scene from Kelso's house to here was one giant puzzle.

She didn't have time to worry about it. From what she could tell neither Kelso nor Ava were among the dead, and neither of them were in the house. She had used the Sorcerers as unwitting bait to draw them out earlier, yet no one had come forth to meet them as they yelled obscenities and threats from the street.

So, where were they?

"Ok, let's go," she said shortly, and led them back to the waiting truck. Once there, she noticed a stampede of footprints heading north. A large mass of bodies had moved that way very recently—in haste, by the look of it, which meant a chase.

She smiled. The Spider absolutely adored chases.

# Chapter 19

The Witch arrived fully at last. Her power was a physical thing that blew all the snow away in a blinding sheet as she flitted forward to engage the vanguard of the Other. Her peerless Dark, the essence of her true strength, followed in her wake trailing wings of obsidian and ash. She was Death Incarnate.

The Ebon Knight was her emissary, his ensorcelled bullets winnowing those who dared to approach his Princess from her sides, her back, her peripheries. His guns cracked again and again until they were empty, each bullet claiming a combatant. Holstering at last, the Knight drew batons and waded into the breach his Ava had made for him.

Engaging those few that got past her initial rush, the Knight meted out his disdain with finality and skill. His silvered and warded short staffs blurred as the Knight crushed throats, shattered bones, and broke the heads of their enemies—always following the Witch as she pushed deeper and deeper into the horde.

With armored hands and feet, with magic, she tore into their ranks, biting deep. The Princess was an avenging goddess of shadow and lightning. Her Dark exploding out of her in tendrils of grasping night as she rampaged among them, face cold and expressionless. Lightning bolts of pitch pulsed from her body in random strikes, killing impersonally and savagely.

In some far off and unknowable realm, the Other spent the lives of its hosts extravagantly and without pause. That rush of bodies—a wall of mindless flesh controlled from afar with cruelty and spite—eventually became too much and slowly turned the tide. Ava's advance was finally halted, and she fought desperately to avoid being pushed back.

The Knight was a whirlwind of silver and white, his ghostly armor bruised and battered as the battle went on. The Witch threw Fel Spikes in a wide arc around her and more of the Other died. But more took their place, standing on the bodies of those previously released.

It came upon him slowly, inch by inch, moment by moment—the realization that they were inexorably losing. Such was their prowess that they were each winning their individual battles, over and over, while the war continually slipped away from them, nevertheless. His armor was flickering, and no matter how fast he struck, how nimble his retreat, there were just too many.

Ava had expended much of her Dark and she was tiring. Kelso felt like he had already pulled or strained every known muscle in his body—plus a few he hadn't known about. There were no quick kills now, and he dueled two or three at a time, while Ava fought double that.

The Dark Witch was incredible, but her power had its limits. A turn, a twist, and Kelso's eyes fell upon Ava as she grabbed an infected Knight by his helmet, ignoring the grey shock she received in return. Fel Lightning leapt from her fingers and directly into his face, arcing his back as she literally fried him on his feet.

The Witch released the thoroughly dead man and stumbled

back towards Kelso. His resolve hardened at her vulnerability, but she recovered immediately. With a growl of frustration, she caught a sword with an armored glove that had been seeking his head. She crushed the blade in her hand, and it shattered in a metallic spray over the bodies of the dead and dying.

The Ebon Knight's spinning retort slammed both batons against the side of his would-be assassin's face, breaking the neck and turning the head grotesquely backwards. As that enemy dropped, Kelso bull rushed a Knight taking aim at Ava with a bow, knocking him off balance right as he let the arrow fly. They both tumbled to the ground for a moment, and Kelso locked eyes with him... with *it*.

"I'm winning," it said with a small snicker.

Kelso said nothing, but even as he beat the life out of the Knight underneath him, his blood ran cold in acknowledgment of the truth in the Other's pronouncement.

"I will not fall to these puppets," vowed Ava in a cold voice. At her declaration the mist of Dark around her again pulsed out, knocking several of their enemy to the ground. Kelso immediately stowed his weapons and began to reload his guns, hands sure and practiced.

"My lady," Kelso said in an even voice, broken only by his panting, "we need to retire from the field. Now."

"Run from these... marionettes? I think not." She stared at him imperiously, but the Knight could see that she was much diminished—perhaps by half of what she was at the start. Dozens lay around them dead, but dozens still stood. It was madness to speak such, but he knew that it was not Ava talking to him, or at least not entirely.

"You may survive," he admitted, "but I won't."

She flinched at his words, eyes boring into him even as their enemies regained their feet.

"I'll stay with you," Kelso promised, "but we're losing."

"At least one of you knows it," laughed a woman, once a sleeper, her arm twisted and broken where it hung useless at her side.

"You could join me," suggested another, "or lay down Argenta and walk away. Either would suffice this night."

The Witch laughed. "My Knight," she crooned darkly, bloodlust rising in her eyes, "don't despair. Our enemy wishes to parlay when it's winning? I think not."

Kelso blinked and looked around at the field with new eyes. Yes, many still stood, but most were sleepers, and nearly all were wounded.

The Witch turned in a circle, trailing Fel Dark that wafted from her in ever increasing waves. Faster and faster she spun and from within the maelstrom her voice issued forth, cold and vicious. It rang through the storm, nowhere and everywhere. "You *all* need to die. You threw my Furies away like they were trash, like they were not worthy of even your control. I grieve for them, but they are now free of you. My vengeance will be swift and final on these, your remaining puppets, but I will come for the puppet master soon enough."

Even as the remaining combatants converged on them once more, Ava was gone, and in her place a Dark blur launched itself, trailing shadow and lightning, leaping from infected to infected. And where the Dark Witch went, death followed. The Knight stood transfixed for five seconds… and in five seconds, it was over.

He blinked, and she was suddenly there in front of him, completely stilled and covered in gore. Around her those that she had visited began to topple—heads severed, hearts or throats removed, bodies folded backwards upon themselves, their spines shattered. Even as she stood looking into his eyes, around him his enemies dropped to the ground in silence.

They stood alone and victorious, surrounded by close to three hundred of the enemy, all dead.

Ava smiled wanly at him… and crumpled.

***

The Spider was deeply impressed.

They had come upon yet another massive battle, with hundreds of dead. All over the street they lay, in various stages of mutilation. Many were in pieces and were grotesquely maimed. Whoever had done this had been powerful, vengeful, and enraged. As she and her small band stepped among the dead, the Spider couldn't help but admire the brutality.

Jesslyn was certain that the unknown killer of these wretches had made it personal—and she could really respect that.

"Tracks leading north", announced one of the Childer. "Only one set of footprints, heavy, probably male."

Jesslyn hurried over to his side and studied the tracks herself. Although she was not a professional tracker by any stretch, she had hundreds of years of experience in hunting down her prey. The Spider agreed with his assessment.

"Load up; let's go," she ordered, turning to make her way back to the truck. As she did so, her foot brushed one of the dead. She glanced down in disinterest, just intending to keep her shoes clear of blood, when she halted—and smiled.

A bullet had blown through this one's head: a neat hole in front, a large, jagged wound in the back at its exit, skull shattered and open to the snow. A bullet...

The Spider laughed delightedly; Kelso lived.

She looked around; barely any snow had accumulated on the bodies. They were close behind him, possibly only minutes.

Jesslyn started to hustle back to the truck and then hesitated. How could she keep the five with her from falling on the Knight if they caught him? He might be wounded. In fact, he *should* be wounded after such a fight. Further, the Spider herself was still weakened from the injuries she had sustained last night, and had enlisted two Sorcerers to accompany her because of that. She would not be able to hold them back sufficiently if they found what she suspected they might.

She had two choices, one of which was to kill them all now while they were unaware. The Sorcerers first, Berserker after, then the Childer. It had its charms, and she almost went with it. At the last moment, only steps from catching up to one of the Sorcerers, she changed her mind and instead brushed past him to stand at the driver's door.

"These enemies are strong, and one in particular might be more than a match for us," she started, picking her words carefully. "I will scout ahead, you will follow me slowly... and if I tell you to hold, you will."

One of the Sorcerers laughed. He sneered when he responded, voice nasally and arrogant. "One against all of us? Theres no need for stealth. Let's just go kill him before he gets away." Several of the others nodded in agreement.

*He was lucky she was on the hunt tonight,* the Spider mused, *or he would be tonight's entertainment.* She *loved* making overly confident tough guys weep.

All she said was, "Caution is warranted; the hundreds of dead lying around should be enough for you to see that. Let me add context, though, since you are all apparently too stupid to put two and two together."

"We are hunting my sister, the one some of you know as the Dark Witch. She is lethal, and I believe she has been at least partly responsible for the carnage we have so far witnessed tonight." Jesslyn raised an imperious finger in warning as the Sorcerer opened his mouth to protest. "Yes, I know it appears that a male is the only one who walked away from this. Heavy, like he is carrying someone—probably my sister."

All five looked at her in various stages of boredom or bloodlust. She could actually understand that mixture of emotions very well. "Here then is our other quarry, the male. I know who he is, and we don't want to tangle with him yet. I need to ascertain if he is wounded, and how badly, before we engage."

The Sorcerer snorted. Jesslyn resolved then and there to kill him by morning light if he still breathed. If he did, that would most likely be because she had failed in her tasks. She would need someone to vent her frustration on, and a part of her *almost* hoped she got the chance.

"You are a fool," she said to him instead. "Attend me and listen well. I believe the quarry we now track is the Ebon Knight."

All five froze at her words, and even the fatally overconfident Sorcerer paused.

"I will track him; you will follow. Is that clear?"

They nodded.

"Once I have ascertained his condition and his destination, I'll make the decision to attack or not. Understood?" She spoke mainly to the Sorcerer, staring him down as she explained the plan.

Once again, they all nodded mutely.

"Give me a minute head start, leave your coms open." She keyed her throat mic once and heard the click from their ear buds.

"Mic up, remain alert."

Turning, she ghosted out into the snow, quickly fading from all perception as only she could. She picked up the tracks and started following, running through the storm after the Knight.

# Chapter 20

Carmen looked up from petting Charlie at a soft knock on her door.

Mrs. Rodriguez was sleeping soundly in one of two small beds in their room. Carmen had Charlie on her bed, playing with his ears while he snored like a chainsaw. The big bulldog was also hogging up all the space on the small single mattress, so Carmen was awkwardly curled around him. She hadn't even wanted him up on her bed, but the soulful look he'd given her when she said he couldn't had broken her heart.

She was a sucker for the dog, obviously. And to add insult to injury, she'd actually had to get *out* of bed to lift him up... and then he instantly flopped down right where she'd been lying, taking up the exact center. She stood there in disbelief, hands on hips, and was about to scold him a little—if she could stop smiling first—when he looked up at her wonderingly as if to say, *"What? Come on, it's time to sleep."*

What could she do about something like that? So, she crawled back into *her* bed, wrapped herself around him, and tried to sleep too.

It didn't come.

Thoughts of her parents tormented her, and tears flowed in an unbroken stream down her face. The only small mercy Carmen had been granted was that she had not been awake and aware as they were put to death by Jesslyn—who was apparently Ava's own sister.

How two people could be blood related yet completely, diametrically, and irrevocably opposite from one another was a mystery. One she loved, one she loathed... and feared.

With a sigh, she got up and went to the door as someone knocked softly again. Chandra stood beyond the threshold with Jae and Misima lurking behind. They seemed grim and twitchy. Sad. A large part of Carmen was grateful that she was not a full Sister. From what she could gather from them, their exit from the Dark was going very poorly—catastrophically so.

"How are you, dear heart?" asked Chandra, voice pitched low so as not to disturb Mrs. Rodriguez, although how any noise could reach her past Charlie's thunderous snores was beyond Carmen's understanding.

"Fine," Carmen answered. "I was just trying to sleep."

Chandra reached up and thumbed both sides of Carmen's face clear of tears. "Not very well, it seems."

"No," the younger woman admitted. "There's just been too much, too fast. I can't even grieve properly for my parents. I'm lost."

"We all are, Carmen," Misimia offered from the shadows. She was holding hands with Jae, and Carmen realized she had been wrong—they were not merely sad, they were completely broken with soul-wrenching grief.

"We've lost more than half of our numbers tonight," Chandra

breathed, almost as if she could not wrap her head around it. "Thousands have fallen. We may never recover."

Carmen didn't know what to say to that since she wouldn't be welcome as part of that recovery. She still felt for the women though; these three were her friends.

Chandra nodded in understanding at Carmen's silence. "Carmen, we must fight tonight," she began. "All the Sisters we left at Kelso's house are missing. Gone from our consciousness."

"All?" Carmen said in surprise. "Inside the house and outside?"

"Well, the ones inside left our shared consciousness of their own accord." Chandra paused. "But I assume that if all the ones guarding the house have been… removed… then it would be safe to assume the sleeping ones are gone too."

"What do you mean by *gone* and *removed*?" Carmen asked hesitantly. "Are they dead?"

"We don't know," Jae said softly. "Every previous Sister that has disappeared from our knowing ended up being a part of the Other. It is happening the world over. Many Sisters are dying while many others become blank to us. Unknowable."

"Ok, so we fight," Carmen said firmly. "Give me one minute to get ready."

"Wait," said Chandra, holding the door open. "*We* are going to fight. Not you."

Carmen hesitated. "You don't trust me?" She couldn't hide the hurt in her voice. How could she explain to them the reasons why she had turned on the Furies in the barn, and why she would never do that to them?

"Oh no, dear one," Chandra said, her accent thick. "We trust you. We know you."

"Then, why?" Carmen asked, voice trembling.

Chandra was silent, struggling to find the words. Jae spoke up, "We have reports, from everywhere. Those that have been stolen from our ranks become pawns of the power that took them. They infect yet others and then those infect even more."

"A wildfire is rushing through the Sisterhood," Misima said in a tremulous voice, "and we can't trust ourselves... or you... around the maddening music that seems to cause it."

Chandra reached out and smoothed back Carmen's hair. "We can make ourselves immune, we think, should we need to. We can heal from what must be done to make that happen. You, though? You are too young, in both years and power, so we can't ask you to do what we can do. Does that make sense?"

Carmen came to the realization then. "You would... maim... yourselves?"

None of the three answered.

Carmen gasped. "That's awful! How do you know it will even work?"

"We don't," Jae responded, "but it might. We can heal from damage like that in an hour or so. No one in the Conflict is so resilient as we. It's unpleasant to think about, to consider, but we are warriors and will see it done."

Carmen shook her head. "So, if you can't hear the song... " She trailed off. "And you wish to spare me from having to do that?"

"Yes," confirmed Chandra, "but only because it could take you a day or more to heal from it—if you could at all. We *think* you can, but we're not completely sure."

"Because I'm not a full Sister," Carmen finished for her. "I see."

"There's more," Misima said softly, real compassion in her voice. "If you hear it, you still must try to become immune to it—immediately. If you can't..." She trailed off, uncomfortable.

"If I can't what?" Carmen asked, though she had an inkling about where this conversation was going.

"If you can't," continued Chandra, "you will have to make a choice. Quickly. You may have just seconds to do so. Will you live as a slave to the Other? Well, for as long it deigns to let you live is more like it, but would you really be Carmen still? I don't think so. I think that what was you, what made you unique, what made you Carmen Salazar, would probably be eaten, discarded, destroyed."

"You're saying I should kill myself?" Carmen asked calmly, face unafraid and eyes steely.

"If you cannot fight it or resist it, then we believe it is better to die while you are still *you* than to let it feast." Chandra's voice was quiet but resolved. "Try blocking it first, two Fel spikes, thin, in each ear. Immediately. Block off the wounds with more Dark as a buffer. If that doesn't work, then you have a choice to make—a choice only you can make for yourself."

Carmen nodded, glancing over her shoulder at Mrs. Rodriguez.

"What about her? She has no hope of defending against the Other." Carmen turned back and looked up into Chandra's dark eyes. "What would you do if you were me?"

Chandra didn't hesitate as she smiled gently down at the much shorter and younger woman. "I would have mercy on Mrs. Rodriguez and keep her safe before I followed."

Carmen nodded again. "I understand."

\*\*\*

Kelso ran as he had never run before.

That he could even run at all was a miracle. Even so, the run was hard, exhausting, and frantic. The Knight carried his Princess in his arms, her face slack, eyes closed, her Dark spent. Through the waist-deep snow and the fury of the storm he raced north as fast as he could, legs and arms straining, his Light struggling to keep him upright, moving, running.

Through a nightmarish landscape did the Ebon Knight flee with the Dark Witch. He hoped that at the other end of this journey he would find friends and shelter. At best guess, he was about a mile away, maybe a little more. Burdened as he was, battered too, and wading through deep snow, it might as well have been ten miles.

It didn't matter; he ran. Not for himself: he ran for Ava, his true love. For the sake of the one that had rescued him last night did he strive with everything he had to make safe harbor. If need be the Knight would run until he died to keep her safe.

Ava was completely unmarked with no visible damage anywhere. She had fought and killed hundreds of supernaturally enhanced foes this night without blemish or bruise. On the other hand, the Knight was a stumbling wreck of flickering Light, wounded and battered—not seriously—but enough that it sapped his strength and added to the burden of running.

Kelso had no idea what he would do if he encountered more enemies. He was loathe to drop Ava, but it might be his only option. The Knight would need his hands free to draw his guns, and if there were more than he could shoot down then he felt it likely that he and the Princess would die. Their story, just begun, would end.

He was nervous and jittery over that possibility, and it weakened him further. With reluctance, he drew back into himself again. He needed clarity of thought, of purpose, and unyielding—even stubborn—determination. No sooner had he fortified himself than his sixth sense kicked in and warned him that he was being followed.

Not close yet, but something was tracking him. How easy it would be, he mused, to just follow along in his wake, chasing him lightly through the path he'd labored to make through the snow.

"*I hate to give credence to your paranoia,*" murmured Argenta in his mind, "*but I think you're right. Someone is following you.*"

"*I appreciate the confirmation,*" huffed the Knight, so exhausted even his thoughts were tired. "*But I don't suppose you could warn me when whatever it is gets closer? Would you do that for me?*"

The Knight felt it was a vain hope and a foolish request, but he made it anyways—more to check it off his mental list than for any other reason.

Argenta surprised him,

"*I will,*" the sword promised quietly. "*Now, move, damn you! Go!*"

"*I am,*" he protested. "*I feel like my heart is going to burst.*"

"*Less bacon from now on, more fruit and veggies,*" Argenta snarled back, and even in his state the Knight couldn't help but chuckle. For a moment the sword was silent at his mirth, then barked a short laugh inside his head too. "*I seem to have become quite motherly with you, haven't I?*"

"*Kind of what I was thinking, yeah,*" thought the Knight back, blinking away dark spots that had formed in front of his eyes as he labored to bull his way through the snow with Ava in his arms. "*You're just a short step away from telling me to wash behind my ears before bed.*"

310

*"Well,"* his sword drawled, *"I didn't want to say anything first, but..."*

Now it was Kelso's turn to bark a short laugh, and Argenta joined in for a moment before she stopped suddenly.

*"Halt! Whatever it was just went around you and is in front of us now. Prepare for battle, Knight."* Her thoughts were calm and assured.

*"How could it get in front of me? I would have seen it wouldn't I?"* He thought back even as he pulled up to a stop.

*"Whatever it is must be cloaked—and quite well, I would add."* Argenta paused. *"I might be able to boost your senses a bit."*

Another layer of sight seemed to drop over the Knight's eyes, and the world sharpened in ways that he really couldn't explain. It wasn't like he could see *better*, but he could see *more*. And what he saw was terrifying.

Not three feet to his right, someone had run past him without his notice, forging their own path through the snow so close that he could have touched them... or them he. Snow dislodged in the wake of whoever had passed him clumped to the sides and even in front of him. Thirty feet ahead, the trail that had somehow been blazed without him consciously seeing it disappeared behind a vehicle.

He felt coldly certain that something waited in ambush there.

Without hesitation, the Knight swung Ava up over his left

shoulder and drew a gun with his right hand.

***

The Spider was at a loss for what to do.

It had been a simple matter to shadow the Knight, and right off she had ranged up to just a few feet behind him to ascertain he carried Ava and that she was not dead. That would not do at all, and Jesslyn had been terrified upon first spying her sister's lolling head and freely swaying arms as he ran.

Jesslyn had stolen up close to peer at her, nearly over his shoulder, and her relief at the life still evident in her youngest sister's body was immense.

She had plans for that body.

Falling back, she had clicked the mic and ordered her companions to stay far behind. The Spider didn't want to alert the Knight that he was being followed yet until she figured out her next move. The simplest plan would be just to steal up behind the Knight again, kill him, and take Ava. Jesslyn would not do that, however, and discarded that course of action as soon as she considered it.

She had plans for the Knight too.

*Kelso,* she reminded herself sternly. *His name is Kelso.*

A brief chuckle from the exhausted man in front of her caught her attention. How he could express any merriment was beyond her. Jesslyn could easily see that he was running forward basically to keep from falling down—his legs barely kept him

312

upright as he doggedly plowed through the snow.

The Knight had been in a pitched battle tonight, probably a long one. He had also been heavily wounded last night, and the healing process in and of itself was exhausting. Kelso must be dead on his feet, yet still he ran on. His perseverance was impressive, and she found herself admiring him anew.

New plan. She would come up behind and poison him—a little—just enough to make him fall, convulse maybe, but with no lasting damage. While he was incapacitated, she would steal Ava away and be gone. This course of action had merit. She just needed to be certain that he didn't see her face, or he would *not* be amenable to her approach later.

As she moved forward to execute her plan, a hollowness already forming in her belly over the thought of finally having Ava in her possession, Kelso suddenly laughed. It startled her and Jesslyn's concentration slipped for just a moment—but enough that his shoulders squared in immediate recognition that he was not alone.

Quickly, she blew by the Knight and ran ahead, forcing her way through the rib-deep snow. She crossed his path some thirty feet up and then hid behind a car, resting.

She hunched there, a drop of poison on her fingernail. Carefully she considered it, making sure it was not too much, nor too painful—which was a monumental first for her. Satisfied it was strong enough, but not too strong, she waited. And he stopped.

Peeking around the corner of the car, still wrapped in her gift, she saw his eyes widen as he somehow became aware of her trail, and when he looked up towards where she now lay in wait for him…

Her mouth ran dry.

The Knight had a solid sliver of Dark that ran from his forehead to his cheek, directly through his left eye. It was like the night had marked him for its own. He was absolutely beautiful in the stark examination of his surroundings. Kelso had one of his guns in his right hand, but she barely noticed it because she was so captivated by his face. He looked positively sinister.

The Spider wholeheartedly approved.

She ducked back behind the car and took a shaky breath. Jesslyn came up with another plan then, one that was perhaps unwise, but she really couldn't help it. She *had* to talk to the Knight, to see him examine her with his falcon gaze, to be able to look back into those clear eyes and lose herself—just a little.

Jesslyn had been intrigued by the Knight from the moment she first saw him on his dramatic flight from the casino's rooftop. He should have died, but he didn't. Then Jesslyn had almost killed him on his way back home, but she didn't. Then she had lured him out to be killed by Furies, but they didn't. So many opportunities to be killed, and yet he still stood.

In the course of his many near misses, she had become *very* interested in Kelso, and he featured prominently in her future plans. Would Jesslyn pass up this golden chance to talk to him?

She just couldn't.

The Spider wanted to parlay with the Ebon Knight.

No sooner had she decided this than she ducked behind the car fully and dropped her cloak. "Hello," she called out into the storm. "Don't shoot me! I come to talk, not fight!"

With those words, Jesslyn stood and rounded the car.

# Chapter 21

Kelso was coldly surprised by the strawberry-blonde beauty that came into view when she cautiously rounded the car. Her armor was deep black and impressive. Not quite as formidable as Ava's, but reasonably close.

That she was powerful and of the Dark was indisputable, which was why he was confused by her temerity in approaching him directly even though his gun was pointed at her chest. The Knight would have chalked it up to the arrogance of those that had not yet been exposed to his ensorcelled bullets, but she actually appeared to be reasonably cautious. Her eyes flickered from his eyes to the gun several times.

She took a few steps forward and stopped, hands raised to shoulder level in surrender. She paused and waited for him to do something, though Kelso had no clue what that should be. The woman was clothed in off-white battle dress fatigues, basically camouflage, accessorized with tactical-level gear and multiple web pouches.

The white of the woman's outfit as seen through the deep black of her armor blended surprisingly well against the snow, especially at night. It would be easy to lose track of her in the storm. She had shoulder-length hair, held away from her face by a clip at the back of her head. Her eyes were hazel and very direct in the moments their eyes met—when she wasn't looking at his gun barrel. No. At his trigger finger.

She was prepared to dodge the moment he tensed, and that,

along with her gear, marked her as an experienced combatant. *Why had she approached him then?*

"I know you think we're enemies," he began, "but believe me when I tell you there are much greater concerns right now than a grudge match between the Dark and the Light. I need you to clear out and leave." The Knight's face was hard and unyielding— laced with just a touch of menace.

The beautiful woman in front of him flushed lightly and swallowed. "I don't think we're enemies. Far from it. I'm a friend, and I have come to help you... and Ava." At Ava's name, Kelso saw her eyes dart to the Princess hoisted over his shoulder. "Is she hurt?"

Kelso didn't answer immediately, his brow furrowed in thought and suspicion.

"Who are you," he demanded, gun steady, voice frigid, "and how do you know Ava?"

"My name is Maigan." She paused. "And I have known Ava since her birth. In fact, I have been searching for her for years. I swear it."

"How did you pass by me without detection? Is that part of your gift?" Kelso felt time slipping away from him. He was perhaps half a mile from safety, and he needed to get Ava out of the storm and into somewhere defensible. He really didn't need this.

"Yes, I can make myself invisible to most." She nodded and smiled. "May I put my arms down?"

"No. Look, Maigan." He quickly glanced back the way he came, still with one eye on her—giving her a chance to make her move. She didn't. "I have to keep going. I can't stand here talking to you all night."

"I understand." She sounded downcast. "It's just that I have searched for Ava a long time, and I am loathe to leave her so easily. As I said, I have known her since she was a child." She thought for a moment, lips pursed. "Could I accompany you? I'll walk off to the side…"

"No," the Knight said again firmly. "I can't spare the energy to watch you. Please, just step aside. When Ava wakes up, I'll let her know you're looking for her. Fair?"

"Sure, that's fair," Maigan said dejectedly and stepped back behind the car and out of his way. "Could I come visit her though? When she wakes up?"

Kelso started forward again, angling into the middle of the street to give the woman a wide berth. "I don't know how possible that will be since the world is careening into chaos. Ava probably won't care much about childhood reunions."

"Are you sure?" asked Maigan intently. "Don't you think she might like to gather all the allies she can find if this is truly a time of upheaval?"

"*I don't trust her,*" broke in his sword, "*and I suggest you not turn your back on this one.*"

"*Like I couldn't already tell something is off with her?*" Kelso snorted in his head at Argenta. "*Just a little credit would be nice once in a while."*

*"I'm sure it would be. Do a couple of things right in a row and I'll consider it."* Argenta paused. *"I have different senses than you, and I'm intrigued by her... and not in a way you would like. As you know, I am what I am."*

"*So... evil,*" Kelso thought.

*"Yes, pretty much, at least by your standards."* Argenta hesitated again. *"But the one in front of you is evil too. Different than me in most respects, but still wicked. I would probably get along with her famously, even if she is a little twisted. You though? Not so much. Do not be fooled by her looks; a monster stands before you."*

Kelso couldn't remember the last time his sword had named anyone evil. It chilled him, and he looked anew at the fresh-faced blonde as he started forward again while angling into the middle of the street to give the woman a wide berth. There was something in her eyes. A sickness, or perhaps a hunger, that could not be sated. Whatever it was, he knew Ava would never be close to someone of that type.

He stopped several feet short of her and extended his gun arm, pointing his revolver directly at her head. She sighed and looked down in defeat.

"So, what gave me away?" She raised her eyes back to him, and they were amused. "Bravo, Kelso!" she crowed, and clapped her hands together rapidly like an overcome schoolgirl. "You have proven your worth yet again! I would've been disappointed if you'd actually turned your back on me. And it's not… healthy… to disappoint me."

"Who are you, really?" Kelso asked, his finger light upon the trigger, ready to pull. "One of her family, I bet."

"Oh, Kelso. I am so proud of you! Yes, yes, I'm her older sister, Jesslyn." She smirked. "And I have come for her."

"You can't have her," Kelso said flatly.

"No? But—"

The Knight fired without warning, but she was already moving before the bullet left the barrel. She dove behind the car, and he fired again, this time into the vehicle, his ensorcelled bullet easily punching through its length and impacting the snow behind.

"Now, that's not very nice!" Jesslyn admonished from behind the car and flitted away yet again as he fired at the spot where her voice had issued. She laughed. "Direct and to the point! I can respect that!"

Kelso considered his options for a moment, then turned and ran, bulling his way through the thick drifts of snow. The Knight charged towards the allies he knew were just up ahead, running as hard as he could. Adrenaline and determination armored him against exhaustion, and he fairly flew from the crazy one hunting his Ava.

"Hey, Kelso?" she called. "Where you going? Let's talk some more, handsome. You have nothing to fear from me." She laughed again.

The Knight wasn't listening. With his left arm, he steadied Ava on his shoulder as he ran, his hand anchored on her back. His other hand still held his gun because he didn't trust himself to holster it. His enemy was fast—very, very fast—and Kelso wasn't sure he would have the time to draw it again when she attacked.

And he knew she would.

*"Can you heighten me at all?"* Kelso thought desperately at his sword. *"She is almost as fast as Ava."*

*"I'm still weak from last night, Kelso,"* Argenta replied with heat. *"Just how many desperate fights do you have to get into this week? I'm all for mixing it up, but you have never drawn me, so I'm power starved."*

*"Is that a no?"* Kelso didn't have any inclination or energy to engage in a debate with Argenta. He needed to bend every ounce of his strength and attention to running.

*"Kind of,"* Argenta grumbled. *"I'll do what I can when she strikes, but it won't be much."*

\*\*\*

The Spider was annoyed with herself.

All her careful planning had been thrown away in an instant. The Knight was just *so* damn intriguing, and her sister was *so* helpless… she just couldn't stop herself from goading him a little. She actually thought she might drool in front of him, such was her desire for both him and Ava. While many might be turned on by the sight of a beautiful, stacked, and oh-so-wicked blonde in obvious heat, the Knight was apparently not one of them. Pity.

Her impulsive actions would complicate things in the future when Jesslyn came back for Kelso, but she could perhaps still make it work. She would be required to get him addicted to her own special brand of poison—one that she often used on sleepers to make them willing and eager participants in their own destruction. In the back of her head, that had always been plan B with the Knight. Now, it was plan A.

Jesslyn ran along easily behind him, wrapped in her gift, thinking gloomy thoughts and wishing she had just kept out of sight. He was a smart one, so rather than follow directly behind, she went through the extra effort of blazing her own path a few feet perpendicular to his.

Her caution was rewarded when he suddenly whipped his hand straight back and fired his six-gun dead center down the path he was clearing. The Knight didn't even turn around or pause as he did so. The Spider's admiration soared for the Knight! He was truly a cagey man, well worth the energy and time it would take to tame him. If Jesslyn had been running directly in his wake, she would have been shot in the upper chest or neck.

She loved it!

The Spider's eyes kept coming back to rest on Ava's hair. It trailed down to the snow and dragged behind the Knight as he forced his way through the deep drifts. Her sister's hair was thick, beautiful, and glossy black. What should Jesslyn do with it? Cut it off or pull it out by the handfuls? Maybe shave Ava bald? There were several possibilities, and it wasn't merely pain Jesslyn would be going for with Ava: it was humiliation too. The Spider well knew that humiliation would cut the Dark Witch most.

And there would be *plenty* of that—along with pain and degradation—over the next few weeks. Just thinking about it made her giddy... and greedy.

The Spider was tired of waiting; she wanted her prize now.

Even as the thought crossed her mind, she leapt gracefully through the snow, bounding like a leopard towards the Knight. Her right-hand fingernail coated with poison as her left hand stretched out to yank Ava off his back.

***

Misima stiffened when she heard a shot ring out within a hundred yards of her position. The damnable storm confused her perceptions, but she was fairly certain it had come from the street directly in front of her. Covered as it was by the deep drifts of snow, it was still the only road that led up to the corner of the wrought iron fence that protected the cemetery.

Hidden here and there among the gravestones which were mostly obscured by that same unrelenting snowfall, Ghouls roused themselves and made ready. Misimia could feel her Sisters as well, but they were spread out across the sprawling property. They would not come closer to her until it was clear she wasn't being turned, the plan being that if one got infected, the other two would have advance warning and could do what needed to be done before engaging.

Misima had no doubt that the shot had come from one of Kelso's deadly guns, and he was coming in hot.

Without thought, she leapt the eight-foot fence in front of her, followed on each side by a Ghoul. Their armor was much thicker than hers, and they were swarthy and hulked lower to the ground. Their limbs were powerful, though, and their faces had taken on a dire pallor, teeth glinting.

There was not a hint of the chaotic music that heralded the Other, but something was attacking Kelso, and by extension, the Princess. Misima raged and launched herself across the snow while the two Ghouls burrowed through it at her sides.

Whoever was attacking the Knight was in for a surprise.

***

Masoni Vance had waited around long enough.

The shots had put him on edge, and his Dark swirled around him in agitation while he was forced to sit in the truck following Jesslyn at a snail's pace. There was fighting up there, and he wanted to get to it.

He glanced over at the other Sorcerer, and their eyes met for a second before that worthy gave him a small nod.

"Punch it," Masoni growled to the idiot Childe who was at the wheel of the truck.

The bearded man opened his mouth to protest, but Masoni cut him off. "Something happened and she could be in trouble. Let's go—*now*." Not for one second did he think Jesslyn was in trouble, but Masoni knew that if she got upset by their interference he could just blame it on the driver and the others would back him.

All of them wanted to get into the fight. There were marks to be gained and blood to be spilled. Masoni's eyes glinted in anticipation as the Childe floored the gas pedal, and the truck lurched forward in pursuit.

Whoever was attacking the Spider was in for a surprise.

# Chapter 22

Something alerted the Knight at the last moment and he dodged to the right, just out of Jesslyn's reach. She wanted to snarl in frustration, but all thoughts of anger disappeared along with a good chunk of her armor when a bullet slammed into her right shoulder.

Kelso had literally brought his gun up behind his head and fired blindly at Jesslyn, never stopping, never turning. If the shot hadn't rocked the Spider so hard and knocked the breath out of her, she would have complimented him. What a worthy mate he would be once she'd weaned him off her poison!

Spinning sideways from the bullet's impact, she sidestepped through the snow to regain her balance and leaped again, closing the distance fast. Jesslyn did so boldly because she knew he had only one bullet left. The Spider was confident that she could take another shot, although it was going to sting.

Again, just as her hands reached for him, he dodged her, but this time he blinked away entirely. Suddenly he was forty feet ahead and tumbling, turning to face her as he did so. Unbroken snow led up to where he was busy crashing through the drifts. She smiled in real admiration. He had teleported! The Spider had seen him do that once before, and she had been curious to see if he would—or could—do it again.

*What a cool power!* She figured it was something that Argenta gifted to its bearers, since she had heard rumors of previous Ebon Knights doing similar. The Spider was slightly jealous, and then… slightly alarmed.

The Knight was skidding backwards into the drifts, Ava slipping off as he did so and rolling end over end into the embankment. Kelso had let her go because he had drawn his second gun, and both were aimed at Jesslyn even as he fell, launching huge arcs of snow out from the sides as he went.

He pulled the triggers, and she dodged one clean. The other impacted on her left breast right over her heart, and the armor there shattered. Jesslyn rolled backwards with the impact, not struggling against it, and fell on her back in the snow as another bullet sizzled through the air above her. He was out of bullets in his right handgun, but she had the left handgun to contend with now.

Jesslyn continued to roll backwards and came to a crouch before launching herself sideways as yet another bullet tore the air where she had been—but a half-second too late. The Spider was so impressed! She couldn't remember the last time someone had done so well against her in single combat. A part of her knew that if he wasn't already exhausted and battered, he could probably take her flat out. That was a *huge* turn on for her, so she wasn't going to penalize him for losing this fight—and he *was* going to lose, very shortly now.

Well, as long as he didn't draw Argenta.

If he did, all bets were off, and she would need to run away at full and desperate speed. Jesslyn was confident that he wouldn't release the sword, though, because Ava's life would be forfeited as well. As Jesslyn hurriedly burrowed under the snow, she was grateful that he had no clue what she had planned for his precious Princess—because if he did Argenta would be freed. The Spider had no doubt that the Knight would much rather end Ava himself than let her live through the indignities Jesslyn had planned.

Her gift enveloped her at last, and she boldly popped out of the embankment, invisible and undetectable to all. Sure enough, the Knight was still on his back and scanning for her with his left gun. Ava was lying face down in the snow. As Jesslyn stood, fully intending to fetch Ava from under his nose and be away before Kelso even realized his Princess had been taken, the impossible happened.

The Knight flicked his barrel over to her and fired.

This time the bullet caught her in the neck, where it punched through her weakened armor with ease and out the other side. She was launched backwards by the impact, blood billowing, and completely stunned.

She landed on her back hard, momentarily spared another bullet, but she knew he would follow up immediately. Jesslyn desperately rolled to the side, not even bothering to staunch her neck first, and another bullet peppered the snow she had landed in. Only one bullet remained in his gun, but there was no way she could risk another hit.

Jesslyn ground her teeth in frustration and pain as she raised both hands to her neck and pressed. Her Dark was already working to stop the flow, and she knew it wasn't fatal—but it *really* hurt! The bullet hadn't gone through her throat, which would have shattered her spine, too. Instead, it had passed through the fleshy part a few inches over.

Jesslyn was lucky and she knew it.

*** 

The Knight could never remember being this tired.

Kelso struggled to his feet blearily, gun trained on the spot where Jesslyn went down. He had to blink his eyes rapidly to even see at all, though his gun hand remained rock steady.

Movement to Kelso's rear alerted him that someone was coming, and he turned backwards to see an enraged Fury sprinting at him, holding a Fel bow with an arrow already nocked as she came. One figure paced her on either side, but they ran low to the ground, like dogs or apes, burrowing into the snow and popping up, loping, leaping. They seemed absolutely savage. Even though he knew the cavalry had arrived, he had a moment of worry that the three incoming and clearly incensed warriors would mistake him for an enemy... or perhaps conveniently forget that he wasn't one.

Kelso thought his fear was coming true as the Fury raised her bow and let an arrow fly, not aiming anywhere near where the woman had fallen. It was then that he saw the snow was illuminated from behind him, and he spun just in time to see a truck as it leapt up the snow drift, missing Ava's body by mere feet.

The arrow that whispered over his left shoulder shattered the windshield center mass and into whoever was driving it, and the truck careened out of control. That was all Kelso had time to recognize before he was flung into the night by a bone-jarring impact. He had a moment to watch his Light wink away entirely as he blacked out, still in the air.

***

The Spider heard the truck enter the battle, and she knew her companions had joined the fight. She was enraged and grateful at the same time. Enraged because they had disobeyed her, grateful because she was losing. The shattering of glass and an impact against the hard charging truck caused her to cautiously poke her head back up out of the snow once she was sure her gift had wrapped her again.

She was only looking for the Knight. He had pierced her veil somehow, so if he still stood she would have to retreat at once. She didn't see him, but she did see Misima. The Japanese woman had summoned twin katanas and had leaped onto the hood of the truck, neatly decapitating the sneeringly overconfident Sorcerer as he attempted to exit on the passenger's side. The driver, too, was dead, a Fel arrow through the sternum.

One of the truck's back doors was kicked off its hinges and flew a dozen feet before crashing into the snow. The female Berserker bailed out after it, clutching a huge axe in her hand. On the opposite side, the other Sorcerer and the remaining Childe also exited—the Sorcerer holding a length of coiled Dark in his hands.

Something swept past Jesslyn and a muscled... thing... launched itself at the Berserker's throat. The large but stupid woman had just enough time to register the attack before it was latched on to her neck, tearing and ripping while its hands tore at her body with claws of Dark. Jesslyn had never seen anything like it, and she stood in shock when she realized it was a Ghoul.

But not like any Ghoul she had ever seen.

The Berserker was too enraged and stupid to die, and she grabbed the Ghoul's neck with one massive hand and brought her axe down into the things back. Thick armor protected the Ghoul, but it buckled under the blow even so. It ignored the axe and furiously tore at the woman's throat with its huge teeth and ripped at her muscle and flesh with clawed hands. Black blood flowed freely from the Berserker, armoring as it came, yet the Ghoul still somehow found purchase against it and tore deeply.

Another Ghoul had launched itself at the remaining Sorcerer, but this one was ready. He whipped the coiled Dark in his hands out like a rope, and it caught the Ghoul and wrapped around it instantly like a snake, pinning the Ghoul's hands at its sides. The Sorcerer stepped out of the way as the flying missile of teeth and claws sailed by him, and a gurgling scream ripped from the Ghoul as bones broke and sinews snapped. The Sorcerer's Dark squeezing its victim to death like a python.

The Childe summoned throwing daggers of Dark and threw them at Misima. She batted both out of the air in quick succession with her blades before reforming her left-hand sword into a throwing spear, which she promptly launched at the man. It blasted through his armor with ease, and he sagged sideways into the open door of the truck, clutching at it with a gasp.

The Spider stared at Misima with hate-filled eyes for a

331

moment before beelining to where Ava was still face down in the snow. Jesslyn roughly turned her over and saw Ava's eyelids fluttering—she was coming to! Quickly, Jesslyn looked around for Kelso and found him sprawled out in the snow another forty feet back. He looked dead. Even as wounded as she was, Jesslyn's heart sank.

As for her own injuries, her Dark was stemming the blood and working to heal the wound at her neck. She didn't want to slow down the process, but if Ava woke, she would kill Jesslyn in seconds—of that the Spider had no doubt. So, Jesslyn concentrated for a moment and formed a vicious globule of poison, making it large and thick. When satisfied, she plunged it into Ava's neck without delay.

Ava's eyes instantly flew open as the poison entered her bloodstream. Her right hand whipped up and grabbed Jesslyn by the throat, crushing her delicate fingers through the wounds at the Spider's neck. Jesslyn saw stars and poured another desperate dose of poison directly into Ava again. What she had already deposited in her youngest sister would have killed several humans by now, but Ava's eyes just narrowed, and she merely grunted at the fresh burst of numbing agent that washed through her body.

A roaring in Jesslyn's ears alerted her to the fact that she was in real danger of collapsing into unconsciousness. Fresh blood was soaking her front and dripping onto Ava's face. The hatred and disdain in Ava's eyes were sharp, accusatory, and vengeful. Again, the Spider pumped another round of poison into the Dark Witch—everything she had left, in fact.

Ava's hand finally lost its strength and her eyes rolled back in her head. The youngest Princess of the Dark fell back limp into the snow, and the oldest Princess of the Dark almost followed her down. By inches Jesslyn staved off unconsciousness... and thus death.

Wearily, she looked up at the battle and saw that the Berserker was on her back, the Ghoul on top, both moving weakly. The Ghoul's teeth looked to be worrying the Berserker's throat from the inside, but the Berserker's axe had broken through the Ghoul's armor and was six inches deep through the spine. The Ghoul's arms and legs were canted at weird angles, and it was obviously paralyzed—except for its head, and more importantly, its jaws. Jesslyn felt confident that neither combatant would survive.

There was no sign of the Childe that Misima had impaled, but Jesslyn assumed he was dead too. The remaining Sorcerer and the lone Fury were locked in a death spiral of their own, but the Sorcerer seemed to be winning. He had wrapped his Dark around Misima's throat, but she had caught it with one clawed hand before it could strangle her. With her other hand, she had skewered the Sorcerer through the collar bone. Even as Jesslyn watched in a half-daze, weak from her own blood loss, Misima turned the weapon ninety degrees and the Sorcerer screamed in pain.

His Dark redoubled its attack, and the Fury's massive hand was forced closer to her throat. Misima was snarling with the effort of holding the Sorcerer's rope at bay, but she was losing. Jesslyn looked back over at Kelso and saw his hand twitch. It was still holding the gun.

*Time to go.*

Jesslyn strained to lift Ava out of the snow and almost fell over with the effort. Finally, she snugged her prize over her shoulder and headed out into the dark.

Slowly, painfully, but steadily.

# Chapter 23

Kelso snapped awake with a start.

Argenta was hollering in his head for him to wake up, to rise, to hurry. He couldn't think straight, and he couldn't even fully understand her words, but the Knight understood her tone. Something was happening that he needed to stop, but Kelso didn't know if he had anything left. In front of him he heard a strange keening sound, like a scream and a snarl all at once.

The Knight had never heard anything quite like it, but it seemed similar to when Carmen had leapt to his defense in the barn. She had sounded a little like the noise now coming from close by: desperate, angry, sad.

Was it Carmen? Was she in trouble?

It took everything he had, and everything he didn't, to find the will to sit up. What he saw confused him for a moment before adrenaline shocked him with dread-filled realization.

A Fury was dying not twenty feet in front of him. A rope composed entirely of Dark had lashed itself around her neck, head, and shoulders. It was clearly squeezing the life out of her. Holding the other end of the rope, a man with a horrible wound in his shoulder was grimacing in triumph and hate, sweat beading on his brow as he bent all his will and power towards throttling the struggling woman.

The Fury had one clawed hand pushing back against the rope as her other tried to pull it away, but she was losing. The keening she made was coming from her in shorter and shorter bursts as her strength failed, and she was seconds from being strangled to death or having her neck snapped.

Kelso stared dumbly for a moment, and then, without conscious thought, raised his weapon and shot the man in his head. The Sorcerer's forehead disappeared; gore and brain matter erupted out of the back of his skull. Kelso pulled the trigger again, and his gun clicked empty. He pulled the trigger again as the Sorcerer came to rest in the snow. Another click. And another. The rope around the Fury winked out and she immediately fell to all fours, breath rasping and shaking in relief. It had been very, very close.

Kelso pulled the trigger again. *Click.*

At the sound, the Fury looked up at him and he recognized her. Misima. One of Ava's Furies and a personal guard to his Princess. Ava. *Where was she?*

Kelso looked back to where he had dropped Ava just a minute ago, and she was gone. The Knight's world tilted as he tried to stand up. Something was wrong with him; his body just couldn't do what he wanted it to do. He dropped his gun hand down to his lap, staring mutely around for his Ava.

*Where had she gone?* Something was bothering him. There was something important he was forgetting.

Misima leapt down from the truck hood as she tracked his gaze over to where he had first looked. The Fury landed at the spot and scooped up some blood that had pooled on the snow there and brought it to her face. She sniffed it. Suddenly, Misima's eyes flew open wide in recognition, and she howled into the night. Or was it a scream? He wasn't sure.

From nearby, two answering howls of unimaginable pain and anger answered Misima. The Fury collapsed in the snow where Ava had lain at the battle's start, her large body shaking as she buried her face in her hands. Two other Fury's raced in, both larger than Misima, and they immediately went to where she lay huddled and started communicating amongst themselves with whistles, growls, and—now—wails. Something was *very* off, and they seemed stricken with grief. What it could be he had no idea, but he felt sorry for them.

*Where was Ava?* She needed to find out what was wrong with her Furies and fix it. His Princess could fix anything; he knew it in his heart.

Several other figures rushed onto the battlefield—hulking shapes that slid along the ground, never standing to their full height. They looked dangerous and feral, and several of them swept the area quickly. A quick scream sounded from behind the car where one of the newcomers found someone still alive. A bone cracking snap ended the scream quickly and silence fell again.

A face floated in front of him: it was a female with impressive, gleaming teeth and a necklace of coffin nails. Her hair was pulled back in a ratty ponytail, and the look she cast him was one of concern and sorrow.

*Why was she looking at him so?* He looked down at himself,

trying to see if he had any entrails hanging out of his stomach, or if he was missing a leg or something. The look she favored him with would only be appropriate if he had a wound like that. A grievous wound, one that would challenge the bearer of it to even find the strength to keep breathing...

A wound where the bearer would rather die than suffer it.

"*Kelso*," said his sword with pity and nothing more. The Knight had never heard Argenta say anything with pity before; he had not thought it possible. But why was she pitying him now?

*Where was Ava?*

The Furies had returned to human form, and all three wept unabashedly, hugging each other. One of them, Chandra, looked over at Kelso and the heartbreak in her eyes included him in it. She wept partially for him, but...

A distant buzzing started in Kelso's ears, and a strawberry blonde's face flashed in his memory. A beautiful face with cruel eyes—no, with insane eyes. She had come for Ava, his Princess. His fearless soulmate, she of the magnificent blue eyes and quick wit. The Dark Witch who caused the wicked to fear and who punished those that transgressed against the weak and defenseless. She who was hunted by her evil, sick, and twisted family—marked for death.

The depths of Ava's disquiet when she talked about her family struck him anew then, and he realized that she didn't fear the death part... she feared everything that would proceed it.

He screamed suddenly and the world rushed in on him.

Darkness came… and Kelso welcomed it.

*** 

Jesslyn trudged through the snow with her prize.

Her Dark had finally plugged both holes in her neck, but she was in excruciating pain. Just putting one foot in front of the other was difficult and she had trouble even focusing. After a grueling mile she moved off the street and sat in the snow, dropping Ava in a heap next to her. The Spider flexed her shoulders in relief and then nearly passed out from the pain as her blasted-apart neck muscles flared in agony.

She almost screamed.

The blood had stopped about a half mile back, which was good, because her pursuers would have nothing more to follow. Her aura would confuse their senses up close, but the path she left—and the blood—would be easy for them to track.

That there were pursuers was of little doubt.

No sooner had she thought this than a shape loped by in the middle of the street, frantically looking from right to left. It was a Ghoul. A few seconds later, another one appeared on the farthest side, also searching desperately. And then another passed not fifteen feet from her. It was a thick-set man with the huge teeth that gleamed dangerously in the Ghoul's mishappen face. He ran crouched over, occasionally leaping and jumping with grace and power.

The Spider was dumbfounded and a little frightened by these

Ghouls. Never had she imagined that they could move or even *look* like they did now. Jesslyn remembered very well how brutal the Ghoul had been that took out the Berserker in single combat back at the truck. If that was how a typical Ghoul could fight, the entire balance of power within the Dark armies would be upended. And if the Furies and the Ghouls were now allied— which seemed to be the case—then the Spider feared that the Dark was in real trouble.

Unlike the Furies, the Ghouls were extremely numerous and could be found pretty much anywhere throughout the world. Any decent-sized town had a cemetery, and Ghouls haunted such. Jesslyn thought that there could easily be over one hundred thousand worldwide, but she might be guessing low. Obscenely low.

The Ghouls had appeared at about the same time the Furies did but were quickly deemed useless. Jesslyn had tortured and killed several over the last few hundred years trying to figure out what made them tick, or if they had any redeeming or interesting qualities. They didn't. Or at least she'd *thought* they didn't.

Now she wasn't so sure.

A small voice whispered in her head that if the Ghouls could actually fight as well as it appeared they could—that if what she had witnessed tonight heralded an unknown side to them—the Dark would soon be battered by an unending tide.

As Jesslyn sat there in the falling snow, she wondered what to do. Or, more precisely, how to do it.

The Spider had finally ensnared the Dark Witch, but how safely did she actually have her? Ava had woken up when Jesslyn poisoned her, and even though the young Princess had nothing left of her tremendous power, she'd still almost killed Jesslyn—one handed. That Ava had done so with no visibly manifested Dark was scary and almost unbelievable.

Jesslyn glanced over at the Witch. There were only a few light wisps of visible Dark surrounding her even now. The Spider had been forced to use three times more of her own Dark to subdue Ava than she had estimated she would need—and that was without Ava even being fully awake and nowhere near combat ready. Jesslyn worried that keeping Ava sedated enough to transport her back to the Dark Court would be close to impossible. In her current state Jesslyn just didn't have the power to spare.

Also, Jesslyn kept remembering how Ava had looked at her when she'd had the Spider by the throat. The Princess had not seemed frightened or worried, but instead angry and vengeful. Perhaps even more concerning, the Dark Witch had not seemed surprised at her sister's appearance. It was almost like Ava had expected to see Jesslyn and then did her level best to kill her the moment they locked eyes.

It was something to consider.

As wounded as she was, not even visions of the horrors she wanted to inflict on Ava could cheer her up. Instead, dark thoughts and worries chased themselves around and around in her head.

She was deeply disquieted by how well the Knight had managed to fight, and how he had pierced her veil. Only her parents had ever done that in all the years of Jesslyn's life. How had he seen see through her gift?

Again, her thoughts returned to the Ghoul's apparent entrance into this new war and what that could mean to the greater Dark. As she watched the three disappear down the street, she shivered over the implications of their arrival.

And she was terrified by how strong Ava was. Jesslyn now knew that she had grossly underestimated her youngest sister. Did she even have the power to keep Ava quiet? The Spider wasn't sure.

For the first time in her long life, a saying that had never made sense to her suddenly seemed perfect for her situation.

Jesslyn had caught a tiger by the tail.

# Epilogue

The consciousness that was known as the Other was incensed. Well, as much as it could be. It wasn't totally sure that *incensed* was the right word for the way it... felt. If that was even possible for it, but somehow it thought it might be.

All of it had been wiped out in Reno and Sparks, and it had none of itself in reserve to quickly rebuild its strength there. The closest of it was in Las Vegas, and even though there was a lot of itself there, it was still not close enough to make any difference. The battle had been lost.

The Other needed to ponder.

It had spent eons pondering, actually, and it had once been very good at it. Now, it seemed like its understanding of this world, its inhabitants, and the Conflict increased at such dizzying speeds that it could barely keep up with its own evolution.

With each new host, new memories assailed it, new experiences and beliefs, new sorrows. One soul's beliefs stood diametrically opposite to another's, and other souls might stand against the beliefs of the first two. As it experienced more and more of what it meant to exist for these beings, a few things happened.

The first was that its appetite had become ravenous. The more it experienced, the more it wanted to experience. It knew the concept of drugs and addiction now, and it felt that its need for new hosts bordered on that—an aching desire that could not be quenched. With every existence it ate, its need expanded. As it cast the tiny sparks of its hosts into the maelstrom of itself, their lights only briefly illuminated more mysteries before fading away into nothingness.

It was maddening because it wanted to explore those mysteries and plumb an understanding that just *barely* eluded it.

It was aware of many worlds, many planes, many timelines in which souls uncountable waited for it to come. That it should come for them was a given, because without it those sparks would flame out and rekindle somewhere else an unfathomable distance—or timeline—away. All those original experiences would be lost and forgotten. It was such a waste, really.

What the Other took, it kept. Each of those thousands of fireflies it had already collected would now live forever in its memory and as a part of its consciousness. Immortality for all, in some ways. Few had the power to stand against it, and the Other knew that the champions of the Light and the Dark were its only true adversaries in this world.

Which brought it to its second understanding.

It had underestimated the resistance it would face, and in so doing had tipped its hand to those that would stand in the way of its progress throughout the multiverse of worlds and realms that lay waiting. This fundamental mistake would not be repeated. Where it had thrown hundreds before, it would now throw thousands—tens of thousands if need be.

It had been weak, timid, and perhaps too crafty for its own

good. Now? It would use a wave of empty flesh to win the day. Where once it had taken years, then months, then weeks to consume its hosts, now it took days for some, minutes for others. It would expand itself exponentially in readiness. The next battle would lead to a final war, and when that war was won it would cast its consciousness out towards the next conquest. It would be stronger, smarter, and more experienced when it came for the worlds after this one.

And it would win. *Everything.*

The last lesson it learned tonight was that even though it had lost, it had gained insights into how it might succeed in the future. Some were immune to its beautiful dirge and that could not be allowed to stand. Even now, at its base of operations in the enclave once known as the Temple of Light, it was mobilizing to start the purge that would be required to wipe out those that could resist its call.

The Paladin had been insane—many of the experiences and thoughts of those it had eaten tonight confirmed that. The Other had somehow healed him in a sense, and whatever disease or malady that had crippled the Paladin had been cured while he could stay close to its song. It had raged over this turn of events because that meant that a small sliver of this world's inhabitants would be immune to it when it came for them.

If it could not have them, it would end them. And in Las Vegas, where the Temple resided, that cleansing would start immediately.

To balance out that weakness, it had found an unexpected

strength. The Furies were extremely susceptible to its song. They could have been fierce warriors in opposition, so this was a welcome development. The Other suspected that they easily fell to its overwhelming consciousness because they were already wired for it.

The Furies shared a larger connection among themselves already, and this had apparently opened up pathways within them that allowed the Other to take them over rapidly and completely. If it could be said to have a favorite *food*, the Furies would be it.

The obvious pain and anger its predilection caused in the one called the Dark Witch was a bonus. The Other felt a sinister pride at hurting her, at provoking her, and thus hurting and provoking the Ebon Knight. That it could even feel these things meant it had advanced in its understanding to an unimaginable degree, much further than it had ever felt it could when it first stirred to consciousness just a short moment ago—to its reckoning, at least.

The Dark Witch and the Ebon Knight would be brought into the fold or killed, but it needed to be ready this time. It would not allow itself to fail again. As a first step, it would consolidate its power and add to its ranks while simultaneously reaping those who could resist it.

Now.

*** 

The bustle of the day was finally drawing down in the Temple, and Isaac Gillian was pleased that he had served the Light to the best of his ability once again. The proudest moment of his life was the day he had ascended into the Conflict; the second proudest was when he had earned his station as a Priest in the ranks of the Light.

After fifty years, his kind manner and steadfast faith had been noticed and he had been given the opportunity to work for the Council of Mages. He had moved to Las Vegas a few years ago, marveling about how an entire hotel/casino could be scrubbed from the memory and notice of everyone that lived in, worked, or visited the city.

He often sat outside on the stone benches and watched the oblivious pass by minute after minute, hour after hour, all day, every day. It was a testament to the strength of the Light that they could do such, in what was often thought of as one of the wickedest cities on the planet. He often wondered what the sleepers saw—or if they saw anything—as they passed the large, gleaming white structure in the heart of downtown just one block removed from The Strip itself.

Did they see an empty lot? A parking garage? A casino under renovation or obviously abandoned? Someday soon he was going to make himself known to some of the passersby and ask them. His curiosity knew no bounds.

His musing was interrupted by a piercing scream.

Looking up with his fellow front desk companions—another Priest, a couple of Knights, and a Paladin—he was surprised to see a female Priestess that he recognized running at top speed for the front doors. She had a wild look in her eyes, and she seemed to be muttering "No, no, no, no!" over and over as she beelined for the exit.

Her name was Yasmine Scot, or "Mother Scot" to those of the Priests order—and she was the head of it. She had entered the elevators earlier tonight with Mason Wistel, who led the Knights. Mason was sauntering after her, completely unconcerned by her flight, and with him were five others.

Isaac blinked. The five remaining Mages of the Council accompanied him, and Isaac fought off the immediate urge to lower his eyes in deference. Something was off.

By all accounts Tich Issan was the most powerful of the Mages, yet he walked in a group with the other four as if they were all equal. In fact, Mason acted the same—it was like the Knight believed he was an equal member of that illustrious group, which was preposterous.

Amazingly, a few of the dozens that were in small conferences around the large lower-level floor followed the Mother out. *Why would they do that?* Perhaps seeing the head of the Priests running away from the group making their way to the exact middle of the mammoth space had goaded them to flight too.

*Should he run?*

Well over two hundred of his fellow warriors in the Light stood frozen in various states of distress or alarm as the six who had exited the elevator stopped. Isaac suddenly became aware of a jolting, discordant, and mind splintering sound. It reached out from nowhere it seemed, from distances vast beyond reckoning, from an alien place beyond understanding.

The song froze him in place.

For a few minutes, as Isaac was held there immobile, he realized that everyone left in the cavernous room was as paralyzed as he was. He had arched up onto his toes, mouth open and screaming soundlessly as his mind fractured and fractured again.

When he fell back down to the balls of his feet once more he was no longer Isaac Gillian.

He was much, much greater.

With a smirk, the Other immediately walked the one who had been Isaac out onto the street. The rest of it dispersed all around on various tasks. Without hesitation, this part of the Other approached the first group of tourists it encountered, and it became visible to them when it was but ten feet away. They stopped in surprise at its sudden appearance, and the father stepped in front of his wife and their two young children in alarm.

The Other hated children; they didn't have much to offer it in the way of experiences, wisdom, or memories. It smiled anyway.

"Hi, folks, sorry," it said with a winning grin, "didn't mean to startle you. I have a question to ask if I could just borrow a moment of your time?"

The father looked at it with suspicion but nodded shortly.

"Awesome, thanks!" The one that had once been Isaac was thrilled. "Tell me, what do you see?" The Other pointed at the

Temple it had just exited, watching the man's eyes track to the large building and glaze over.

"Uh, nothing?" the man said. "It's a fenced off lot, maybe for parking? I don't know."

"Ahh," said the Other, disappointed. "Ok."

The family started to move past it before the Other asked, "By the way, what do you *hear?*"

It smiled as all four of them suddenly stiffened. Down the street, the Other spied a group of men drinking out of some paper sacks and joking loudly. The former Priest of the Light laughed delightedly and started their way.

Beyond them, it saw a couple walking hand in hand.

The Other was excited to make all of their acquaintances tonight...

***

Las Vegas had more than its fair share of psychiatric wards.

Melissa Zapatos knew this without a doubt; there were literally dozens if you counted the larger full-time institutions and the smaller outpatient or temporary hold facilities. Why, then, did it seem like every time there was an inspection by the state it seemed to be at hers? And why was she invariably the head nurse on duty?

She was seriously considering a transfer. The pay at Jeffries Inpatient wasn't *that* much different than some of its smaller rivals; and she wouldn't have to put up with half the inspections, she bet. Jeffries handled its fair share of alcoholics that had lost control, gamblers that had hit rock bottom, and washed-up entertainers or wanna-be entertainers that had become suicidal as they realized their real (or imagined) glory days were far behind and forever out of reach.

They had all of those, yes, but they were all basically sane people that had just come to the end of their rope. The problem was that Jeffries also had *two* wards full to bursting with the criminally insane or those so far off their rocker that new words should have been invented to describe their afflictions.

It was these two supermax wards that attracted state inspectors like flies to… honey. And she was sick of it. Newsflash! Some of the inspectors themselves were almost as damaged as the patients they came to ogle at. Case in point was tonight's inspector.

He was a dark-skinned man dressed strangely in old-fashioned khakis and a billowy shirt tied at his waist. He literally carried a pouch on one side of his belt and a large knife on the other. His head was bald, and when matched with his wicked goatee and tapered eyebrows, he gave off a slightly sinister vibe. He had told her assistant, Julia, that his name was Melhmut, of all things, and that he was here to "inspect the insane."

Melissa had asked Julia why she and the male orderlies had allowed him into the waiting room with a knife. Her subordinate had seemed flustered by the question and ran off to the ladies' room. Well, Melissa wasn't taking any of that, so she summoned two of her largest and had them arm up with the tasers they were not supposed to have and pepper spray—also frowned upon.

She didn't care. Melissa was *not* walking into a room with a man that looked a lot like Emperor Ming from that old Flash Gordon movie while he was in possession of a knife—particularly without her own protections. Period.

If this *Melhmut* was perhaps deranged himself, and thinking he was quite clever to break into a psychiatric hospital—whether it be for fun or curiosity—he was shortly going to find out the error of his ways. She would have that knife safely put away in a weapons locker and a three-day hold for its owner within the hour—if he wasn't on the up and up, that was.

Melhmut was waiting for them in the secured room just off the hallways that led deeper into the bowels of the hospital. When she entered with the two huge and unsmiling orderlies behind her—all businesslike and no-nonsense—his peculiar, fixed smile never wavered for an instant. It was like his face was just a mask, and the emotions and thoughts that made him human were absent.

*This guy is a cinch for lock up,* Melissa thought as she looked him over with a practiced eye. *I'm going to need that knife though.*

Stopping just inside the door, with the two orderlies flanking her, she merely stared at him for a moment, trying to make him sweat. He didn't.

"Mr. Melhmut," she began, "how can I help you?" Her tone left little doubt that she didn't believe she could.

His smile remained unchanged. "I'm here as a test. I'm something of a... musician... you see, and I'm curious to see how your patients react to my songs."

"You want to play them music?" Melissa asked in suspicious disbelief. Next to her, both men lightly dropped their hands to their tasers at the same time. Some sort of an annoying tune had come to her attention, and she found it very distracting. Worse, she had no clue where it was coming from.

"Yes, that's right." He shrugged. "It's important."

"I see." Her tone slipped into detached professionalism. "And why did you bring the knife?"

"Oh, well, if they don't like my music, I'm going to kill them all—each and every one of them." His smile never slipped. "No, I'll let your hand kill them instead... as a welcome gift. How's that?"

"I don't like that plan very much," she murmured, sweat breaking out on her brow. Both orderlies had pulled their tasers but held them unsteadily. Something was throwing off her concentration, and she was having trouble thinking straight. The damn music was *everywhere,* and her vision blurred as she strained to keep herself together.

"Give it a minute," the Other urged, "and you'll be all in. Trust me."


**The End**

The adventure continues with the next installment in the Chronicles: "The Arch Mage"

*Please* remember to review my books on Amazon, GoodReads, etc.!

# Author's Notes

This second book sprang organically and easily from the first. As those of you that read my first book know, I had the idea that eventually became "The Ebon Knight" kicking around in my head for many years before finally taking the plunge and writing it. I knew the whole story from beginning to end and figured I could get it all out in just one book. Yeah, right.

As I continued to build the adventure, more and more ideas came to me, and interesting characters presented themselves and demanded a place on the page. Thus, my plans for one book quickly turned into three. If you enjoy my work, then that is a win for you. For purposes of the overall story arc, I believe it was the only option. "The Dark Witch" flew out of me and onto the page, too! I literally wrote the entire book in about two months, and I'm SO proud of it! I hope you loved reading it as much as I enjoyed writing it.

So, again, what now?

As I mentioned before, if the first three books of the Chronicles are well received, I would feel blessed to be able to continue to write full-length novels in the world of the Ebon Knight and the Dark Witch. I will also continue to add short stories exploring some of the pivotal and/or more interesting minor characters—regardless. I might even put those stories on Amazon, but for now: if you want more, there is more at authorjamesdwood.com.

A completed short story is already available on my site called

"The First Fury" which explores the events of Kelso's ascension through the eyes of Kiasa, the legendary Fury alluded to several times throughout the series. My second short story will be called "The Lord Commander" and is about the pivotal moment that pushed Marcus Dain down a dark path. Look for that story in mid-2024.

I'm eager to take on a horror project that has been plaguing me for several years too, and so some decisions will be made about my next project shortly. If you like my writing, then it shouldn't be a stretch to look me up in the horror categories in 2024, right? If you get scared easily, don't worry they will be totally bland... and I'm totally lying. Ok. So, they might be a *little* scary, but they will be well crafted, so if I go that route please check them out!

As I promised at the end of book one, I will keep writing either way.

I sincerely hope you enjoyed "The Dark Witch" (as you apparently did "The Ebon Knight") and remember to look for "The Arch Mage" next, which will conclude this arc of the story. All three books will be presented in both eBook, print, and audio versions on Amazon. Check my website occasionally for the launch dates and for the next product announcements.

Thank you for reading! I am beyond grateful for your support and please remember to review my work on Amazon and Goodreads!

Nov 11, 2023

# About the Author

Being born in Detroit, Michigan, but raised in rural Nevada could be whiplash-inducing for anyone. I prefer to think of my formative years as a "boot camp" of sorts that prepared me for all of life's challenges after I moved to California and met my wife. After twenty years with her and four kids, three dogs, one cat, and one fish, I realize I wasn't prepared half as much as I thought I was.

I write urban fantasy with a touch of humor and a smidge of romance—well, maybe more than a smidge. Firmly believing that evil is evil and good is good, I promptly went out to write a series disproving my beliefs... cause that's just how I roll. I have three books coming out in 2023/2024, collectively called "The Ebon Knight Chronicles," along with several short stories in the same universe. I was interested in writing a series that explores the vast grey landscapes that exist between the shining white Paladins on the one hand (boring) and the darkly maniacal Wizards on the other (lame). If you think everyone has a little heaven and hell in them, then you will enjoy the Ebon Knight Chronicles!

My favorite authors are Stephen King, Dean Koontz, Jim Butcher, Jonathan Maberry, and John Conroe. If you like any of their books, they influenced mine.

If you want to join my newsletter and get my short stories for

FREE, then go to **https://authorjamesdwood.com** and sign-up! I have a welcome story for all who join called "The First Fury," and I plan to add new stories to the world of the Ebon Knight at least twice a year. My website also has pictures of Charlie, who is one of my real-life English Bulldogs—I lent him to Kelso for the duration of the series because he was eating me out of house and home. If you enjoyed reading about Charlie, then put a (fuzzy) face to the name and check out "The Nine Faces of Charlie" on my website.

You can also look me up on Facebook to check out songs I like for some of the characters or chapters and just assorted zaniness at https://www.facebook.com/profile.php?id=100094581420780 or search for "Author James Wood." There are a couple of other authors with the same name, though, so if you don't see something about "The Ebon Knight Chronicles" you went to the wrong page.

Printed in Dunstable, United Kingdom